# Hidden in the Dark

## Every Family Has Secrets - Some Are Worth Dying For

RaShell Lashbrook

ISBN:0998691704
ISBN-13:978-0998691701

# DEDICATION

This novel is dedicated to my grandmother, Dorothy May Longhofer Pope, who always believed in me no matter how crazy my ideas were. She bought me my first Writer's Handbook in 1997. I know that she is watching me from heaven and smiling right now. Also, this book is dedicated to my mother, Marcia Pope Weller, who has an incredible imagination and entertained me with great stories when I was a child. I am sure that she was a writer in a previous lifetime. And last, but definitely not least, this novel is dedicated to my father, Lyle Lashbrook Sr., who taught me to work a little harder and a little longer than everyone else. He is the embodiment of hard work, determination, and courage.

# CONTENTS

# ACKNOWLEDGMENTS

Thank you Jen Bell, Rocio Burkhead, Kris Jackson Keeling, Shelly J. Moore, Sandy Nitcher, Gary "Will Power" Rapp, and Susan Reed for your invaluable input on the first edition manuscript of this novel. Without your feedback, Hidden in the Dark would not be possible. I am forever grateful for your time, attention to detail, and your incredible patience with my numerous questions.

Thank you to my family and friends for supporting me during this process and allowing me to ramble on incessantly about the novel without bashing me over the head. I appreciate your great restraint.

Thank you to my son, Grant Harris, for always being willing to read whatever passage I've recently written to make sure it sounds "okay".

# CHAPTER 1
## GENNY'S GOLDEN YEARS

### August 2011

"YOU are the monster!" Randall spat the words out while poking her in the chest to emphasize each one. Genevieve didn't know what to say to him. She never did.

"And you wonder why your girls don't come around? They can't stand your two-faced, lying ass either!" He ran his hand through the top of his unruly hair. "But I have to put up with you, don't I? Until death do us part!"

Genevieve remained quiet even though she felt like her heart was going to break through her chest cavity with its wild thumping. She'd used up all her tears a long time ago. Tears are pointless, she thought.

"What? Now you've got nothing to say? Well you were sure full of words earlier!"

Genevieve knew that Randall wouldn't stop until she gave him something. It was always the same when he got like this. If she ignored him, he would continue until she had to defend herself. Might as well get the inevitable over with, she thought.

"Randall, please! You're drunk. Let's just go to bed and everything will be better tomorrow." She pleaded in the most gentle, submissive voice that she could summon. If she could just get him through the night, things would be calm in the morning. She'd held on for eight o'clock in the morning more times through the years than she could count.

Years ago, she would've placated him with sex, but those times were over. His age, along with the excessive drinking, had made the act nearly impossible. He couldn't maintain an erection long enough to do anything

1

other than to remind Genny of the past. She guessed that his inability to perform made him even angrier.

"I'm not drunk yet! But I'm gonna be now!" Randall staggered to the freezer to fill his tumbler with more ice and liquor. He exaggerated his movements to make as much noise as possible.

Genevieve sighed. She thought that Randall would've given up alcohol by now. But here they were, in their sixties, doing the same old song and dance that they did in their twenties and thirties. Only somehow it was worse now. Or maybe she was just tired. Men were supposed to mellow with age, weren't they? Instead, Randall had become even more belligerent in his so-called golden years. And retirement had taken away his reason to be sober for at least part of the day.

"I'm going to bed." It was after midnight. She started to walk toward the staircase when Randall grabbed her upper arm, preventing her from leaving the room.

"No, you're gonna stay and finish this!"

"Finish what? We're done! I'm not even sure why you're mad!"

"Like that's a surprise! You don't understand much, do ya?" His breath was disgusting – new alcohol layered on top of the sickly sweet underlying smell of the booze from earlier in the day. She hated it, hated him, when he put his face up to hers. Genevieve turned away but she didn't try to wiggle loose of his grip. She knew better.

"I think we should call the girls right now," he hissed into her ear, "and ask them why they don't come around. Maybe then you'll get it through that thick skull of yours!"

Genevieve put her free hand between his hot breath and her ear. Randall slapped her across the mouth.

"You better not hit me again!" Randall released her arm and shoved her backward in one motion.

"I didn't hit you!" Genevieve touched her swelling lip and pulled her hand back to see the blood on her fingers. She ran up the stairs and locked herself into the bathroom.

She looked into the mirror and saw the image of a very tired, emotionally bruised old woman. She didn't know if she could take much more.

# CHAPTER 2
## RAINE TO THE RESCUE

Raine thought about everything except the paper in front of her. She hated her job, but without a college degree her chances of finding anything better were slim. She'd contemplated going back to school but decided it would be too much work. The money was good, so she stayed even though she was bored off her ass. At the age of twenty-five, Raine was stuck in a rut that most people waited until their forties to find.

Stifling a yawn, she scanned the document on her desk for mistakes. Proofreading insurance policies was one of Raine's duties as a customer service representative for Seth, Jones, and Pringle Insurance. The office was trapped in a windowless suite on the twentieth floor of a dreary building, which was located smack-dab in the middle of downtown San Antonio. To make matters worse, the old air conditioner did nothing to keep up with the oppressive August heat. Little beads of sweat trickled down her back under her camisole.

Her boss poked his oily head into her gray cubicle and barked, "Aren't you done yet?"

Raine jumped, nearly biting her tongue. Keeping her tone polite, she repressed a surge of adrenaline fueled anger, triggered by the scare. "Almost, Mr. Kendall."

Putting up with her boss's bullshit was another requirement of her position, although this wasn't included in her job description. Raine had been with the agency for four years and had worked closely, much too close for her liking, with Mr. Kendall for three of them.

Mr. Kendall was short, fat, and practiced questionable hygiene. Top producing sales agent for six years running, the agency partners forgave him for his less than appealing appearance. Raine often wondered how Mr.

Kendall managed to attract so many clients when he seemed to repel nearly everyone else.

"He's such an ass," Raine grumbled to herself. She tucked her pale blonde hair behind her ears and continued to check the rest of the policy. She stopped for a moment to rub her strained eyes. The outdated florescent lights were placed too far apart, but the cheap agency heads refused to add more fixtures. She took a deep breath and refocused on the file.

Once she was satisfied that the policy was correct, she slipped it into the fancy agency folder which would be delivered to the client. Hoping not to catch his attention, Raine sneaked into Mr. Kendall's office and put the folder on his massive desk.

"Raine!" Mr. Kendall bellowed before she could escape.

She took a deep breath and rearranged her expression before turning around to see what Mr. Kendall wanted. She'd learned to control outward signs of her irritation. If her boss sensed that she was annoyed, he became even more demanding than usual.

"Yes Mr. Kendall?" Raine glued a plastic smile onto her face and imagined the old guy in full makeup. Picturing her boss in drag was a handy little technique Raine used to distract herself from the overwhelming urge to smash his face in. She couldn't help but grin at the thought of false eyelashes and heavy eye shadow underneath Mr. Kendall's bristly eyebrows. It was even more amusing to imagine bright red lipstick on his crinkled old lips.

"Finish up the McAllen audit, and call it a day," Mr. Kendall didn't bother to look up from the newspaper that he held in his meaty paws.

"Sure thing Mr. Kendall." Under her breath, she added, "You pompous old troll." The rest of the office staff had been gone for over an hour now. Staying late was normal for Raine. Part of the job, she told herself. She finished up the audit and left it sitting in the out box on her desk.

Twenty minutes later, Raine opened her apartment door to a very friendly and hungry cat. Jinx welcomed her home by wrapping himself around her legs, almost tripping her in the process. At least someone is happy to see me, she thought.

Raine didn't mind living alone, despite the occasional boredom. She was ten years younger than one of her sisters and fifteen years younger than the oldest of the bunch. She might as well have been an only kid for most of her childhood.

Her phone beeped with a text from her friend, Noelle. "Ready to go? I'm on my way."

Raine grimaced. Noelle had pestered Raine until she agreed to a girls' night out. Partying wasn't exactly Raine's favorite thing to do. She felt out of place in the clubs. Sometimes she lessened her uneasiness by imagining that she was a famous actress, out on the town, surrounded by her admirers.

"Be ready by the time you get here," Raine texted back.

After taking a few moments to touch up her neutral make-up and brush her shoulder length hair, Raine was ready to go.

Noelle arrived decked out in a shimmering off-the-shoulder silver mini dress. She gave Raine the once over and twisted her pretty features into an exaggerated expression of disgust. She unbuttoned the top two buttons on Raine's blouse. "Find a shorter skirt."

"Really? I'm not trying to impress anyone, Noelle. I'm only going to keep you out of trouble!" She'd known that Noelle would have something to say about her appearance. Noelle fancied herself to be a fashionista.

"No protesting, Raine! You look like an old lady!" Noelle interrupted Raine's words of objection before she could even get them out of her mouth.

"All right, if it'll get you to stop pestering me!" Raine gave Noelle a fake pout as she obediently went to her bedroom to change. Glancing at her reflection in the full-length mirror, Raine admitted to herself that Noelle was right. *I look like I'm going to church.*

Raine found a mid-thigh length black skirt way in the back of her tidy closet. The skirt still had the price tag attached to the waist because Raine hadn't found the courage to wear it. In fact, she couldn't remember buying it. She tore the tag off with her teeth and slipped out of her dowdy skirt. Raine carefully pulled the shorter skirt up over her long, slender legs. For Noelle's benefit, she strutted like a supermodel out to the living room and did a little twirl.

"Now that's what I'm talking about! Much better!" Noelle gave her stamp of approval and they left for the club.

A ringing sound startled Raine out of a restless sleep. The gnawing throb behind her left eye reminded Raine that she had knocked back way too many shots of tequila the night before. Swimming around in Raine's head were foggy memories of a struggle to put her house key into the lock. She hoped that Noelle made it home safely. Noelle hadn't been much better off than she was when they parted ways last night.

The ringing continued and Raine realized it was her cell phone. She switched on the bedside lamp and looked at the digital alarm clock, which read 4:00 am. She prayed she hadn't given her number to any guys. Sometimes, to cope with her crippling shyness, she would imagine herself to be a famous movie star named Serenity. Unfortunately, she had given her phone number out (on more than one occasion) while pretending to be Serenity but didn't remember doing so.

"Raine, I'm so sorry to bother you honey! Were you sleeping?" Mother spoke in a whisper.

"Yeah, it's okay. What's wrong?" Mother only called in the middle of the night for one reason.

"I wondered if you could come get me." She added, "If it isn't too much trouble for you."

The sound of her mother's tear-thickened voice twisted Raine's stomach up into knots. This phone call meant that Daddy was drinking again. She wasn't surprised because her father had yet to stay sober for more than six months at a time.

"What'd he do to you?" Raine wasn't sure why she bothered to ask. Mother had a tendency to downplay Daddy's bad deeds. She'd tried to understand why her mother stayed. Sometimes, Raine couldn't decide which one she hated more - her father for treating her mother like shit, or her mother for putting up with it.

Raine was ten years old before she realized that not all fathers drank every night. She'd gone to a sleepover and was shocked that the girl's dad didn't drink himself into a stupor. Raine hung out with her classmate as much as possible over the following two years. She felt like a different kid at her friend's house. She felt normal.

The girl's dad was eventually relocated for work, and Raine's refuge went with them. She fantasized that the family would come back for her and beg her to move away with them. For the first two weeks after they moved, Raine's heart leapt with hope every time the doorbell rang. For a small moment, Raine would imagine that it was her rightful family coming to save her from her sad, gray life. Eventually, Raine settled into the understanding that she wasn't going to be saved by anyone. She tried to escape by reading novels and sketching imaginary worlds.

"Raine, please come get me!" Mother's hushed voice interrupted Raine's thoughts. "I don't think I can do this anymore."

"I'll be there in thirty minutes" Raine reassured Mother as if she were speaking to a frightened child.

Raine threw on her old gray sweats and sneakers in a hurry. She cupped her hand around her nose and mouth, and huffed out. Her own breath almost knocked her over. I'd better chew a piece of gum, she thought, for Mother's sake if nothing else.

Still off-balance from the alcohol, Raine jammed her thigh into the sharp corner of her dresser as she scurried out of her bedroom. She rubbed her wounded leg while she searched for her misplaced purse. Finally, she found the black leather purse upside down between the sofa and the wall with its contents dumped out. Cursing, she shoved her wallet and cosmetics back into the handbag as fast as she could. Raine locked up her apartment with shaking hands and went to rescue her mother.

# CHAPTER 3
## IN THE BEGINNING

Genevieve placed the phone on the receiver and tiptoed from the kitchen to the small bathroom. As she washed her bruised face, blood mixed with the running water to make little swirled patterns in the blue porcelain sink. The cut on her lip was deeper than she'd initially thought, and the small amount of movement caused it to break open again. She patted her face gently with a towel and proceeded to smooth her gray hair into a simple bun.

Out of habit she wiped the counter and sink down with the hand towel. Randall never cleaned, but he was the first to complain if anything was out of order.

She grabbed her worn purse and sensible brown shoes and hid them in a dark corner by the back door. If Randall knew she was trying to leave the house, he would stop her, and it wouldn't be pleasant. Better to let him think she'd gone to bed.

Heart pounding and hands shaking, she tried to pull her thoughts together. After turning in circles for a few moments, she went up to her closet to pack a few changes of clothing. She couldn't decide what to gather up to take with her to Raine's house. She wasn't sure how long she'd be gone. Maybe forever.

She fit as many pieces of clothing as possible in her little suitcase and did a quick scan of the small room that she had shared with Randall for over forty years. It was strange, she thought, that the bed held the only decent memories she had with Randall.

She looked at her wristwatch and guessed that she still had about five minutes before Raine arrived. A quick glance into the den confirmed that Randall was still sitting in his chair, motionlessly facing the television. She felt a sad sort of tenderness looking at the back of Randall's balding head. And for a moment, she was deeply sorry for her husband.

Genevieve had thought that by this time in their lives, the kinks would've been worked out between them. But happiness didn't seem to be in the cards for them. She'd never been able to please Randall. No matter how hard Genevieve tried, there was always something she forgot to do. Or something that she didn't handle to his liking.

Although it was forty years ago, she remembered the first time Randall hurt her like it happened yesterday.

## June, 1971

Genevieve stood in front of the kitchen sink, anxiously watching out the window. She hoped to see that familiar dust cloud from Randall's car speeding up the long dirt drive. They'd been married for six months, and Randall had never been late before.

Genevieve had made certain that dinner was ready on the table every night by six o'clock sharp. On this particular day, she'd already put dinner back into the oven because Randall was over an hour late. She chewed the inside of her bottom lip while wavering back and forth between fear that he'd been in an accident and suspicion that he was doing something he shouldn't be.

Horrible thoughts crept into her head. Over and over again, Genevieve tortured herself with the images of Randall and some faceless, slender woman wrapped in each other's arms.

She didn't want to believe that Randall would do such a thing, but with each vanishing minute her suspicion seemed more likely. After all, Genevieve's own daddy had cheated on her mother.

Genny was starting to think that her growing belly might be a turn off to Randall. He didn't make love to her as often since she'd begun to show. Genevieve had felt only slightly reassured by an article she'd read in the doctor's office, which explained that some expectant fathers are afraid of harming their unborn child during lovemaking.

Genevieve had conceived almost immediately after their wedding. Now that she was six months along in the pregnancy there weren't very many lovemaking positions that were comfortable, let alone possible.

To take her mind off the panic that she was feeling, she picked up her knitting. Several mistakes later, Genevieve tossed the unfinished baby blanket into the basket beside her. It was no use; she couldn't rip her thoughts away from Randall. The sky had taken on a dusky hue and still there was no sign of him.

The closest neighbor was over a mile away. Genevieve knew that if she didn't begin the lengthy walk to the neighbor's house to use their phone, she would be resigned to a long night of fretting. She pulled her thick, shoulder length hair up into a ponytail and put on her sensible shoes. She left a note on the kitchen table for Randall, in case he came home while she was gone.

Her shoes made a nice crunchy sound on the gravel road. The evening air had started to cool, and the gentle breeze was refreshing. The setting sun brushed brilliant shades of purple and orange all over the horizon, reminding her of the previous summer's walks with Randall. She missed those walks. Randall had been so in to her. Now, he ignored her half of the time. She hoped Randall was okay, hoped that he'd only had a flat tire or ran out of gas. *Maybe he's walking home right now.*

Genevieve was relieved to see Mr. Ashland in his rocking chair on the front porch. She hadn't thought about what she would have done if the Ashlands weren't home. She supposed she would have sat and waited a while.

"Hello little lady! What brings you here this evening?" Mr. Ashland's kind eyes crinkled into a smile. The pleasant aroma of cherry tobacco from the old man's pipe wafted down the porch steps.

Genevieve thought that Mr. Ashland looked like Santa Claus. She didn't visit the kind-hearted Ashlands as much as she should. I'll have to come back for a proper visit, Genevieve thought.

"Oh Mr. Ashland! I'm terribly worried about Randall! He hasn't made it home yet tonight. He's never late!" She walked up the steps onto the shaded wrap-around porch and rested her hand on the white painted railing.

"I wondered if I could use your phone to try to reach him at the office."

Mr. Ashland stood up and waved her toward the door. "Of course, of course! Come on in. Mrs. Ashland is right inside."

Mr. Ashland ushered her toward the kitchen where the telephone was located. Mrs. Ashland sat at the breakfast table with piles of flowery fabric and pattern pieces spread all around her. She looked up from her sewing machine with a puzzled look on her plump, pink face. Mr. Ashland explained the nature of Genevieve's visit.

"Oh dear!" Mrs. Ashland warbled, "I do hope Randall is alright!" She abandoned her sewing project and stood by the phone as Genevieve dialed Randall's office.

Randall's office number rang and rang. Of course, no one answered; it was hours after closing time. Genevieve's throat tightened. "What do I do?" She sighed and massaged her own temples. All this worrying was giving Genevieve one hell of a headache.

"Poor darlin'! Why don't you try callin' the hospital to be sure there hasn't been an accident?" Mrs. Ashland looked genuinely concerned.

Several phone calls later; one to the hospital, one to the police department, and one to Randall's buddy George's house, Genevieve felt worse than when she started. No one had seen or heard from Randall.

Genevieve accepted Mr. Ashland's kind offer of a ride home. The sky had grown completely dark. There was no sign of Randall at home so she waited up on the sofa, not knowing what else to do.

# CHAPTER 4
## STAND BY YOUR MAN

"I'll keep an eye out for 'em, Mrs. Carter." Sergeant Williams reassured her in his gritty old voice. He hung up the phone and turned to the station dispatcher.

"Poor kid," Sergeant Williams said. He puffed on his cigar and shook his head with sympathy. "Her husband is probably out getting plastered, and she's home alone worried. And expectin' a baby, to boot."

"Is that the Carter boy you're talkin' about?" the dispatcher asked.

"You betcha! Takes after his old man, I reckon." Sergeant Williams put out his cigar and took his time getting up from his chair. His knees didn't work as well as they used to. For that matter, neither did the rest of his body.

"Guess I'll head on over to the bar to see if that boy is there."

"Better you than me. Enjoy yourself." The dispatcher had a reputation for going out of his way to do as little as possible. He'd been with the force even longer than Sergeant Williams so no one in the station complained.

*Damned drunks.* Sergeant Williams had been tracking down drunks for far too many years in his book. He'd be a rich man if he had a dollar for every inebriated fool he'd hunted down over the last forty years.

There were only two drinking establishments in town. One was the VFW and the other was aptly named The Watering Hole. Sergeant Williams ruled out the VFW and drove over to the Watering Hole. Sure enough, Carter's orange Chevrolet was in the parking lot. Sergeant Williams parked his cruiser out back and lumbered up to the tavern door.

Barely lit by a few neon signs, the inside of the bar seemed darker than the night outside. A lone couple swayed on the dance floor to Tammy Wynette's "Stand by Your Man" playing on the jukebox. A few of the regular patrons sat on their usual seats at the bar.

"Hey Sergeant!" The bartender waved hello. The town of Boerne was small enough that everyone knew everyone else. "What can I do ya' for?"

Tipping his hat and nodding his head, Sergeant Williams said, "I'm here on business, Mac."

Sergeant Williams scanned the dim, smoky room looking for the Carter boy. Unsure of what he was seeing, the officer walked toward the booth farthest in the back. As he got closer he could make out two bodies twined together, lips locked and all.

Ugh, he thought with disgust. This was one of the many things he hated about looking for missing persons. He often found them doing things they shouldn't be. And most of the time, they weren't particularly happy to be found.

"Can I speak with you son?" Sergeant Williams tapped on Randall Carter's shoulder. Startled, Carter turned around and stood up abruptly.

"Whoa, easy there, fellow! No big deal, we'll just have a little talk over here." Sergeant Williams led Carter over to the entryway to the restrooms.

"What's this about Sergeant?" Carter slurred, wobbling a little.

Sergeant Williams lowered his voice, casting his eyes over to the made-up blonde at Carter's table. "Your sweet little wife is lookin' for you, son. She's worried something awful. I think you oughta head home now."

Red-faced, Carter clenched his jaw. He sat back down at the booth and whispered in the girl's ear. She smiled and nodded in response. Chomping on a wad of gum, bright red lips open; the girl made an obnoxious "look at me" kind of giggle as they walked arm-in-arm up to the bar. Carter pulled out some crumpled-up bills to pay his tab. He cast a dirty, backwards glance at the Sergeant as he walked out into the warm night air.

# CHAPTER 5
## IT'S ALWAYS 20/20

Even though she hadn't thought it possible, Genevieve dozed off. The sound of the back-door knob startled her awake. She waited a moment for the grogginess to pass and went to meet Randall in the kitchen. The clock over the breakfast table indicated it was three thirty in the morning.

"Thank God you're here! Where have you been?" Frantic words spilled out of her mouth.

Looking Randall over carefully, she could see that he was disheveled but there were no signs of an accident. She reached out to embrace her husband, and the familiar stench of liquor assaulted her nose. The odor brought back painful memories of Daddy's disgusting breath, too close to her face. Genevieve leaned back to look into Randall's eyes. "How could you? You know how I feel about liquor!" she cried out.

He reacted as if she'd slapped him with her words and shoved Genevieve away with all his might. She couldn't regain her footing quickly enough and fell backward into the corner of the sturdy oak kitchen table with a thump.

Stunned, Genevieve sat still for a moment, trying to make sense of what had happened. She took Randall's outstretched hand, thinking that he was going to help her up. A flood of disbelief washed over her as Randall swung a balled-up fist down onto her head with his other arm.

Unsure of where she was at first, she slowly regained consciousness. Genevieve looked up at the underside of the table and realized she was lying on the cold linoleum floor. She gingerly touched the back of her head and felt the bump that seemed to be the source of excruciating pain.

Next, she caressed her belly. Fear gripped her heart when she didn't feel movement from the baby right away. As if to reassure her, the baby gave

Genevieve a little kick. Tears of relief stung her eyes. Calibrating her ears to the stillness around her, Genevieve listened for signs of Randall. The silent house did not betray his whereabouts.

Cautiously, she stood up, testing her weight to be sure nothing was broken. Once assured her limbs were in working order, she tip-toed toward the living room. Only the yellow glow of the porch light illuminated the front room. As she made her way to the staircase, she heard the couch springs creak. Randall's stretched out silhouette on the sofa was barely visible in the dim light. She paused for a moment and held her breath. Thinking him to be asleep, she continued to the first stair step.

"Think you're pretty clever, don't ya'!" Randall's voice cut through the darkness, sending a jolt of fear through her body.

Turning her back to the flight of stairs, Genevieve sized up the situation before her. Randall made no move to get up.

"Made me look like a fool, you bitch! Think it's funny to send the police after me?" Randall's words were low and venomous.

"No, no, no! I swear I don't think it's funny! I was scared you'd gotten into a wreck or something!" Almost unable to talk through the lump swelling up in her throat, she pleaded with him.

"Save your lies for someone else, you sniffling, whining bitch!" Randall screamed in a voice she'd never heard before. "Get the fuck out of my sight!"

Genevieve nearly ran up the flight of stairs. She locked herself in the room that they were planning to use for the nursery. Randall had helped paint the walls in pale yellow, and she'd sewn curtains to match. The crib stood unassembled in the corner, waiting for Randall to put it together. The floor would've been too hard to sleep on with her pregnant body, so she positioned herself in the rocking chair that Randall's mother had given to them.

Although she desperately needed rest, Genevieve wasn't able to sleep. She knew she couldn't go to her mother. Grandma would be her only assured place of refuge but her grandmother's home was at least twenty miles away. On foot, that distance would've been impossible for Genevieve to manage at that stage of her pregnancy.

Sneaking out while Randall was still sleeping would be her safest plan of action, Genevieve figured. But what if he awoke while she was trying to leave? She concocted every possible scenario that she could formulate in her mind. In the end, she hoped and prayed he would leave for work like normal. Having Randall out of the house would give her time to pack a few things, take a little bit of money out of the spare change jar, and walk to the Ashland's house to call Grandma.

The night dragged on painfully slow. Finally, morning light began to peek through the bright yellow curtains. Normally, Randall would be showering and having his first cup of coffee at that time. The house was lifeless.

She needed to use the bathroom so badly that she thought her pregnant bladder was going to explode. She quietly opened the nursery and looked up and down the hallway in both directions. Their bedroom door was shut. Thankful for a clear path, Genevieve quickly tiptoed to the bathroom.

While washing her hands after relieving herself, Genevieve looked in the vanity mirror. A swollen, tear stained face peered back at her. *At least my face isn't bruised.*

Leaning her mouth under the faucet, she swallowed big gulps of tap water. After taking a deep breath to calm herself, she opened the bathroom door to discover Randall standing right in front of her. Arms crossed and head cocked to one side, Randall looked at her with an expression of concern. "Did you get up early?" he asked.

"No, I've been in the nursery all night," she replied, shaking her head. Genevieve felt like she might faint.

"Why? What's wrong?" He appeared sincere.

"Randall, don't you remember last night?" Genevieve asked timidly.

Randall rubbed his chin, a gesture he made when pondering something. "No, Genny, I can't say that I do."

In between big gulping sobs, Genevieve told Randall what he had done. Randall wrapped his arms around her and held her gently. He whispered soft promises and words of sorrow. At that moment, Genevieve chose to believe it would never happen again.

The rest of their first summer as a married couple was good for Genevieve. She busied herself tending to the vegetable garden and keeping house, finding pleasure in the simplest of tasks.

And Randall kept his promises to Genevieve that summer. He never touched her in an unkind way and came home to her every night. Genevieve's fears of Randall gradually melted away. The beating started to seem like a bad dream.

After making love, she would lie awake for hours watching her husband's sleeping face illuminated by the white gold glow of the moon. Genevieve had never felt more complete than when lying next to Randall, his child moving softly inside of her, feeling the warmth of his seed running out of her.

Genevieve had her first orgasm that summer. No one had ever talked about orgasms to Genny but she'd been given a copy of "Human Sexual Response" by Masters and Johnson at her bridal shower as a prank. She laughed about the gift in front of everyone, but she devoured the book in private. Even though the book was written in a clinical way, reading it made Genny aroused.

While lying in bed together on the Fourth of July, watching fireworks off in the distance through the open windows, Randall began to lightly stroke Genevieve's ripening belly. His touch gave her delicious goose bumps. Tired from the day, she closed her eyes and gave in to the relaxing sensation of Randall's caresses. Randall slowly unbuttoned her white cotton nightgown, pausing in between buttons to kiss her bare skin.

Randall whispered, "Keep your eyes closed."

Currents of excitement moved through her spine. Randall's lovemaking usually had a sense of urgency. His deliberate restraint was a decided change from the norm.

A cool breeze from the open window rushed over Genevieve's body as Randall opened her nightgown completely. Her swollen nipples hardened in response to his hands lightly brushing the cotton nightgown off her skin. Randall gently nudged her thighs open with his legs. She expected to feel him enter her. Instead she felt his hot, wet mouth latch onto her nipple.

In response to his suckling, creamy wetness ran out of her. Her inner thighs ached with desire for him.

"I want you inside of me," she moaned.

Randall hushed her with his kisses. Then he began to make a trail from her breasts to her belly with his tongue. When he reached her lower abdomen, he began to separate her swollen nether-lips with his fingers. Randall groaned in appreciation of her tightened, engorged vagina as he penetrated her with his finger.

She moaned with pleasure as he moved his finger in and out of her. Exquisite sensations washed over her, making her light headed as Randall traced circles around her hardened clitoris with his tongue.

Pulling his finger out of her, he began to lap up her juices with his hungry mouth. Genevieve thought she would die with desire. She tried to pull him to her, begging him to enter her. He pushed her hands away and continued to suck and massage her clitoris with his tongue. She writhed in beautiful agony until she climaxed.

Never before had she felt something so perfect. Her womb tightened with her orgasm. Sweet waves of contractions carried her climax out as Randall thrust his erect cock inside of her.

Randall forcefully moved in and out of her, making her climax again and again. Randall looked like a god to her as he came. She could feel his semen mixed with her fluids pouring out of her as he finished. Genevieve knew she would always be bound to Randall by this moment in which she belonged to him completely.

## September 1971

Randall and Genevieve's first-born child arrived on a warm day in early September. She was hanging freshly washed laundry out to dry when she felt her first contraction. Twenty-four hours later, Genevieve and Randall were the proud parents of a beautiful baby girl. Genny marveled over her tiny little fingers and perfect rosebud lips. She thought that Lillian Grace looked just like a porcelain doll.

The first week after they brought Lillian home, they were overwhelmed with visitors. Well-meaning church ladies came in droves, armed with casseroles and advice.

"You should give her a little dark Karo syrup," said one busybody, "to keep her from getting constipated."

"Don't overfeed her," another cautioned. "You'll make her fat!"

"Don't pick her up too much – you'll spoil her!"

"You can't let her cry. She'll feel abandoned and grow to be an unhappy child."

All the conflicting advice had given Genny a continuous headache. She was relieved when the visits slowed down to a trickle. Now, I can get something done, she thought.

But it wasn't long before she started to miss all the visitors. At least when the church ladies were there, Lillian had someone to hold her all the time. Left alone, Genevieve realized that she was more than a little afraid of her own baby. She'd never cared for an infant before. The parenting books she read while expecting didn't reassure her that she was prepared for such an important job. Tiny Lillian cried very big tears. Her piercing wails made Genevieve feel helpless, and sleep deprivation left her feeling irritable and forgetful.

Randall grew impatient with Genevieve. As all seasons do, their summer of warmth and love had passed. Gone were the hot nights of lovemaking and days of carefree happiness. Genny was focused on the baby, and Randall started to come home after work later and later.

Genevieve cried almost as often as baby Lillian did. She was fat, tired and frustrated. Desperate for help, she eventually broke down and called her grandmother. "I don't know what to do with her!" Genny wailed over the phone line.

"What's the matter, love?" Grandma always had time for Genevieve.

"She cries all the time! I can't seem to make her happy! I really don't know what I'm doing wrong!"

"Are you changing her diaper often enough?" Grandma asked.

"Of course I am Grandma!" Genny knew that she must sound a little rude. "I change her diaper every two hours whether she needs it or not! I'm constantly feeding her! I hold her every time she cries! And she cries all the time! I don't know what I'm doing wrong with her! I'm so tired."

"Well, maybe you should stop nursing her and give her a bottle. You aren't very busty; maybe you're not making enough milk. You're probably starving her!"

Genevieve didn't argue with Grandma, but she knew she was making more than enough milk, little boobies or not. She thanked her grandmother and hung up feeling even more frustrated. She'd never felt more alone. She didn't know if she could muscle through the crying much longer.

The very next week, Genevieve found salvation at the doctor's office during Lillian's one-month checkup. Genevieve had been reduced to tears during the drive into town. The baby's shrieking cries from the back seat made driving almost impossible.

When they arrived at Doc Harding's office, Genevieve realized that Lillian had pooped through the waistband of her diaper, soiling her darling little pink dress. Of course, Genevieve had forgotten to pack a change of clothing for Lillian. She took the soiled clothing off and cleaned Lillian up the best she could in the backseat of the car. Walking quickly from the parking lot with her naked baby wrapped in a blanket, Genevieve literally ran into her savior.

"Oh God, I am so sorry!" Genevieve apologized to the ginger- haired young woman she had plowed into. She looked into sparkling hazel eyes that belonged to a young woman about Genevieve's age.

"Are you okay? Can I help with anything?"

"No, I'm fine," Genevieve sniffled, shaking her head. "I'm late already, and I can't seem to deal with anything lately without crying! I'm fine, really."

"It's just the baby blues, honey. You'll feel better in another month or so." She shifted her smiling toddler from her right hip to the left.

"This is Kimmy, and I'm Carol. Nice to meet you!" Carol stretched out her right hand.

Genevieve liked the feel of Carol's handshake. Not too firm, not too soft and definitely not clammy like her own. A calm feeling settled over Genevieve.

The two young ladies walked together into Doc Harding's office. Visiting in the waiting room with Carol, Genevieve couldn't shake the sensation that she'd known Carol for years.

"Did you grow up here?" Genevieve asked.

"No, Jim and I grew up near Tulsa. We moved here two years ago, to help out with his uncle's ranch. We like it just fine here but I sure do miss my momma." Carol gave little Kimmy a squeeze. Kimmy was sitting on Carol's lap, humming and looking through a picture book.

"How about you? Did you grow up here?"

"Close, in Kerrville." Genevieve bounced Lilly on her lap to calm her. She was overdue for a feeding but Genny wasn't comfortable nursing in public.

"What led you to San Antonio? Work?"

"No, Randall's family is from here. They had a farm about five miles outside of Boerne. When his daddy died, his momma moved into town and we moved in." Genevieve rocked Lillian side to side to keep her asleep.

"We don't farm it or anything; no one does anymore. His daddy gambled it all away except for the house and a few acres."

"Ah, that's a real shame to lose family land. Jim's family has owned the same ranch for almost a hundred years. His uncle is the only one that wants to keep it running. But everyone's glad it's still in the family."

"I think Randall got so sick of working on the farm when he was growing up that he's happy to be stuck in an office all day. Even the long drive into work doesn't seem to bother him. I'd like to have a milk cow and some chickens though. Maybe someday I'll convince him it's a good idea."

After Kimmy and Lillian's appointments, they stood in the parking lot and continued to visit for a few minutes. Looking at her wristwatch, Carol said "I've got to go, but we'll have to make a date for lunch soon!"

Genevieve looked forward to their weekly visits. She could talk to Carol about anything. Genevieve had never felt so at ease with another human being. Carol's friendship made everything seem better. Even the knowledge that Randall was drinking again didn't bother Genevieve that much.

# CHAPTER 6
## BETTER LATE THAN NEVER

### August 2011

A soft tap at the back door transported Genevieve out of her thoughts of the past. Raine's apprehensive face peered through the glass, tugging at Genevieve's heart. She was grateful and ashamed at the same time.

No child should have to rescue her mother, Genevieve thought. She supposed this moment was a small thing compared to the other atrocities her children were made to endure through the years.

Genevieve grabbed her small suitcase and slowly turned the doorknob, so as to make as little noise as possible. She held her breath as she stepped over the threshold, terrified that she would be yanked backward by Randall's iron grip. Daring not to look back, she kept her eyes anchored on her daughter's face until she pulled the door shut.

She didn't take a real breath until they were safely speeding along the interstate. Soft music on the radio blended with the hum of the tires on the highway to create a calming sound that Genevieve found soothing. Apparently not in the mood for music, Raine flipped the radio off after a few minutes.

Genevieve rolled down her window and let her thoughts disappear into the early morning air. For the first time in forty years, her future was wide open. In her secret fantasies, this moment of freedom was always imagined to be dramatic and confrontational. She'd even memorized what she would say to Randall.

It was Genevieve's plan to rip him apart with her words, to reduce him to a trembling mess of sorrow for all the pain he'd caused her through their years together. She had relished in the thought of Randall begging her for mercy, in the same way she'd begged him all those years. After letting Randall plead his case for a while, she would calmly inform him that it was too late. Then, she'd walk away without so much as a backward glance.

When Genevieve was a young woman, the fantasy had also included a prince charming type with whom she would fall madly in love. Prince Charming would also fall in love with her and her children. And they would live happily ever after in a picture-perfect little cottage surrounded by a white picket fence.

Genevieve's "Prince Charming" chapter of her fantasy dissolved along with the passing of her youth. She understood that Prince Charming didn't save gray haired old ladies. No matter, Genevieve thought, living alone will be far better than living in hell.

The morning sun was just beginning to light up the day as Raine pulled her car into the apartment parking lot. Immaculately kept lawns surrounded the newly constructed buildings, and brightly hued flower beds were strategically placed throughout the complex.

"This is really nice, Raine." Genevieve had never been to Raine's apartment. She wondered how much rent on an apartment as nice as this one was.

"Thank you, I'm glad you're finally able to see my place." Raine opened her car door before adding, "I was starting to think you'd never come to see me."

"Oh honey, I'm sorry. I really wanted to. I did. But Daddy worried if I was gone for very long. And he had the car most of the time."

Randall became agitated if Genevieve was gone longer than necessary. Necessary was defined as a weekly trip to the grocery store and scheduled doctor appointments. To keep the peace, she had skipped lunch invitations from her daughters, shopping trips to the local thrift store, and garage sales. She'd missed out on doing those things, but ultimately, causing Randall anxiety wasn't worth the joy of the moment.

Genevieve felt out of sorts when she walked into Raine's apartment. Raine had created a life that Genevieve had no place in. She took some time to examine the blind-darkened room. There wasn't much to give an indication of Raine's interests. Tastefully decorated with neutral colors, the sitting area strongly resembled a waiting room in an office. Genny hesitated to mess up the perfect vacuum lines etched into the carpet. She wondered if Raine had a cleaning lady. There wasn't a speck of dust or disorder in sight.

Touching a framed print on the wall, she half expected it to be screwed down for security purposes. A small photograph on the end table caught Genevieve's attention. It was an enlarged copy of a snapshot of the children, taken several weeks after Raine's birth. Fifteen-year-old Lillian held Raine, and ten-year-old Miranda gazed lovingly at her baby sister.

Genevieve remembered how the girls doted over Raine. It was as if they were trying to do everything in their power to make up for Randall's disappointment in the birth of yet another daughter. Randall had wanted a boy so much that he had suggested they have a third child. The day that Raine was born would always be a bittersweet memory for Genevieve.

"It's another beautiful baby girl! Congratulations Mr. and Mrs. Carter!" Doc Harding held Raine up for both to see.

"She's gorgeous. Praise the Lord!" Genevieve choked up. It was an incredible relief to see that her newborn was healthy. She turned to Randall and her smile quickly faded. Randall looked angry.

"I reckon we've got enough girls already. I was hoping we'd have one with outdoor plumbing this time."

Doc Harding gave a nervous laugh, and said "Oh come now Mr. Carter, you can't ever have too many girls!" Randall didn't bother with a reply.

He disappeared for hours after Raine's birth. Genevieve never once asked where he'd gone. She'd learned to not ask questions. It was better to let Randall reveal what he wanted on his own time. More often than not, he didn't disclose anything.

Gently tracing with her finger around the edges of the brushed nickel frame, Genevieve's gaze settled back on Miranda's angelic face. At ten years old, Randi still had a beautiful light in her big blue eyes. By the time Randi had turned twelve, the light was all but gone.

Genevieve had chalked it up to normal teenaged girl behavior. She told herself that it was just a phase Randi was going through. Genevieve had even speculated that her temperament had something to do with being a middle child. She'd read about birth order and middle child syndrome. That seemed as likely an explanation as any other did. And it felt good to have some sort of reason that her sweet girl had transformed into a sullen young lady.

Rather than grow out of it, Randi became more distant and angry. By the time Randi entered high school, Genevieve could hardly stand to be near her.

Randall, however, had taken an interest in Randi. He coached her softball team and took extra time to help her with her game. They practiced for hours on her form and took lots of walks together. Randall's attentive involvement in Randi's life made it easy for Genevieve to detach from her daughter.

Genevieve was ashamed by the little stabs of jealousy she'd felt when Randall paid attention to Randi instead of her. No matter how hard she'd tried to squash her petty thoughts, she couldn't shake them.

Now, at the age of thirty-five, Randi wasn't on speaking terms with either of her parents. She hadn't contacted them in almost ten years. Genevieve couldn't think of anything that would have caused the estrangement. It had been so long since she'd seen Randi, Genevieve wasn't sure she would be able recognize her daughter in a crowd. "Have you heard from Miranda?" Genevieve asked Raine.

"No, not lately." Raine gave her typical answer. Lillian and Raine offered nothing when asked about Randi.

# CHAPTER 7
## RANDI

Randi took the last drag off her cigarette and smashed it out in the bedside table ashtray. Standing up into a stretch, she caught sight of herself in the smoke-stained dresser mirror.

*Not bad for thirty-five.* Sucking in, she inspected her flat tummy. Turning slightly, Randi pulled her shoulders back and stuck her chest out. Doing so made her breasts almost look like they belonged on a twenty-five-year-old.

The sleeping figure behind Randi's reflection startled her. She'd forgotten she wasn't alone in bed. Looking at him in the morning light, Randi felt as if she'd never seen the man before. Strange how people look so different in the bar light, Randi thought. She decided he wasn't a bad looking guy, as she examined his thick dark hair and muscular broad shoulders.

Randi shook the edge of the mattress with her bare foot. "Time to go man!" She no longer bothered with the niceties of the morning after. Pretending to be anything other than a piece of ass was pointless. The type of men she hooked up with weren't interested in breakfast, getting her phone number, or knowing her last name.

Randi lit another cigarette while she watched him dress. "Wham, bam, thank you Ma'am," Randi said under her breath as he was leaving.

Moving dirty laundry out of the way with her feet as she walked, Randi made her way to the kitchen to start some coffee. Flies were feasting on three days' worth of unwashed dishes piled up all over the stained countertop. *Must have a hole in the screen door again.* She moved dirty dishes out of one side of the sink and began to fill her coffee pot with cold tap water.

The ritual of drinking coffee made her feel that she was starting her day with a purpose. For a few moments of each morning Randi felt like she might actually accomplish something. Her sense of determination went downhill from there on most days.

Randi had been searching for a way to make her mark for years now. She'd tried every get-rich-quick scheme that came across her path. She'd even started to write a novel but couldn't seem to finish it. Nothing had panned out so far. Probably never would, Randi suspected. She was starting to accept that her life would never be spectacular.

She checked her cell phone and saw that Raine had called earlier in the morning. Curious, Randi listened to her voicemail. Raine didn't call Randi very often. Whenever they did speak, Raine's distaste for Randi was palpable. Randi didn't give a damn what anyone else thought of her, but Raine's disapproval hurt. Raine had been her little baby doll when they were kids.

"Randi, its Raine. I don't know if you care or not, but I wanted to let you know that Mother left Daddy. She's staying with me if you want to see her. Call me."

Unexpected tears welled up in Randi's eyes. Randi had figured she'd never see her mother again. It was hard to believe that her mother had left her father.

Hands shaking, Randi poured a cup of coffee. She pulled a folding chair up to the worn out old table, sat down and lit another cigarette. She thought about the last time she'd spoken to Momma. Friends from group therapy had convinced her to talk to Momma about Daddy. "Randi, you have to tell your mother! It's the only way to move on with your life. Do it for your inner child."

Randi had bought into all their psychobabble crap and made the call. She could still hear herself stutter, "Hey Momma, are you busy right now? Is Daddy home?" Randi had picked a time to phone Momma when she thought her father would be at work.

"No honey, what is it? Do you want me to have him call you back?"

"No, I wanted to talk to you." Randi was so scared that she felt like the air was being squeezed out of her lungs. Her voice sounded raspy and hollow.

"Momma, I need to tell you about something that happened with Daddy when I was a kid."

Randi misunderstood her mother's silence to be encouragement to continue speaking. "Do you remember how Daddy spent so much time with me? I need to talk to you about that."

"Randi," Her mother interrupted her, "whatever your relationship was with your father really isn't my business. You're a big girl now and you don't owe me any explanations."

She was unprepared for her mother's dismissive words. Every ounce of bravery drained from Randi's body. Ears ringing and throat dry, she made polite small talk, said her good-byes and hung the phone up.

Randi swore to herself that she'd never tell anyone again. She stopped going to group therapy. The others in the group were witnesses to her secrets. To continue going to group would mean that she couldn't pretend it didn't happen.

Sometimes, Randi wondered if she had imagined the whole thing. After she moved out of the house, Daddy had treated her politely, as if she were a stranger. He didn't seem especially interested in her or her life any longer.

Randi was around eleven years old when Daddy started to spend extra time with her. Their private walks together had become a daily routine. She remembered feeling very important to her dad during that time. Daddy never asked Lilly or Mom to go on walks with him.

Randi had liked that Daddy cared enough about her to ask her how she felt about things. She could tell Daddy things that she couldn't tell Momma. Daddy told her things too. She and Daddy had a very special relationship.

Looking back, Randi wondered why her mother didn't question her about those private walks.

# CHAPTER 8
## LILLIAN

Lillian scrubbed the stainless-steel sink with a vengeance. They were already cutting it close this morning, and she knew that she should skip the breakfast cleanup. But coming home to the mess would irritate her. Six-year-old Caleb came barreling through the kitchen, nearly knocking a plant over in the process.

He was the reason that she'd packed up all her gorgeous Nampeyo pottery. During one of his sprints through the house, he'd toppled an entire table and destroyed a piece of pottery worth at least one month of Gabe's salary. When she was in a mood to feel sorry for herself, she looked through old photographs to remember how beautiful their Hacienda-style home had been before the children were born.

"Caleb! Goddammit! Slow down!" Irritation burned between Lilly's eyes. Laney began to cry from her playpen. Lilly had forgotten the baby was asleep for a moment. Letting out a huge sigh of frustration, Lilly slammed the sponge into the sink. Glancing at the microwave clock, Lilly realized they should have left ten minutes before. She grabbed Laney out of the playpen and yelled for Caleb.

"Come on Caleb! We're late!"

"Okay Momma!" With his backpack dragging behind him, Caleb ran to the car. Going full speed was Caleb's specialty.

Twenty minutes later, with Caleb safely delivered to kindergarten, Lilly was on her way back home. A quick glance in the rearview mirror told her that Laney was sleeping again. The vibration of the car and warm sun on her face always did the trick. She could feel some of the tension draining out of her neck and shoulders.

Good, maybe I can get something done for once, Lilly thought. There

27

was never enough time in a day, she marveled, and yet the days were always too long. She carried the car seat, intact with a still sleeping Laney in it, into the kitchen and carefully sat it in the playpen.

She turned on the radio to an alternative rock station that she'd recently discovered. Gabe hated the new stuff, but Lilly thought that listening to new music kept her in touch and made her younger somehow. It was really starting to bug her that the mothers of some of Caleb's classmates were born the same year that she got her driver's license. She caught herself looking in the mirror more often than usual, checking for signs of wrinkles.

One of her new favorites, a song by Foster the People, was playing, so she turned it up and started cleaning out the refrigerator. She was just getting into a good groove when the phone rang. She almost didn't answer it but saw that it was Raine.

"Hang on," She turned the music down. "Hey sis, what's up?"

"Mother left Daddy." Raine's voice was almost monotone.

"Are you serious?" Raine wasn't the joking type, but Lilly couldn't conceive of Mother leaving Daddy. She had always figured Mother and Daddy would be together until one of them bit the dust.

"Yeah, she's here with me. I picked her up early this morning."

"Is Daddy furious?" Lilly also couldn't imagine Daddy remaining calm. When she was growing up, there was always hell to pay if things didn't go Daddy's way.

Raine sighed, "Don't know yet. He's probably still hung over. Is there any way you can come over today? I think she needs our help."

After hanging up, Lilly argued with herself about whether or not to go to Raine's house. She had a long to-do list, but she felt obligated to be with Raine and Mother, at least until they knew how Daddy was going to react.

She took her secret stash of Camels from the canister labeled "Tea", walked out to the patio, and lit a cigarette. Lilly ignored Laney's indignant shrieks as she sucked down the whole cigarette. Smoking was a guilty pleasure for Lilly. No one knew that she smoked except for a few acquaintances from her part time job. The taste was disgusting and she hated the way her hair smelled afterward, but she loved the way smoking made her feel, rebellious and defiant. And because she only smoked once in a while, she didn't consider herself to be a smoker.

She stamped out her cigarette and hid the butt behind a rose bush. Inside, Lilly tried to erase the traces of her secret habit by scrubbing her smoky hands in the kitchen sink and popping a piece of spearmint gum into her mouth. She finished off the cover up job by misting a cloud of vanilla body spray over her head. Lilly poured the last of the coffee into her travel mug and decided she'd be selfish if she didn't go to see her mother.

# CHAPTER 9
## DADDY'S GIRL

Time followed no rules after Randi listened to Raine's voicemail. She sat on her kitchen floor, criss cross applesauce in her pajamas, for what might have been several hours. Three different times she dialed Raine's number but hung up before the calls went through. Randi wasn't ready to talk to Momma yet.

Even though the topic of the day was Momma, Daddy bullied his way into her thoughts. One particular memory continued to force its way to the surface. For some reason, it was the memory that always made her feel the guiltiest.

It was summertime, and Randi was somewhere between eleven or twelve years old. She and Daddy had reached the end of one of their walks, and Randi was getting worried. "It's probably time for dinner," she thought aloud "Momma is gonna be wondering where we are".

Daddy laughed at her, "We can't go home with poison ivy all over us, can we now?" He tousled Randi's hair and pointed to the pond behind the barn.

Confusion set in. Randi didn't realize they'd walked through poison ivy. She'd gotten into poison ivy before and certainly didn't want it again. Obediently she walked with Daddy behind the barn. Kneeling at the edge of the pond, Randi began to rinse her hands and face in the water.

"No, Randi" Daddy instructed, "You need to get in all the way".

A little embarrassed, Randi slipped her sneakers and socks off first. Daddy made the motion with his hand for her to continue. Randi turned and shimmied out of the rest of her clothes and made a beeline for the pond, submerging herself up to her ears in the murky, chilly water. Moments later Daddy was in the water behind her.

Daddy's hand on Randi's back startled her at first. He began to make rubbing motions up and down her back. Each time his hand would reach her waist, he would rub a little lower. He held her steady with his left arm as he washed her bottom. His breathing became more uneven as he rubbed inside of her private parts.

Momma had told Randi to never let strangers touch her there. Daddy wasn't a stranger. Even though Randi felt uncomfortable, the touching felt nice. Her tummy and thighs got a funny tingly feeling that Randi liked very much.

After Daddy was done washing her, they got out and dried off. Daddy never told Randi to not tell anyone. Randi just knew that she shouldn't.

# CHAPTER 10
# A PLAN

"What should I do with my things?" Mother asked after Raine hung up the phone. She looks pitiful, Raine thought. Mother sat on the sofa with her hands folded together in her lap. Sitting on the floor next to her feet, Mother's small suitcase looked as worn and tattered as she did.

"You can put them in the office. It'll be your room while you're here." Raine's old daybed was in the office. She'd slept on it up until a few months ago, when she'd decided it was time for a grown-up bed. It wasn't very comfortable but it would be better than the sofa.

"Lilly's on her way. She has to drop the baby off at the sitter's," Raine added as her mother reached the office door.

Mother looked troubled. "I don't see any reason for her to rearrange her day. Both of you girls should keep your normal schedule. I'll be fine by myself."

"It's okay, I've already called work." The hangover was the main reason she'd called in but Mother didn't need to know that.

"Honestly Raine, it's not necessary. I can manage myself today."

"I don't think you should be alone right now. We'll help figure out what to do next." Raine was worried that her mother would cave in and call Daddy. Mother needed support right now. She'd never made this big of a stand against him.

Before Mother could argue some more, a knock interrupted the conversation. Lilly stood at the door with a big mug of coffee in her hand, hair and makeup perfectly in place, and a determined look in her eye. She first doled out perfunctory hugs and then pulled a long to-do list out of her leather bag.

"Okay, let's think about what we need to do first. I've got this so far;

hire an attorney, check on your bank accounts, find an apartment, transportation, think about what property you want in the divorce, health insurance, life insurance, and retirement assets. Can you think of anything else?"

"What about a women's crisis center for counseling?" Raine asked. Lilly, per usual, had thought of almost everything.

Nodding, Lilly agreed, "That's a good idea." She added Raine's suggestion to her list.

"Anything else you can think of, Mother?" Staring out the window, Mother didn't appear to be paying attention to the conversation.

"It's so much to think about at one time. I'd like to have a day or two to figure out what I want to do."

"There's no reason to wait to find an attorney. You'll want to have the upper hand in the divorce. If you wait, Daddy might file first." Lilly cautioned.

"She's right. If you wait, Daddy might get the best of you." Mother's hesitancy irritated Raine. The hangover headache wasn't helping Raine's mood either.

"I appreciate your help, but it's too soon! I'm sure it can wait until Monday. And besides, I don't think your father will be thinking about divorce yet."

"We're both here to help. I've taken off work and Lilly hired a sitter. Can we at least get some of this list taken care of?"

"You're both ganging up on me. I guess I don't really have a choice, do I?" Mother didn't look very appreciative. In fact, she looked downright mad.

"It's not as bad as you think, Mother. I already have a list of attorneys for you to contact." Lilly pulled her phone out and began to copy a list for her mother onto a piece of notebook paper.

"And my boss gave me the name of an attorney this morning. It's the same guy that handled his divorces; said he's the best. He even offered to set up an appointment." Interjecting, Raine knew she'd one-upped Lilly on this one. She had something better to offer than Lilly's list of names and numbers – she had a referral from an actual client. She studied Lilly's face, hoping a little for some sign of annoyance.

Cool as always, Lilly moved on to the next item on her list. "Do you know what you have in your bank accounts and more importantly do you have access to them? Checks? Debit cards?"

In an undeclared competition to see who could be the most helpful, Raine and Lilly tag-teamed their mother until she pleaded for a break. "I have a terrible headache. I need to take something and lie down. Do either one of you girls have aspirin?"

"I do." Lilly checked her watch and said, "I should be going anyway, it's getting late." She unzipped her purse and pulled out trial sized bottle of aspirin.

"Thank you dear." Mother took the bottle and gave Lilly a hug. "And thank you for your help today. Give the babies a kiss for me."

Raine gave her sister an air kiss and shut the door behind her with great relief. Lilly's sheer flawlessness always left Raine exhausted. *Who can keep up with that? No wonder Mother has a headache.*

# CHAPTER 11
## CAROL & A CHRISTMAS MEMORY

After being strong-armed by her daughters all day, Genevieve found herself thinking about her friend from so long ago. Carol was the best friend she'd ever had. *Hell, who am I kidding? She's the only friend I ever had.*

Genevieve had been relieved when Carol's husband and Randall hit it off right away. The few friends that Randall did have weren't married or going with anyone. Genevieve was happy to be included in Randall's social life for a change. Jim and Carol had invited the Carters over for dinner and cards every Saturday night for almost a year before the big blow up.

The last time that they visited Carol and Jim was late autumn of 1972. Whenever she thought about that night, Genevieve could still remember the way the air smelled while they stood waiting on the front porch of Jim and Carol's tidy little house, crisp and clean and laced with fireplace smoke.

"Come on in you two!" Carol had taken the casserole dish out of Genevieve's hand and hugged her tightly before pulling her into their little foyer.

Jim shook Randall's hand and offered to take their coats.

"Jim, I brought us a little somethin' special." Randall held up a bottle of whiskey. "Tonight, we celebrate."

"What's the occasion?" Jim didn't usually drink anything stronger than beer.

"Got that promotion today. Been waiting on it for over a year." Randall's smile alarmed Genevieve for a reason that she couldn't put her finger on.

"Want to give me a hand?"

Genny sat Lillian down in front of Kimmy and her pile of toys and followed Carol into the kitchen. "What can I help with?"

"You can slice up the roast." Carol pointed to the knives and cutting board.

Genny tried to distract herself from thinking about Randall by making small talk with Carol. But under the surface, uneasiness nipped and nibbled at her guts.

"Got any shot glasses?" Randall poked his head into the kitchen.

"Sure, over there with the wine glasses." Carol pointed Randall in the right direction.

Randall rummaged around in the cupboard and found a couple of small souvenir shot glasses. He returned to the den to Jim. Carol gave Genevieve a questioning look.

"What is it, Carol?" Genevieve could guess what Carol was thinking, but she decided to play dumb.

"Randall's drinking hard liquor again?"

"Not really. He's been staying away from it; just has a beer now and then." Genevieve paused, thinking about how long it'd been since Randall last bought a bottle. Things had been fairly peaceful around the house for some time.

"It's been at least six months since he's had the hard stuff. I guess the occasion calls for it."

"Hmm, I don't know." Carol's voice trailed off in a judgmental way that annoyed Genevieve. She wished that she hadn't told Carol so much.

As Carol and Genevieve prepared dinner, they could hear raucous laughter coming from the den. Although the words were indistinguishable, Randall's voice had an aggressive energy to it. Ignoring Carol's skeptical gaze, she kept her worries to herself.

"Let's eat, gentlemen!" Carol called the men to dinner in an overly cheerful tone. Randall had his arm thrown about Jim's shoulders when they entered the dining room. Genevieve could see the strain on Jim's face as he sat down.

"Mmmm, this sure smells delicious, ladies!" Jim complimented Carol and Genevieve. "Randall, you'd better dig in!" Jim held the platter of roast beef up to pass it to Randall.

"Did you make this Carol?" Randall smirked. Genevieve felt a squeeze around her heart. She didn't know what he might say next, but the expression on his face indicated it wasn't going to be good.

"I did." Carol must've sensed something too because she quickly added, "Your wife made the cheese and potato casserole."

"Well, then," Randall's words dripped out as slow and deliberate as cool molasses, "I'll be sure to fill up on your roast beef." Head tilted back slightly and eyelids partially closed, Randall grinned at Carol in a slow, seductive manner.

"Oh now, Randall, aren't you the cut-up?" The flush in Carol's cheeks gave away her discomfort. Jim looked irritated. Genevieve flinched with embarrassment for everyone at the table. She busied herself with making Lillian's plate.

"Jim, you are a lucky man. Not everyone is blessed with such a talented and beautiful wife. How did you convince this amazing woman to marry you?" Randall smiled at Carol, looking at her as if she were the only woman in the room.

"I am a lucky man," Jim nodded in agreement. "You didn't do so bad yourself, my friend." Jim gave Genevieve a sympathetic look. "You have a lovely wife too; and if I remember correctly, she makes a pretty mean meatloaf."

Randall snorted and downed another shot of his whiskey. Genevieve wished that the chair would swallow her whole. Her ears were hot with humiliation. Randall had purposely embarrassed her, but she wasn't sure why. The only thing that she was sure of was that her heart was crushed into a million pieces.

Except for the sounds of the children eating, silence filled the dining room. Carol pushed her food around on her plate, and Jim painstakingly cut his roast into miniscule pieces. Genevieve willed the tears that were threatening to spill out of her eyes to stay in place.

Finally, Carol spoke in a gentle voice. "Randall, I think you hurt your wife's feelings." She waited for a response but Randall said nothing at first.

Genevieve knew that Carol had just made everything much worse. Randall did not tolerate anyone calling his behavior into question. Genevieve cringed on the inside, waiting for the bomb to drop.

When Randall finally spoke, his words forever changed the path of Genevieve and Carol's friendship. "Is that right? Well, Carol, you don't have to live with the bitch."

"That's enough Randall! You're out of line!" Carol turned to Jim for reinforcement. Normally mild-mannered, Jim paused before saying anything.

"Randall, you've gone too far. Maybe the whiskey's gone to your head." Jim kept his tone congenial. "Why don't you apologize to the ladies, and we'll enjoy the rest of our evening."

"You gonna' let your wife speak to me like that, Jimbo?" Randall's words became more slurred. "I'd say she's out of line, speaking to your guest like that. She should learn to keep her place."

"She is in her place! As my wife! You should learn how to treat a lady!" Jim's face turned a shade of purple.

Grinning, Randall said, "I guess I don't see any ladies in the room with us." He stood up and mockingly looked around the dining room. With a chuckle, Randall said, "Get the baby, Genny. We're leaving."

Genevieve made a weak apology to Jim and Carol through her tears. Carol grabbed Genevieve's hand as she got up to follow Randall. She squeezed Carol's hand.

"Stay with us tonight, Genny! At least let us keep Lilly with us until Randall calms down; she can sleep in Kimmy's room." Carol pleaded with Genevieve.

"It's really no trouble." Jim echoed Carol's sentiments. His kind face was etched with worry lines.

"It's okay, we'll be fine." Genevieve whispered to the couple as she gathered up Lilly and her purse. She knew that if she were to stay, Randall would view her actions as disloyal to him.

She hurried to the car where Randall was already waiting. The car made a low rumbling sound as it sat idling. She had barely gotten Lilly settled into the back seat when Randall hit the gas.

"No Randall! Stop! Oh, God!" Genevieve's scream dissipated into the air as Randall drove away with the back passenger door ajar. With legs made of lead she tried to chase after him. "Stop, please! Lilly's gonna fall out!"

It was unlikely that he'd heard Genevieve's shrieks but Randall stopped the car at the end of Jim and Carol's long driveway.

Genevieve's ragged cries of horror must have been loud enough to catch their attention because Jim and Carol rushed out onto their porch. Jim realized what was happening and sprinted to the end of the driveway. Genevieve prayed that Randall wouldn't take off again before Jim could get to him. The back door was still open slightly and one-year-old Lilly wasn't buckled in.

Instead of going to the driver's door, Jim quickly grabbed Lilly and ran back with her toward Genevieve. "Take her inside! Go!" Jim ordered. "Call the police!"

Carol called the police while Genevieve soothed Lilly. Jim stayed outside with Randall until Sergeant Williams arrived. Sergeant Williams took Randall to the station where he spent the night in jail. No charges were filed, and even if they had been, Genevieve wouldn't have testified. She was too terrified of Randall. She would pay dearly for his night in jail, even though she wasn't the one who had called the police. To testify against him was unthinkable.

Carol stayed in touch for a while, but the Carters were never again invited to Jim and Carol's home. Genevieve knew that Randall wouldn't have gone anyway. He couldn't abide the company of anyone who questioned or doubted him.

Randall no longer approved of Genevieve's only friend. Although he didn't tell her that she couldn't spend time with Carol, he assassinated her character with his toxic words every chance he got. To escape his disapproval, it became easier for Genevieve to avoid Carol.

Carol eventually stopped trying to be a friend. Over time, Genevieve had almost persuaded herself that Carol was a bad person. *It's less painful to lose something if you can convince yourself you didn't want it anyway.*

And through the years, Genevieve got quite good at convincing herself that she didn't want anything. Genevieve's mother hadn't been a part of her life since she was just a girl. Grandma passed away when Genny was pregnant with Miranda and after that, there was no one else to point out how abnormal Randall Carter was. No one on the outside of the Carter household ever got close enough to notice that something was very wrong on the inside.

Genevieve's life was a series of disappointments chased with hope. Randall was her god. Whatever he gave, he could also take away. There were good times (she told herself) but each moment of happiness was followed with deep despair. At one point during the marriage, Genny had gone to counseling at the church. She figured maybe Randall was right and that she was the screwed up one in the relationship.

"You should pray for strength. God gives us nothing that we cannot bear." The pastor had listened to her entire dilemma before speaking. "Perhaps you could volunteer at our crisis center so that you can appreciate the life that your husband provides."

Instead of feeling grateful for her life, she recognized herself in women who came to the church crisis center for help. Although she wasn't beaten as often as some of the women she met, her stories were much the same.

"My husband doesn't let me see the bank account," one woman answered when asked what amount of money she might have access to.

She looked embarrassed, and Genevieve knew the woman's pain. Genevieve didn't have a clue how little or how much money they had in the bank. Randall had everything mailed to his office. Once she'd asked him how much money they had saved.

"*We* do not have anything saved," he had sneered"; *you* do not work; therefore, *you* have nothing saved." He'd finished with, "What I have saved is none of your business."

She understood it was like to be isolated from family and friends too. She knew what it felt like to not have one single person she could talk to about their marriage. It was so much easier to shun close friendships than to cause collateral damage.

After just a short time volunteering, she could pick them out in a crowd. They were the women who lived in the same quiet hell that she did. They were the ladies who looked like their life was together, if you didn't look too deeply. Always watching their husband as if to gauge his mood; they had the same demeanor as a whipped dog. They carefully guarded their words and smiled in a way that never reached their eyes.

She stopped volunteering because it was like having a mirror held up to her face each time she counseled another woman. Clinging to the raft of hope, she resigned herself to riding the waves of Randall's moods.

~ Not So Happy Holiday Memories ~

The girls were out of their minds with excitement during the days leading up to the Christmas of 1982. Randall didn't normally acknowledge Christmas other than to give himself a bottle of whiskey. That year, he surprised them all by bringing home a real tree two weeks before Christmas day. It didn't take much for the children to get in the spirit of the holidays, but Genevieve was a little more reluctant. She didn't want to get her hopes up.

Genevieve had spent the morning of Christmas Eve baking pies and rolls for their Christmas dinner. Lilly sat at the kitchen table cutting out snowflakes with Randi.

"Like this Randi!" Lilly tried for what seemed like the hundredth time to show her five-year-old sister how to fold the paper.

"Lilly," Genny warned, "watch your tone."

"I know, but she's just not paying attention!"

"I am so!" Randi argued.

"Are not!"

"Am too!"

The girls argued back and forth, each trying to drown out the other.

"For heaven's sake! Enough!" Genevieve yelled over the both of them and pointed her finger to the door. "Get out of this kitchen!"

Lilly grumbled as she stomped out of the room. Randi started to cry. Genevieve ignored them and went back to rolling out her pie crust.

The rains had been heavy, and the ground was too muddy for the girls to play outside. They began to chase each other around the partition separating the kitchen from the living room. They're a little noisy but at least they aren't fighting, Genny thought. She continued rolling out her pie crust.

A large crash, followed by an ear-splitting scream startled her out of her daydreams. Brushing the flour off her hands onto her apron, Genevieve ran to the living room. The entire coat tree was on its side, with Randi underneath.

"What on earth happened?" Genevieve picked up an armful of coats and lifted the coat tree off Randi. She looked scared but didn't appear to be banged up.

"We were running and Randi knocked the coats over."

"I did not! The coats just fell on me!" Red faced and crying, little Randi defended herself.

"Did too! You kicked it when you ran by!" Lilly argued.

"Please stop! Enough with the arguing already!" Genny shouted.

"What in the hell is going on now?" Randall stood at the edge of the foyer. He'd been sleeping, and he most certainly did not look happy.

*Uh oh, here we go.* Genevieve started putting the coats back onto the tree. The day was doomed.

"Go on girls. Go to your room and find something quiet to do."

Genevieve could hear Randall banging things around in the kitchen, presumably making a cup of coffee for himself. She prayed there was still some in the pot. Having a pot of coffee ready for Randall in the mornings was a small peace offering. It was a silly, superstitious idea; the notion that a pot of coffee could change the day.

Randall had spilled a little coffee on the counter and was searching for something to wipe it up with.

"I'll get that, honey." Genevieve offered and got a new washcloth out of the towel drawer.

"I can do it!" Randall yanked the washcloth out of her hand. After he wiped up his spill, he stormed out of the kitchen.

Genevieve was hurt. She was only trying to help. I can't get it right, she thought. *And if I hadn't offered to clean the mess, he'd be mad at me for that.*

Within minutes, the girls' bickering voices could be heard from upstairs. Genevieve winced and hurried upstairs to do damage control but Randall had beat her to it. He was pulling off his belt just as she got to the door of the girls' room.

"Turn around!" He barked at the children. The spankings were relatively light compared to some of the past. Both Lilly and Randi didn't cry much. While sliding his belt back into the loops of his pants, Randall tromped downstairs.

Genny could hear Randall fumbling around in the pantry looking for something. Deep apprehension rumbled around in her gut. She debated whether she should go to him and offer to help find whatever he was looking for or just stay out of his way. In the end, she decided to leave him alone. The top stair felt like a safe distance, so she sat and watched.

Armed with two large black trash bags, Randall scooped up gift after gift from under their beautiful Christmas tree. Genevieve watched in disbelief as Randall took every last present and tossed them into the bags. He cinched the drawstrings up and carried the bagged-up gifts out of the front door.

Next, he jerked the tree away from the corner without bothering to unplug it first. Glass balls crashed onto the floor, shattering into pieces. Precious homemade dough ornaments that the girls had worked so hard on turned to crumbs as they flew off the quaking tree. Randall yanked the light cord out of the outlet and dragged the tree out the front door.

Randall didn't come back into the house. Genny opened the door to the girls' room to find them both huddled up under their blankets. They looked terrified. She was certain that they'd heard the commotion.

"Stay in your room!" she ordered. Lilly nodded, and Randi just continued to suck her thumb. Genny normally would've told Randi to take her thumb out of her mouth, but she didn't because at least she wasn't making noise by crying.

The living room floor was a mess. Fir needles were stuck in the carpet amongst shards of broken glass and crushed dough ornaments. The front door was wide open and to her dismay Randall's muddy footprints were all over the beige carpet.

Genevieve knew better than to follow Randall outside. Instead, she did what she knew how to do best. She began to clean up the mess; as if cleaning the disarray would somehow erase what had just happened. She carefully picked out slivers of glass and evergreen needles from the rug; all the while praying hard that Randall would stay outside for a while.

After picking up clumps of mud, she vacuumed. The carpet would have to be steam cleaned again. To make matters worse, she'd forgotten all about the pies in the oven. Apple filling had bubbled out of the pan onto the bottom, and the sugary burnt liquid filled the entire house with a smoky sweet smell.

Tears clouded her vision as she thought about how she should have been watching the girls better. It never occurred to her that Randall's angry outbursts might not be her fault. She was sure that if she could be a better wife and mother, she might be able to keep him from getting angry again.

Randall left the house and didn't come home until after bedtime. He made no apologies nor did he ever tell Genevieve where he'd taken the gifts. She was so grateful that he wasn't still angry when he came home later that night that she didn't dare to ask him.

The next day Genevieve served the big meal minus the burnt pies. Without a tree, gifts, or even visitors, the day wasn't different than any other day. Over time, that Christmas blended in with all the bad memories and seemed no more and no less than the others.

# CHAPTER 12
## HELLO SERENITY

Raine's head didn't feel so well after Lilly left with all her lists, notes, and advice. The night out with Noelle and the morning with Mother had taken its toll. She crawled into bed and drifted off into a hazy kind of sleep.

A foggy kaleidoscope of lights surrounded her as she moved through the dream. A polished looking girl holding a glass was talking to her, but the words made no sense. Like a television on low volume, barely enough discernable words broke through for Raine to know that the language was English. Raine answered the girl, but even her own words were mumbled. As soon as she'd spoken, she couldn't remember what she had said. She wanted so badly to know what she'd said that made the girl laugh, but she couldn't find a way to ask. Her mouth was frozen.

The tan, wavy haired guy grabbed her and hugged her warmly. He appeared to know her well, but Raine didn't recognize him. He offered to light Raine's cigarette for her. Raine took a book of matches off the bar and lit her cigarette herself. *Wait, I don't smoke.* She inhaled deeply and felt the burn all the way down into her lungs.

In the dream, she continued to converse with the people in the room. *This is important. I should pay better attention.* She eventually slipped into a deep sleep.

~ The Club ~

The cool dark air felt like heaven. She loved this place like a moth loves a flame. The club was a beautiful cocoon secluded from the outside world. Here, she could be with people of her own kind without judgment from those who didn't understand.

"Serenity!" A warm, mellow voice called out to her from one of the plush velvet booths. Blood red satin drapes clothed the booths in sumptuous privacy making it difficult to distinguish where the voice came from.

Chandeliers with real candles lit the entire club. The delicious fragrance of hot wax mingled with the perfumes of the patrons. The smell was intoxicating. Her eyes slowly adjusted to the soft flickering glow. A chocolate hued hand pulled back one of the lavish curtains, revealing the owner of the voice. Abel was one of her favorites. He was always so aggressive and creative.

"I've been wondering when I'd see you again, Angel." Abel's melodic voice was seductive music to her ears. His eyes reflected light, like a panther in the dark. The little smile on his full lips excited her. Raine might have decided to be virginal, but Serenity needed to feel the weight of a man on top of her; the heavier and bigger, the better. And Abel made her feel like a fragile china doll.

"Today is the day." She smiled back. "Do you feel like playing with me now?" She began to look around for a staff member to arrange a private room. Private rooms were expensive, but if one allowed an audience, the room was complimentary.

With his free hand, Abel summoned the waitress who was dressed in only a pair of sheer panties. His other hand was nestled between Serenity's creamy white thighs. She continued to stand, frozen by the exquisite sensation of Abel's teasing fingers.

Settees were strategically placed in the Victorian boudoir to allow for viewing. While a handful of members belonged to the club for the pleasure of participating, the voyeuristic segment made up the larger part of the population. Those who wanted to watch but didn't have the stomach to give or receive were the bread and butter of the club.

Every seat in the house was filled with members dressed in a variety of costumes; most scantily clad. For discretionary purposes, all club members were encouraged to wear ornate masks. Serenity had already put on her mask and was waiting patiently on the bed for Abel. There were a few spectators making themselves comfortable while the wait staff began to take drink orders.

Serenity closed her eyes, opened her legs, and began to stroke herself lightly over her thin panties. She liked to pleasure herself first before allowing Abel inside of her. It helped make the initial penetration less painful and allowed her to reach multiple orgasms.

Heavy breathing from a viewer caught her attention so she opened her eyes slightly. Some newcomer was already masturbating. He won't last long at this pace, she thought.

Serenity closed her eyes and slid her hand inside her panties. She traced half circles around her erected clitoris repeatedly until contractions from her orgasm flooded her panties with creamy wetness. Delicious goosebumps covered her entire body when she felt the bed sink from Abel's weight. She kept her eyes closed and waited for his first touch.

God, he is good, she thought as Abel pulled the crotch of her panties aside and began to lap up her cream. His tongue had the amazing capability of being as soft or as hard as she needed. And he always seemed to know exactly what she needed. He inserted one of his very long fingers inside her swollen, hungry pussy. Serenity loved that she could feel him playing with her cervix, as if he were trying to enter her womb. It was a little painful, but it made her orgasms so much more powerful.

With his tongue forcefully flicking her clit and his finger nearly entering her cervix, he brought her to a violent orgasm. Her uterus tightened up into a small ball, which only intensified the orgasm. With his silky tongue, Abel traced a path up her belly to her breasts. He began to suckle at her left breast while still penetrating her with his finger. She groaned in ecstasy as he inserted another finger inside of her. She could feel the lubricated tip of his erect cock on her thigh.

"Please!" She begged him to enter her. It was so hard to be patient. She ached so badly inside.

"Not yet." Abel moved to her other breast.

"Open your legs wider," he instructed. She obeyed.

She took a very deep breath as he pushed the tip of his erection against her. Slowly he moved in and out, completely filling her up. It was a few moments before she could accept him all the way. The stretching sensation was exquisite. She loved the way he made her forget everyone and everything around her.

# CHAPTER 13
## SACCHARIN LOVE

Lilly waited for him in her car outside of the office building. Every car that passed caught her eye and not even one was his. Her stress level was through the roof after spending the better part of the day with Raine and Mother. She needed a little escape from her life today. *Where in the hell is he?* She only had two more hours before she needed to pick up Laney from the sitter.

A brew of relief and excitement flooded through her body when his Taurus pulled into the parking lot. She waited, impatiently tapping her fingers on the steering wheel. He pulled his duffel bag out of his trunk and locked up. He looked around the parking lot nervously before speed-walking across the lot to the passenger side of her SUV.

"Where do you want to go?" Lilly asked.

"Somewhere south" he replied. Neither one looked at the other until they were on the highway.

Lilly took a familiar exit and drove slowly looking for the motel they had used before. One place looked much like the next, run down and seedy. The motel that she was looking for rented rooms by the hour, cheap and discreet.

The rental was sixty-nine dollars for two hours. She paid with cash and gave the front desk clerk a ridiculous story about needing a place to hang out while her home was being painted. Lilly wasn't sure why she felt the need to lie. The clerk knew why she was there. No one rented a room by the hour unless they were going to get laid.

She held the key up in front of her windshield as she walked toward room number six. As always, he would wait to get out of her car until she was safely out of sight. Lilly thought that his insistence on not walking into the motel room at the same time as she did was a silly precaution. They both knew that if either of them got caught at a motel, it wouldn't matter who they were there with.

After meeting this way eight times now, they had already established a routine. He pulled a can of beer out of his duffel bag and lit a cigarette. She went into the bathroom to freshen up, knowing she would come out to find that he'd already finished his first beer and cracked open the second.

Drinking during the daytime wasn't something Lilly did. His need to drink when they were together was starting to bother Lilly. It felt trashy to her. *As if going to a cheap motel to screw isn't trashy.*

She'd met him through work. He was her district manager at a direct sales company. He'd taken great interest in Lilly's progress, noticing each accomplishment and lavishing her with praise. Lilly felt special for the first time in a long time. It was nice to have a man's attention again. She found reasons to be in the office when he was there. They both found reasons to work late.

It was Lilly's only affair in all her years of marriage. Her exhilaration only slightly outweighed her guilt. Whenever the guilt disturbed her too much, Lilly thought about her husband's past transgressions, as if somehow his mistakes erased her wrongdoings.

The first time was the most painful for her. They had just closed a sale and went out for drinks to celebrate. It was exciting to have a conversation with someone who hadn't already heard all her stories, someone who didn't have her all figured out.

After drinks, he walked her to her car and hugged her too long. Lilly was aware that he was going to kiss her, and she didn't stop him. Struggling to breathe, her heart beat in staccato. His kiss tasted like cigarette smoke and wine. It reminded her of high school days. Driving home afterward, Lilly cried big salty tears. It had been a long time since she'd had sex in the backseat of a car.

Gabe didn't notice her tear-stained face when she got home. He didn't bother to look up from his laptop. Setting the shower on as hot as she could stand, Lilly tried to wash away her disgust and shame.

Later in bed that night, Lilly did something she'd never done before. She seduced her husband with a feverish passion. Lilly wanted to erase all traces of the other man.

Although Lilly hated herself after the first time, she couldn't stop thinking about him. Over the subsequent weeks, the agony subsided, and the memories earned a prized spot in her erotic fantasy file.

Every time she made love to Gabe, the other man was there with them, like a mental orgy. The weeks following her fall from grace were full of the best sex she and Gabe had ever had. The next time she cheated on Gabe wasn't in the backseat of a car, and it wasn't nearly as painful.

The subsequent weeks played out like a parallel universe. Thoughts of the affair distracted her from everything. Although she carried out her days the same as she had before, she no longer felt she belonged in her normal life. Lilly had committed a sin that she'd never thought possible. Even worse, she wasn't sure why she'd strayed in the first place.

She knew that he didn't love her. Lilly didn't love him. And it wasn't because the sex was so great. (The embarrassing truth was that sex with him wasn't great at all.) He hadn't showered her with gifts, expensive dinners, or even offered to pay for the motel rooms. Simply, he listened to her and fed her a few drops of saccharine sweet praise. Lilly had broken her sacred marriage vows in exchange for a few pretty words and the thrill of impressing a stranger.

Standing in front of the stained motel bathroom sink, preparing to sin again, Lilly had the notion that the woman looking back at her wasn't someone she knew. She certainly wasn't someone that Lilly wanted to be. Images of her babies and her husband flashed before her eyes like a near-death experience. Lilly made a decision.

Fully clothed, she walked out of the bathroom and said, "I can't do this anymore."

Not seeming surprised, he tossed his empty can into the trash by the bed and began to load the rest of his six pack into his duffel bag.

She waited in the car while he dropped the key at the front desk. She turned on the radio to fill up the awkward silence during the drive back to the office. He stared out the window, his gaze frozen on an imaginary object in the distance. Lilly kept her eyes firmly on the road. She couldn't get there fast enough.

He leaned over to kiss her cheek before grabbing his bag out of the back seat. She felt relieved as she watched him walk to his car one last time.

Gabe arrived home less than an hour after Lilly did that evening. After giving Caleb and Laney bear hugs, Gabe wrapped his arms around Lilly's waist from behind. She was standing at the sink washing dishes willing her tears to not fall.

Hearing her sniffles, Gabe gently turned her around to face him. "What's the matter, honey?"

"It's nothing really. I'm just upset about my parents." Lilly didn't have the guts to devastate him with the truth.

Over the course of a few days, she developed an irrational fear that Gabe might be able to see her thoughts, as if they were tangible things that could be plucked out of the air. So, she stopped thinking about the affair. Only in the dead of the night did she allow herself to wonder how she could've done such a horrible thing.

She hoped that in time the memories and the guilt would leave her completely. Lilly had always figured that karma would bite her in the ass if she ever did something wrong. But as each day passed, she began to think that her dirty little secret might never be discovered and that she might escape punishment.

"Aren't you going to training tonight?" Gabe noticed Lilly wasn't getting ready to leave for work one evening later that week.

"No, I think I'm done. I've been at it for a while. Let's face it, I'm not making any money. It's a waste of time."

"What happened to perseverance and never giving up?" Gabe winked, teasing her a little bit.

With a wry smile, she said, "Yeah, well…I'm re-thinking that motto." She was re-thinking a lot of things.

Caleb tugged at her arm and smiled, "Momma, are you staying here with us?"

"I am, sweetheart. I don't want to miss you anymore."

Caleb hugged her leg. Lilly patted her little man's back and kissed the top of his silky head. Still rubbing Caleb's back, she turned and kissed Gabe soft and slow.

# CHAPTER 14
## A LESSON FOR GENNY

"Genny!" He had a motherfucker of a headache, and the bitch had done it again. The morning sun was burning a hole into the side of his face. She knew better than to leave the blinds open when he was sleeping in his recliner.

Grumbling, he pushed the lever with his hand and forced the footrest down. The room spun around a bit while he let his head adjust to an upright position. Shielding his eyes from the glare, Randall staggered over to the picture window and twisted the blinds to the closed position. Shade flooded the room and his agony lessoned slightly.

"Genny!", Randall yelled again. "Make some coffee, would ya'?"

She didn't answer, but his head hurt too much to holler again. He overdid it a little last night, but the dumb bitch pushed him over the edge. She really liked to set him off. *Should know better by now old boy, lettin' her get under your skin like that.*

The coffee pot was ice cold, unusual for this early hour. Genny always made a full pot but only drank a cup or so herself. Randall dumped the old coffee, filled the pot up with tap water, and poured it into the back of the coffee maker. His hands shook a little bit, causing him to spill water down the backside of the pot. He fumbled around in the cabinet for a few moments before he found the coffee and filters. He couldn't remember the last time he'd made a pot of coffee.

While he waited for the coffee to brew, he looked around Genny's kitchen. Tucked in between the outdated tile backsplash and the cabinet were paint samples that had been there for at least a decade. Now, he couldn't remember why he'd told her no. Probably just to remind her that he was still the one in charge. Maybe I'll surprise her for Christmas, he thought. She doesn't ask for much.

The old coffee pot spit and sputtered out the last few drops of brew. Randall pulled his cup out of the cabinet and noticed that Genny's was still in its place. He filled his cup and walked up to the bedroom to make sure she was okay. After all, he thought, they were getting older. It wasn't unheard of to just wake up dead.

The bed was perfectly made. Genny's shoes weren't in their normal spot. He pulled the curtains back and could see the car still sitting in the driveway. Irritation started to needle at the back of his eyes. What kind of game was she playing with him? He may have been a little rough on her last night, but he didn't tolerate any pouting bullshit.

"Genny! You will come when I call you!" He slammed the bathroom door open, hoping to startle her. The towels hanging on the rack fluttered from the forced air, but the room was empty. Genny's toothbrush was missing from the cup on the vanity.

Randall's chest felt tight. Genny hadn't tried to leave since the youngest was still at home. *Where would she go? Does she have any friends?* He sat down on the edge of the bathtub because the room was spinning a little bit.

He needed a plan, but first, he had to get rid of this wicked headache. Laughing out loud because he almost yelled for Genny to bring him some aspirin, Randall went downstairs to find the medicine and to make a tall drink to swallow it down with. *Yes siree! A little hair of the dog is just what the doctor ordered!*

Randall spent the rest of the first day sans Genny getting tanked, which wasn't very different than any other day since his retirement. He did come up some brilliant (or so he thought) plans to get her back and then get back at her. First, he had to find her. But that was a job for a sober man. And sober, Randall was not. So, in commemoration of the moment, he decided instead to take something from her.

After downing a half of a bottle of Jack Daniels, Randall took some time to walk around the home that he'd provided for that ungrateful sow for the last forty years. He paused from time to time, first eyeing a grouping of Hummel figurines, and then a set of ceramic thimbles. Although these things were important to Genny, he was looking for something more meaningful to her.

After a complete tour of the house, he figured it out. What could be more precious than a collection of teacups from her dead grandmother? He'd never really liked the old woman, and she certainly didn't like him, so no love lost there.

He picked up the delicate cups, two at a time, and placed them out on the back porch. Once he'd moved all the cups, he searched for something handy to smash them with. He decided that Genny's favorite cast iron frying pan would do the trick. One by one, he crushed her precious little teacups into a powder. He hoped that Genny could feel each blow.

Afterward, he brushed the shards off the bottom of the frying pan with his bare hand and went back into the house. He flipped the porch light off. Maybe Genny will be a little more careful next time, he thought with a smile.

# CHAPTER 15
## A WELL TRAINED WIFE

Genny did all the right things after leaving Randall. She opened her own bank account, she filed for divorce, and upon the insistence of her eldest daughter, she'd even signed up for counseling through the battered women's shelter. All of these actions made her look as though she were making great strides toward independence. Secretly, Genny was terrified. She felt like a child who had broken every rule in the house and was waiting for the hand of God to strike her down.

Everywhere she went, Randall was skulking in the shadows. She couldn't stop thinking about how angry he was going to be with her when he found out everything that she'd done.

Long ago, when the girls were little, she'd needed a little extra money to pay for a perfume that the Avon lady had swindled her into buying. Rather than risk upsetting Randall by asking for money for such a frivolous thing, Genny had the bright idea to get cash back after filling up at their local gas station, and put it on their account. It seemed like a good idea at the time. Genny didn't think that Randall would notice.

"Genny, come here please." The calm sound of Randall's voice scared her. His calm voice was worse than his angry voice. Genny's pulse kicked into high speed, and her mouth felt dry. She put the dishrag down and went to him.

He was sitting in his chair, holding an envelope with his right hand. He gestured for her to come closer.

"Do you know what this is, Genny?"

"No," Genny stammered, "I don't." She wanted to reach for the envelope but didn't dare.

Randall pressed his lips into a thin line and shook his head. He tapped his left palm in a slow rhythm with the envelope. "You thought you were being sneaky, but you can't get anything by me."

"I don't know what you're talking about." Genny tried to recall what she could have done to upset him. She had a hard time predicting what might set him off. Once, she'd answered a survey over the telephone without asking his permission. Randall was furious when the follow-up letter, thanking her for her time, came in the mail.

"If I can't trust you with the little things, how can I trust you with the big things?"

"Randall, I honestly don't know what you're talking about!"

He laughed, "That's a funny word for you to be using! Honestly!"

She swallowed her tears and waited. Randall wasn't finished. He'd barely begun. Genny stood in front of him, doing her best to look submissive. Any hint of anger on her face would magnify whatever Randall had in store for her.

"Who earns the money in this house?"

"You do." She focused on a small piece of string lying on the floor, near Randall's left foot.

"And who makes the decisions about what we do with the money?"

"You do."

"I'm sorry." Randall cupped his ear with his left hand and said, "I can't hear you."

"You do." Genny spoke loudly but continued to stare at the piece of string, noticing the way the string zoomed in and out of focus.

"So, why in the fuck do you think it's okay to take money from me without my permission?"

"I don't." Genny's answer sounded weak, even to her own ears.

"Bring me your purse."

"Randall, no!" As soon as the words were out of her mouth, she regretted them. To say "no" to Randall was a bad move. She took one step backward but not soon enough to avoid the backside of his hand.

The girls didn't seem to notice Genny's black eye that evening. Just to be safe, she stayed home from Wednesday night bible study. She couldn't risk the humiliation of people gossiping about her. When she thought about the time that she confided in their pastor, she still felt ashamed. The pastor promised to talk some sense into Randall. After their meeting, the two of them came walking out like a couple of good old buddies, laughing and slapping each other on the back. Nothing about Randall's behavior changed. Pastor Greene treated Genny as if she were feeble-minded, and Randall stopped going to church altogether.

The worst part about Randall losing his temper was the reminder that she was less valuable to him than the family dog. Randall never hit the dog.

She went about her evening as if nothing had happened. Randall had taken her set of car keys, so she made up a silly excuse when one of the girls asked to go into town to get poster board for a school project. Since he'd taken every last penny out of her purse, she wouldn't have been able to purchase it anyway.

Randall spent his night sucking down booze and listening to old records on the stereo. By the time that Randall came to bed later that night, she'd been tossing and turning for what felt like hours. She could hear him fumbling around in the bathroom, whistling, and drumming out a beat on the bathroom vanity. She recognized the tune as one of the songs that he'd been playing too loudly on the stereo downstairs.

Controlling her breath to appear as if she were asleep, she prayed that he would let her stay that way. The smell of his aftershave wafted into the bedroom and her heart sank. She was so tired that she wanted to cry. Maybe, she thought, he'll leave me alone if I just lay still.

"Hey," Randall whispered loudly. "You awake?" He nudged her a little.

She didn't move. Randall pulled her close to him and slid his hand inside her panties. As much as she wanted sleep, her body responded to his touch. She hated the smell of his breath, hated him, at that moment. But his touch was the only thing that she had, and she needed to be soothed.

Afterward, they lay intertwined, and for a few minutes, Genny felt loved. Randall ran his fingers through her hair and touched the cheekbone that he'd bruised. He kissed her gently on her forehead.

"I didn't mean to give you a black eye, baby," Randall said, "but you've got to stop antagonizing me."

Genny fought the urge to stiffen up and pull away. A stray tear rolled down her face onto her pillow. Once Randall started snoring, she untangled herself from him and rolled as far to the edge of the bed as possible. She promised herself not to antagonize him again.

He'd given her a black eye for that little wrongdoing. This was a million times worse. Randall would never forgive her for asking for half of everything. In all the years of being married to Randall, Genny couldn't remember one single time that she'd been able to hide anything from him.

She'd felt so brave at first. She continued, in part, to put on a courageous face because Lilly and Raine seemed so proud of her. But as the days rolled on, she began to fear that she'd started a war she wouldn't be able to finish.

# CHAPTER 16
## TRACKING GENNY

An irritating buzzing sensation between his nose and his upper lip woke Randall from his restless sleep. Without opening his eyes, he swatted at the fly that had landed on his sweaty face. He'd just started to drift back to sleep when the damned thing landed on his eyelid.

He sat up quickly and instantly regretted it. His head was pounding. Using both thumbs, he pressed into his eye sockets to help distract himself from the pain. Once the worst of the stabbing subsided, he opened his eyes to see what time it was. The clock on Genny's side of the bed read "9:17".

Every other morning since she'd left, he hadn't remembered that Genny was gone until he was wide awake. This morning was different. He wasn't surprised by the absence of the smell of coffee. *Gonna have to fix that.*

He took a half-assed shower and threw on some clothes. Normally, he would have shaved and applied cologne. No matter what the night before had been like, Randall always took pride in his appearance.

This morning, all that didn't matter. He had only one focus. He needed to stay sober for the day. She'd been gone long enough, and he was done with her little game. She should be ashamed of herself, he thought, for acting like a child and running from her responsibilities.

It took him a small amount of searching to find Genny's address book. Worn from years of use, there were more names and phone numbers marked out than still existed. He speculated that most had been busybodies from the church that Genny had belonged to for so many years. None of those harpies bothered to come around anymore. Genny was such a wishy-washy twit, she'd probably bored them all to death.

There were only three numbers that he cared about anyway. It took him a minute to remember what Lillian's married name was. He didn't like the guy much, but he had money. It didn't take a lot of brainpower to figure out why his gold-digging daughter went after him. Even in high-school she was a snooty little bitch. *The pretty ones usually are.*

"Dad?" She answered on the first ring, as if she were expecting him.

"Is your mother there?" Randall did his best to speak in a soft voice. No sense in starting out with excessive force, he decided. Women were a ridiculously emotional bunch, crying over the littlest thing.

"No, she isn't."

He waited for a minute, expecting her to elaborate. When she didn't offer any more information, he asked, "Do you know where she is?"

"No, I don't," she said, "but I can take a message for you. I'll give it to her the next time I see her."

Randall's head started to pound again. "No. You'll tell me where she is right now! She's my wife and I have the right to know!"

"She'll call you when she's ready."

"You listen to me! You can't stand in the way of me and your mother!" Randall was yelling, but he didn't care. Lilly knew where her mother was, and she had no right to keep that information from him.

"I'm following Mother's wishes. She'll call you when she's ready. She doesn't want you to know where she is. She needs a break from you."

"If you had any sense at all, you'd be telling me where she is. I've got half a mind to come squeeze it out of you. You're damned lucky that I don't know where you live. Better hope I don't find out!"

"Don't call me again." She hung up on him.

Randall slammed the receiver against the phone as hard as he could, and the old phone made a dinging sound. He needed a little drink to calm himself down. He was a cursed man. Other men had loving wives and sons. Instead, he was stuck with a sneaky, conniving half-wit of a woman and three girls. Not one of them were worth shit to him. He'd provided a good home, protected them, and made sure they never wanted for anything. And this was his thanks.

After he downed a glass of whiskey, he dialed Miranda's number. She was the least irritating of the bunch to him. She had been a real daddy's girl, he thought with a smile, always so soft and trusting. She hadn't pulled away from him like the other two had. He wondered if she would answer her phone. They hadn't heard from her in a long time. She'd just stopped coming around.

Her number was out of service. Disappointed, he hung up. He flipped through the pages and found Raine's number. He'd hoped that he wouldn't have to call Raine. That one has some wires crossed, he thought. She had been a pretty little thing, but she'd turn on a dime. One minute, she'd act timid and submissive, then the next, she'd have an angry gleam in her eye. It made for an exciting time, but he remembered being a little afraid of her.

"Hello?" Raine answered.

"Is your mother there?" No point in beating around the bush, he thought.

"No, why?"

"Is she staying with you?"

"I don't think that's any of your business, Daddy."

"She's my wife, and everything she does is my business!"

"She won't be your wife for long." Raine seemed to be enjoying his pain. He could almost see her expression through the phone line.

"I'm coming for her now. Tell her to get ready." Randall poured himself another glass of whiskey.

"Then, I'm calling the police. She doesn't want you around." Raine hung up on him, just like Lilly had.

"Well, I do believe there is a theme going on here," Randall said to the empty room. He swallowed the whiskey and poured himself another. He had time to figure out the best way to get her back. It would help if he knew where any of his daughters lived. For now, he needed to take the edge off the day.

Randall opened the cabinet where he stored all his vinyl records. Nothing pacified his soul like music and booze. He decided the Eagles would make a good beginning to the afternoon.

# CHAPTER 17
## CALL FROM THE PAST

Lilly's hand shook as she hung the phone up on her father. She should have known that he'd try to find Mother, but she wasn't prepared to hear his voice. She needed to warn Raine.

Raine's number was busy. She paced the kitchen, making up things to do. After a few minutes, she tried Raine's number again. This time, it rang.

"Dad called me." Raine didn't bother to say hello.

"Me too, that's what I was calling to tell you." Lilly felt some sort of relief knowing that she wasn't the only one Daddy had harassed.

"I told him I'd call the cops on him," Raine said. "He said he was coming for her."

"I hung up on him," Lilly said. "He's an ass! Nothing's changed. Do you plan on telling Mother?"

"No way! She's not strong enough to stand up to him."

"True," Lilly added, "The minute he gets ahold of her, she'll back down."

Lilly tried to remember what she'd been doing before her father had called, but she couldn't. She checked on Laney, who was still sleeping, and went out onto the patio. Most of her neighbors were at work by this time of day. The occasional bird call or barking dog broke up the quiet of the day.

The sound of Daddy's voice had taken her back to places she'd hoped to never go again.

~ Dark Days ~

"Lillian, open up!" Daddy banged on her bedroom door with his fist. Mother said something that Lilly couldn't quite understand.

58

"Just a minute." Lilly slipped her pajama bottoms on as quickly as possible and fumbled around in her dresser drawer for the matching top. The tiny lock wouldn't hold if Daddy decided to force it, so she didn't bother to button the top all the way before opening the door.

"Let me see them," Daddy demanded. Mother looked scared but said nothing.

"See what?"

"The clothes that you just took off," Daddy said. "I know you were with a boy."

"Randall!" Mother sounded mortified.

Lilly could feel her cheeks and ears turn hot. She reached into her hamper and pulled out the pair of jeans and sweatshirt that she'd worn to the football game. She handed them over to Daddy.

"No, your underwear too," Daddy said. "Where are they?"

"I'm still wearing them." Lilly forced herself to not cry. She looked to her mother, hoping that she would disagree with her father, but Mother avoided her gaze.

"Take them off," Daddy barked, "Now!"

"Randall, please!" Mother protested.

"You can leave!" Daddy told Mother, pointing to the bedroom door. Mother left the room, leaving Lilly all alone with Daddy.

Lilly couldn't hold her tears in. She obeyed and slipped her pajama bottoms off, then her panties. Humiliated, she pulled her top down to cover herself as much as possible. She placed her underwear in Daddy's outstretched hand.

To her horror, he opened them to expose the crotch. He put his face in her panties and inhaled. She couldn't speak.

"You fucked him!" Daddy yelled. "You little whore!"

Lilly hadn't had sex with anyone that night. She was too shocked to defend herself. The blood rushed out of her head, and she felt like she might faint.

"Turn around!" Daddy was sweating and panting. He shoved Lilly face-down onto the bed and pulled his belt off. He whipped her bare bottom until she finally cried out for him to stop.

"No daughter of mine is going to act like a whore," Daddy said before he left her room.

She cried herself to sleep that night. The next Monday morning, she ignored the nice boy that had taken her to the football game.

# CHAPTER 18
## ALMOST

Raine was certain that Mother wouldn't be able to stand up to Daddy. There had been only one other time that her mother had tried to leave Daddy. Raine was eight, maybe nine years old.

She awoke to the sound of her father yelling. Bits and pieces of a dream were still with her, so she ignored Daddy's voice for a minute and thought about the dream. In it, Daddy was hurting her friend, Shanti. He was doing things to Shanti that Raine wasn't allowed to talk about. Raine was crying in the dream, because she couldn't stop him.

The rest of her dream disappeared, and the darkness of the room was filled by the harsh echoes of Mother and Daddy's fight. Mother cried, and Daddy yelled some more. After a time, Raine could hear them doing the thing that they did after the fighting. She always covered her ears for that part.

Raine fell back asleep and woke again when it was light out. Mother was in Raine's room, quietly pulling clothing out of her dresser drawers. Raine sat up in bed and rubbed her eyes.

"Momma? What're you doing?"

Mother made a "Shhhh" sound with her lips and continued to put Raine's clothing into a duffle bag.

Raine watched Mother without saying anything more. She'd learned to be quiet when told to do so. Her tummy felt uneasy, like she needed to poop. She waited a little longer, then asked, "Can I go to the bathroom?"

"Yes, just be quiet." Mother was using her whisper voice. Raine started to feel frightened.

Raine tiptoed to the bathroom and closed the door behind her as softly as possible. She pulled down her panties and sat on the toilet to do her business.

As soon as she began to pee, she yelled for her mother.

"For heaven's sakes!" Mother whispered loudly, "I told you to be quiet!"

"Momma, it burns!" She matched her mother's voice with a loud whisper of her own.

"You probably have a bladder infection," Mother said. "Make sure to wipe from front to back."

When she was done, she noticed a little bit of dried blood in her panties. She told her mother about it, but Mother was too busy rushing around, packing things, to pay attention.

"Take a few of your favorite books and one stuffed animal," Mother said, "That's all we have space for."

"Where are we going?"

"I'll tell you later. Just be quiet and hurry." Mother looked pale and scared. Daddy was still sleeping. Raine was old enough to figure out that Mother didn't want him to know they were leaving.

Mother packed the trunk and closed it gently. "Raine, please get your pillow and your bathroom things. Put them into the backseat. Remember to be quiet, and don't let Daddy see you."

Raine started to tremble. Once she was in on the sneaking around, she knew that she could be punished for going along with it. But she wasn't about to let Mother leave her alone with Daddy.

Armed with her pillow, toothbrush, and her hair brush, Raine walked down the stairs. She took great care to avoid the creaking spots where the boards were a little loose. She took a great big breath of cool morning air once she reached the car.

Mother was already sitting in the driver's seat. She waited for Raine to put her belongings into the back before starting the engine. "Get in honey. We don't have much time." Mother kept her eyes focused on the upstairs bedroom window that belonged to her and Daddy.

Raine didn't ask questions until they were out on the highway. Daddy didn't have a separate car, so he wouldn't be able to chase them down. Still, she felt superstitious, like maybe he would be able to hear their conversation from the road.

"Momma, where are we going?"

"Someplace safe. Someplace where your father can't hurt you or me."

Raine glanced at her mother's face, looking for signs of a beating. Mother had a funny reddish spot above her lip, but Raine was so used to seeing strange markings on her that she didn't connect them with wounds. Mother always made up a silly reason for the bruises. Until Raine was old enough to connect the dots, she'd thought that her mother was the clumsiest person in the world.

Mother covered Raine's hand with her own. They rode that way for a while, with their hands resting on the seat in between each other.

"Are you feeling okay?" Mother asked.

"I'm okay, Momma."

"I'm sorry for what Daddy did last night. I don't know what he was thinking. He gets stupid when he drinks."

Raine didn't know what her father had done the night before. She didn't ask, either. Mother already looked upset. Raine just smiled at her mother and turned her head to look out the window.

As their car ate up the miles, Raine started feeling a little bit excited at the thought of living somewhere else. Maybe, she thought, we'll even have a place in the city. Then we won't have to smell those stinking pigs every day.

The sun moved into its noon-time position, and Raine's stomach started to grumble. They'd been so busy leaving that they hadn't eaten any breakfast.

"Momma?" Raine asked, "Can we stop to eat? I'm starving."

"Oh, my goodness! You didn't have breakfast this morning, did you?" Mother pulled off onto a frontage road. There were signs for restaurants along the way.

Mother pulled into a McDonald's parking lot and said, "It'll be good to stretch our legs."

Raine hadn't felt that happy in a long time. She couldn't even remember the last time she and Mother had gone anywhere together, other than the grocery store or church. She skipped up to the restaurant door. The smell inside was like heaven to her nose. A mixture of cherry pies, cheeseburgers, and French fries made her mouth water.

"Figure out what you want while I use the ladies room," Mother said.

Raine had a hard time picking just a few things, but by the time her mother came back, she'd decided what she was going to order.

"Go ahead, Raine. Tell the lady what you want." Mother smiled and pulled her wallet out.

"Ma'am, what can I get for you?" The lady behind the counter asked mother for her order.

Mother's chin began to quiver as she looked through her wallet. Then, she started to dig through her purse, pulling the contents out and setting them onto the counter. Raine stared at her mother in disbelief. Something was very wrong. Mother shoved everything back into her purse.

"I'm terribly sorry," Mother said in a thick voice. "I've seemed to misplace my money." She took Raine by the arm and nearly pulled her out of the restaurant.

"I don't understand," Raine said. "What are we doing?"

"We're going back home."

"But why?" Raine couldn't believe that they'd driven all that way, just to turn back around.

"Because your father took every dime out of my purse. He took my ATM card, my checkbook, everything." Mother put the key in the ignition, looked at Raine and shrugged her shoulders.

Raine started to cry. Partly because she was very hungry but mostly because she didn't want to go back home. Maybe, she thought, Momma will just go home and get her money from Daddy. Then, we'll leave again.

They pulled into their driveway around three o'clock that afternoon. Mother hadn't spoken much during the drive back. Raine was so hungry that she felt like throwing up.

The house was quiet when they went inside. Daddy wasn't in his usual spot for a Saturday afternoon. The television wasn't even on. Mother had left all their things in the car, so Raine still had a glimmer of hope that they might leave again.

"Go make yourself a bowl of cereal," Mother said.

Raine was starving. She rummaged around in the pantry and found a box of raisin bran that was still half full. She sat at the kitchen table and ate two bowls of cereal.

Mother went upstairs. Raine didn't hear anyone talking so she assumed that Daddy wasn't home. Dresser drawers opened and shut. She could tell that Mother was looking through everything in the bedroom. She knew that her mother was looking for the money.

Eventually, Mother stopped looking and came downstairs. She had been crying. Without saying a word to Raine, she went out to the car and began to haul their belongings back into the house.


Raine couldn't remember what happened later that afternoon. There were blank spaces in her childhood memories, as if someone had just torn the fabric out and left nothing in its place.

As an adult, she wondered, why didn't Mother just go to the bank and withdraw some money? Why didn't she call someone for help? What was her mother so afraid of that she decided to stay?

She knew one thing about her mother. She was weak. Raine made a pact with herself a long time ago to never let a man get that close to her. If it weren't for Daddy, Mother might have had a chance of being a normal woman. Raine knew that men, in general, were bad news. Sex screwed everything up. Daddy used sex to control her mother. Raine was disgusted, watching Momma letting Daddy rut all over her like that.

Raine was perfectly happy to abstain. She didn't understand the whole "sex drive" thing anyway. The girls in the office would gossip (a little too loudly) about their sexual conquests, and Raine found it repulsive.

Flirting was foreign to her. Whenever her friend, Noelle, would talk her into going out to a club, Raine would pretend to be someone else just to be able to deal with the guys. She never told Noelle that she was pretending to be Serenity, but she was sure that her friend had noticed a difference.

"You're such a flirt when we're out, but you act like a damned nun when we're at the grocery store! What's up with that?" Noelle said to her after the cute produce guy tried to get Raine's number.

The only problem with pretending to be Serenity, is that sometimes she got so far into character, she forgot to be Raine. And when she forgot to be Raine, she couldn't remember everything that Serenity had said and done.

# CHAPTER 19
## SHE'LL BE BACK

The doorbell ringing, followed by a series of sharp knocks, woke Randall from a hazy slumber. He'd stopped keeping a regular schedule since Genny had gone, therefore he had no idea what time it was. If pressed, he wouldn't have been able to say what day of the week it was. The two trips that he'd made to town had been sufficient so far to stock the kitchen with booze, soda, and bacon.

After the rude treatment from his offspring, Randall kept himself on a nice even keel of soused. He was marinating in the booze, marinating in his thoughts. He'd vowed to get her back, but he was willing to wait until the time was right. No sense in rushing a job of that magnitude. And besides, he thought, she was enough of a weakling that she'd probably come crawling back after the real world spit her out anyway. Then, he'd rub her nose in it, just like a dog who'd shit on the carpet.

The knocking continued, so he went to the front door to see what all the fuss was about. A man holding a set of papers was on the other side of the door. Randall didn't bother to open it. He didn't answer for anyone unexpected. The fool was lucky that Randall didn't greet him with his Colt 45. He waited until the man drove away before starting a pot of coffee. The sun was almost in its noontime position. Randall pulled the last bit of bacon out of the refrigerator and dumped it into the cast iron skillet on the back of the stove. The aromas of the coffee brewing and the bacon frying mingled together into a delicious memory of a time when Genny was right where she belonged. Soon enough she'll be back, he told himself, soon enough.

# CHAPTER 20
# CLOSE QUARTERS

Daddy didn't call Raine again. In a way, she would have felt better if he had. The silence was worse because she had no idea what he was up to. The process server hadn't been able to serve divorce papers to Daddy. He hadn't answered the door.

Most days, Mother walked around with a bewildered look on her face. Raine had the suspicion that Mother had no real intention of making a life of her own. Instead, Mother was acting like she wanted to become a stay-at-home-mom again. At first, Raine liked having her laundry done, her meals cooked, and her apartment cleaned. It was nice to have Mother's undivided attention. But lately, all of Mother's mothering was annoying the hell out of her.

"Your clothes are washed and put away, honey."

"Was there anything to wash?" She was sure there was only a few things in the hamper.

"Just want to make sure you have clean clothes for work." Mother smiled and stirred something on the stove. "Dinner is almost ready."

"Thanks, but I'm not hungry," Raine said. "We had a baby shower after work for one of the secretaries."

"Did you eat anything healthy?" Mother asked. "Or did you just fill up on cake?"

"I'm fine." She went into her bedroom to change into her favorite sweats. The sweats weren't in their normal spot, at the foot of her bed. They weren't in her drawers either.

Raine yelled from the bedroom, "Do you know where my sweats are?"

"Which ones?"

"The sweats on my bed."

66

Mother appeared at her doorway. "Those old things? I threw them out. They had stains all over them and the cuffs were getting worn."

"They were my favorite! They were fine!"

"I've been going through your clothes and it looks like it's time to go shopping," Mother said. "Your bras are worn out, and you have almost no dresses."

"My wardrobe is fine!" Raine grabbed some shorts out of her dresser and stomped into the bathroom, slamming the door behind her.

"Raine, honey?" Mother stood outside the bathroom door. "I'm not trying to upset you. I know you've been busy and I can see that you need help."

Raine rubbed her eyes with both hands. The tension was giving her a mild headache. "I don't need a wife! And I'm not a little kid. I can take care of myself!" She waited until she could hear her mother walk away before she opened the door.

Instead of going to the living room to watch her evening television programs, Raine closed her bedroom door behind her, sat down on her bed, and opened her laptop. The daylight was giving way to dark. She liked the soothing blue-gray light seeping in through the partially opened blinds. Not sure what she was looking for, Raine surfed the internet for a while. The mindless activity helped take her mind off her irritation. The longer that Mother stayed, the less she felt at home in her own apartment.

## ~ A VISIT FROM SERENITY ~

Serenity waited until Raine drifted off before she went onto the site. She had to retype the login and password because the history had been erased on Raine's computer. It had been a while since she'd had any freedom at all. With Raine's mother hanging around all the time, she was virtually on house arrest.

Almost immediately, a member of the chat room who went by the name of BigBen69 sent a message, "Turn the lights on baby."

Serenity reached behind her and pulled the cord on the bedside lamp. She typed, "Better?"

"Need more – wanna see your sweet body."

She got off the bed to turn the overhead light on and locked the door. Then, she positioned herself on Raine's bed in front of the laptop and typed, "Can you see me now?"

BigBen69 said, "Let me see your tits."

She slowly unzipped her hoodie, revealing her bare breasts. "Is this what you wanted to see?"

"Touch yourself," BigBen69 typed.

## ~ THE MORNING AFTER ~

"Raine?" Mother tapped on her bedroom door. "You're going to be late for work."

Stretching, she felt the hard edge of the laptop with her foot. *Damn it, I did it again!* This was the fourth or fifth time she'd fallen asleep with the computer. Luckily, she hadn't kicked it onto the floor yet.

"Raine?" The knocking continued.

"I'm up." She sat up and realized that her shirt was missing. Puzzled, she looked through the bedsheets. The hoodie was tossed onto the floor. *Weird.*

# CHAPTER 21
## KARMA

Toward the end of October, the trees began to shed their red-gold leaves and pumpkins made their annual appearances on neighbor's porches. Lilly was getting excited about Halloween. She took the children shopping for their costumes and Caleb picked out a Batman costume. Lilly hunted for a while before finding a darling little cat costume for Laney. The smell of bread, cookies, or pies baking in the oven greeted Gabe almost every evening. Getting ready for the holidays was one of Lilly's favorite things to do.

To make the season even more memorable, she planned Halloween themed crafts for Caleb each day. This was the first year that he was capable of cutting and pasting things without much help. She hoped that he would remember these times when he was older. Lilly didn't have much in the way of happy holiday memories from her childhood. She'd been accused of going overboard by several of her friends, but she didn't care. She was trying to be the kind of mother that she had needed when she was a child.

Caleb sat at their big dining room table happily making construction paper bats and ghosts for several hours one evening. Lilly almost stopped him from making so many. They had enough bats to last a lifetime. She thought better of it though and decided to let him cut to his heart's content.

"Momma?" he asked as he cut out another bat.

"What, Honey?"

"Why don't we have Halloween trees? We have Christmas trees. Maybe we should have a tree for every fun day." His little face looked perplexed.

"I don't know baby, I guess we could." Caleb's perspective tickled Lilly.

The morning of Halloween, Lilly put the ingredients for chili into the crock-pot. She'd won the Chili Division of the Crock-pot Cook-off fundraiser for her Junior League Chapter two years in a row. It made her feel good to have her recipe published in the annual cookbook.

After dropping Caleb off at school, she rushed home to make cupcakes for his class Halloween party. He'd been talking about the party for days.

"Please Momma, don't forget my party" Caleb pleaded with her.

"Don't worry, Baby. I'll be there." Lilly had reassured him with a kiss on his forehead as she dropped him off at school earlier that morning. He was still young enough that he wasn't embarrassed to kiss his mama in front of his friends. Soon enough, he'd pretend he didn't know her in public.

Lilly had young children, but her girlfriends all had teenagers. She'd heard the sadness in her friends' voices when they talked about their kids pretending like they didn't recognize them in public. She imagined that it would be very hard to go from receiving blown kisses at the classroom door to being someone they avoided out of embarrassment.

All the rushing around made Lilly a little nauseated. She grabbed a soda out of the fridge and took a few sips. *Maybe the sugar will help me feel better.* She forgot to eat sometimes when she was busy. Nausea was one of the nasty side effects of low blood sugar. After a few swallows, she began to feel better.

Later that evening, Gabe walked through the door into a flurry of activity. Laney was crawling around in a diaper and cat ears. Caleb was testing his Batman cape by running as fast as he could from one end of the house to the other. Lilly was dumping a mountain of candy into a bowl that she would leave on the porch for trick-or-treaters.

"Hi Honey." Lilly looked up at Gabe from the candy bowl with a grin.

"When are we leaving?" Gabe asked.

"Any minute; the only thing left to do is to put Laney into her costume", Lilly replied as she tossed the empty candy bag into the trash. "I've got chili in the crock-pot for later."

Gabe grinned and rubbed his stomach. "It smells *really* good! I'm starving!"

The evening was perfect for trick-or-treating, not too cold or damp. Caleb flew from house to house, collecting more candy than he'd ever seen in his life. Laney fell asleep in her stroller after the first three houses. Gabe, the self-designated photographer, took their camera along and snapped some cute shots of the kids.

When she tucked Caleb and Laney into their beds that night, Lilly's heart was full. She was grateful in a way that only a newly redeemed sinner could be. She'd been given the second chance of a lifetime. Lilly gave a silent prayer of thanks for everything that she'd almost thrown away.

A wave of nausea woke Lilly the next morning before dawn. She hoped the chili wasn't bad. Having the whole family sick with food poisoning was the last thing she needed. Rolling onto her side she could see that Gabe was still sleeping soundly. Maybe it hasn't hit him yet, she thought.

Lilly slipped her robe on and went down to the kitchen. She sipped on some soda while she started a pot of coffee. Her stomach settled a little and Lilly all but forgot the nausea.

She grabbed the biggest mug she could find and filled it up with strong black coffee. The soft dawn light was just starting to cast a golden glow over her kitchen. The quiet early morning was her favorite time of day. With her planner, she sat down at the breakfast bar to see what the day held in store for her. She flipped through to November 1st and was thrilled to see a completely blank page. Even though Lilly didn't have a job anymore, it was a rarity that she had a day all to herself.

Feeling generous, she decided to make Gabe a nice breakfast. Lilly pulled eggs and bacon out of the fridge. She got her favorite copper skillet down from the rack and set the burner to medium. After a few moments, the bacon began to sizzle. Lilly loved her new gas range. It gave her so much more control over the temperature than the old electric one had. It had cost more, but it was well worth the price. Gabe had spoiled her.

Gabe poked his head into the kitchen and inhaled deeply. "Mmmm! I smell bacon!" he exclaimed. Gabe hugged Lilly from behind, giving the nape of her neck a little kiss.

"It's almost ready!" Lilly turned to kiss Gabe on his cheek.

The aroma was making Lilly feel a little sick. She guessed it was a stomach bug that she seemed to be coming down with. Once Gabe left for work, Lilly woke up Caleb and helped him dress for school. After a brief protest over wanting to eat Halloween candy for breakfast and a frantic search for a lost shoe, they were on their way to school.

On the way back home, Lilly's mind raced with thoughts of how to spend her free day. She decided she'd spend the morning planning homemade Christmas gifts. Although making all the gifts for teachers and friends was a little time-consuming, Lilly thought it was a nice touch.

Lilly put Laney down for her morning nap and began to search Pinterest for gift ideas. The warmth of the sun on her back was making her sleepy. A nap sounded wonderful to Lilly. She put her computer in sleep mode and went upstairs to do the same with herself.

Lilly woke up from her nap feeling queasy again. Little alarm bells went off in her head. The blood rushed out of her head as she sat up in a panic. *How could I have missed it?* Frantic, she tried to recall when she'd last had her period. Gabe had a vasectomy after Laney's birth, so Lilly had stopped keeping track of her menstrual cycle.

"Oh God, please no!" She prayed over and over. She couldn't be pregnant. Unable to catch her breath, Lilly went into the bathroom to splash cold water on her face. Desperate thoughts raced through her mind.

While standing in the feminine product aisle later that afternoon, in a store as far from her house as possible, Lilly compared the early pregnancy tests. She decided on the brand that promised accurate results any time of day.

The cashier rang up the test and smiled at Laney. "Is this gonna be your second baby honey?"

Lying, Lilly said, "It's for a friend".

Barely making it in time, she picked up Caleb from school and hurried back home, hoping to get there before Gabe. She locked herself in the bathroom and opened the box. Carefully, she removed the test from the foil wrapper and sat down on the toilet. Lilly peed on the stick for ten seconds, just like the directions said.

She couldn't bear to watch the test develop so Lilly busied herself straightening the bathroom counter. After several minutes of solid prayer to a god that she wasn't sure she even believed in, Lilly summoned the courage to look at the results.

She heard Gabe's voice and realized he must have just gotten home. She quickly wrapped up the evidence into the shopping bag and stuffed it deep into the bathroom trash under a pile of used Kleenex tissues.

"I'm in here Honey!" Lilly replied to Gabe's calling for her. Picking up a few dirty towels, she walked toward the laundry room. Gabe met her in the hallway with a warm hug. She put her face into his chest and took a deep breath to steady herself.

"Are you okay?" He moved her backward from his embrace to view her face.

Lilly shook her head. "I'm not feeling well" she lied, "I think I'm coming down with the stomach flu."

Gabe gave her a gentle squeeze. "Go to bed honey. I'm sure I can handle the kids for the evening."

Guilt twisted Lilly's heart into little knots but she went to bed anyway. She needed time to think about what to do. She cried into her pillow for nearly an hour. She went through a mental list of options but nothing felt right. She could think of only one person that could help her.

# CHAPTER 22
## AN INVITATION

Randi didn't recognize the number on her caller id. Probably a bill collector, she thought. She silenced the ringer and put the phone back down on the table. Annoyed by the interruption, she found her place again in the John Grisham novel she was in the middle of. Randi didn't own a television. Reading was her main form of entertainment.

A few moments later, the same number called Randi again. She sighed and answered in her most businesslike voice.

"This is Miranda, may I help you?"

"Hi Randi, it's Lilly. Am I interrupting something?"

"Kind of; what's up?" She didn't elaborate that she was reading the same book she'd finished two months before.

"Could we meet for lunch?" Lilly added quickly, "My treat."

"Sure, but I can buy my own." Randi wasn't about to let Lilly act superior to her. Just because she didn't have a wealthy husband like Lilly didn't mean that she couldn't buy her own lunch. "When?"

"Now? If that's not too short of notice."

Randi didn't answer Lilly right away. She could hear the sense of urgency in Lilly's voice and was enjoying having the upper hand for a change, even if it was only for a second or two.

"I can pick you up." Lilly offered, as if to sweeten the deal.

"That's fine, but give me about an hour."

Randi changed out of her sweatpants into something nicer. She didn't know where Lilly might want to go for lunch but she was certain sweatpants wouldn't be appropriate attire. She straightened her dingy little front room. Even though she'd never been to her big sister's house, she was sure Lilly's front room was always tidy.

Once she was done dressing and straightening, she had about twenty minutes to kill before Lilly was due to arrive. Randi went out on the porch to wait for her sister. She sat down on the top step and lit up a cigarette.

Randi wondered what Lilly wanted to see her about. She could count on one hand the number of times that she'd spoken with either of her sisters in the last few years. Randi hadn't even seen Lilly's new baby yet. Randi wasn't the doting auntie type. Hell, she thought, the new baby probably isn't that new anymore.

# CHAPTER 23
## FORTUNE AVENUE

It took Lilly a little longer than she'd expected to find Randi's house. She wasn't familiar with the part of town that her sister lived in. The streets were lined with empty flower beds and unfinished landscaping projects. Partially painted and weather worn, the houses were a testament of unfulfilled hopes and dreams.

She wondered if the owners had run out of money or motivation. *Maybe both.* Lilly thought it would be sad to live in such disrepair. The front yards were cluttered with sun-bleached toys and shards of plastic from playthings broken by years of use. Her own children played on sturdy Little Tykes brand toys, safely encased in a fenced-in play yard. Her and Gabe's lush green lawn was cared for every Tuesday by a landscaping service.

She glanced at the scrap of paper with Randi's address once more to be certain that she had the right place on Fortuna Avenue. Funny name for a street in this neighborhood, she thought. Randi sat on the top step of the front porch smoking a cigarette. She looked out of place with the weathered, worn house as a backdrop behind her. Lilly wondered how Randi had managed to stay so pretty after smoking and drinking so much through the years. It wasn't any big secret that Randi liked to party.

Lilly paused for a moment before getting out of her car. She wasn't quite sure she was going to tell Randi why she'd wanted to see her. Play it by ear, she told herself.

She opened her car door and waved at Randi. Randi put her cigarette out and held her finger up as if to say "Just a minute." Randi locked her front door and walked toward Lilly's car.

"Hey big sis!" Randi smiled and opened the passenger side door of Lilly's Lexus.

"How've you been?" Lilly waited for Randi to buckle before pulling away from the curb.

"You know, just getting by." Randi dug into her bag and pulled out her cell phone. She appeared to be reading a text, so Lilly waited for her to finish.

"So, are you working?" Even though Randi's place wasn't very nice, she figured she must have some income.

"No, not regularly."

Lilly focused on the traffic and tried to think of something else to talk about with Randi. Save for the same gene pool, they had absolutely nothing in common. *I'm not sure why I have to be the one to make conversation.*

"So, how are the kids?" Randi asked.

Lilly smiled. "They're great. Caleb is in kindergarten and Laney is almost ready to walk. They're the best."

"I'll have to see them sometime." Randi looked away.

"Sure, that'd be nice." Lilly lied. She loved her sister, but exposing her children to Randi was the last thing that she wanted to do. For all she knew, Randi was on drugs.

"How's Momma?" Randi asked. "I mean, how's she holding up since she left Daddy?"

"Okay, I guess. Haven't you seen her lately?"

Randi shook her head. "No, not yet. I should, but I'm just not up for it."

Lilly tapped her fingers on the steering wheel and tried to think of a response that wouldn't sound judgmental. Mother wasn't fun to be around, but she didn't deserve to be shunned.

"Can I ask why you aren't speaking to her? It's been something like a decade, right?"

"I really don't feel like discussing it. It's between me and Momma." She fiddled with her phone some more.

"I think it's just between you and you, Randi. Mother doesn't seem to know why you aren't talking to her."

"Drop it okay?" Randi ended the conversation about Mother.

"Fine. Sorry to be so nosy. I guess I can't help being the bossy big sister." She hoped that by making light of it, Randi wouldn't be too offended.

# CHAPTER 24
## FULL OF SURPRISES

Lilly's car was impeccable, as Randi knew it would be. The Lexus was loaded with leather seats and power everything. Randi couldn't even remember the last time she was in a car this nice.

With perfectly manicured hands, Lilly changed the radio to a station with classical music. Randi felt sleepy immediately. She supposed Lilly wanted neutral background noise.

Randi examined Lilly's profile. Even though years had passed, her big sister didn't look much different than when she first got her driver's license. She smiled whenever she thought about that year.

Lilly was fifteen, Randi was ten, and riding to school with her big sister was the coolest thing in the world. The old beater that Dad let Lilly drive had an eight-track tape player in it. The only tapes they owned were Foghat, Led Zeppelin, and Creedence Clearwater Revival. "Oh Suzie Q" by CCR was Randi's favorite song, and she knew it by heart. Sometimes Randi thought she'd give anything to go back to those days - riding to school with Lilly in that old, beat-up Dodge.

The ride today was nothing like those fun cruises from long ago. Lilly tried to make small talk and Randi tried to reciprocate but conversation was awkward. They had nothing in common. She might as well be trying to converse with a stranger in the supermarket, except for the part where Lilly reprimanded her for not talking to Momma. Randi didn't bother to explain to Lilly. She wouldn't understand anyway. They rode together in strained silence the rest of the way.

Lilly pulled into the parking lot of small Mexican cafe. Randi was a little surprised that Lilly would choose such an unassuming place for lunch. She'd figured they'd eat lunch at the country club or some other snooty restaurant.

Piped in Tejano music could be heard at the outside entrance. Inside, the place smelled like fried tortilla chips and cumin. It took a minute for Randi's eyes to adjust to the dark interior before she could see clearly. A doe-eyed girl who didn't look old enough to be working seated the sisters in a quiet booth in the back.

"What can I get you to drink?" The hostess handed them plastic covered menus.

"I'll have a frozen margarita." Lilly surprised Randi by ordering something other than iced tea.

Randi ordered a screwdriver and busied herself looking over the menu choices. The owners had chosen to keep the meals simple, so it didn't take Randi long to decide what she would order. Randi nibbled on the chips and salsa and watched her big sister study the small menu. Lilly didn't look up at Randi until the waitress brought their drinks.

"Do you know what you want?" Lilly asked Randi.

"I'll have the carne guisada y papas", Randi replied.

Lilly ordered the tortilla soup and another margarita. Randi had never seen Lilly drink more than one beer. Her curiosity peaked, she asked, "Okay, sis, 'fess up - what's this about?"

Lilly surprised Randi again and lit a cigarette. To the best of Randi's knowledge, Lilly had smoked only once in her life, years ago, before she'd graduated from high school. She'd threatened to kill Randi if she ever told Mom about it.

"Randi, I need to know this is between you and me." She raised one eyebrow and motioned with one finger back and forth between Randi and herself.

"Ha, who would I tell? It's not like you and I travel in the same circles, Lil." Randi laughed dryly.

"I'm serious, Randi! You can't talk to anyone!" Lilly demanded.

"Okay, Lil! I won't say anything. I swear it." Randi held her right hand up like she was being sworn in on the witness stand. Must be bad if she's smoking and drinking, Randi thought.

Lilly took a long drag off her cigarette and began to tell Randi about her affair.

"That's it? You brought me here to tell me you've been cheating on your amazing husband?" Randi interrupted Lilly. "You're whining because you've screwed around on Mr. Perfect, and you drag me to lunch in a dive for that?"

"God no, Randi!" Lilly's eyes filled up with tears. "It's far worse than that! But thanks for the judgment! I expected more from someone like you!"

"Someone like me?" Randi repeated herself. "Someone like me? What exactly would someone like me be? Someone not like your prima donna, country club friends?"

"No, Randi, someone who understands what it's like to make mistakes!" Lilly must have uttered the words before she had a chance to think them through.

"That's perfect! My perfect big sister fucks around on her husband and needs to make a confession. Is that it, Lilly? Can't tell your spotless friends? What, will they ban you from the next bake sale?" Randi stood up and threw a twenty-dollar bill on the table.

"Better not touch that, I probably earned it stripping!"

"Randi, wait!" Lilly begged. "I didn't mean it like that! I'm so sorry! Sit down, please!"

Randi realized she had the undivided attention of all the patrons in the restaurant and sat down. She lowered her voice to a loud whisper, "What, Lilly? What else did you need to confess to me?"

What Lilly said next surprised Randi for the third time in less than an hour.

# CHAPTER 25
## LILLY'S SECRET

"I'm pregnant." Lilly couldn't believe she was continuing to tell Randi her secret after the outburst. She had nothing left to lose. The worst was already said.

"It's not Gabe's. He had a vasectomy after Laney was born."

Randi looked appropriately stunned. Lilly continued. "I don't love the baby's father. I'd give anything to take it back. It was a huge mistake." Lilly could feel the margarita she'd just downed threatening to come back up.

Randi sat quietly for a moment. Lilly couldn't read her expression. After what felt like forever to Lilly, Randi spoke.

"So, what do you want from me?"

"I don't know. I don't want to have it. I thought maybe…" Lilly let her words trail off. It was so hard to say it out loud.

"I thought maybe you knew someplace that I could, you know, get this sort of thing taken care of. You know, discreetly."

"Do you mean abort it, Lilly?" Randi asked in a very gentle voice.

"Yeah, I don't know what else to do. I'll lose Gabe; I'll lose everything." Lilly felt like her heart was being squeezed into pieces.

Randi lit a cigarette and chewed on her bottom lip. Lilly tried to imagine what Randi was thinking.

"Lilly, I don't know what you thought I could do for you, but I don't know where you could get something like that done. And even if I did…" Randi's voice trailed off.

Randi leaned across the table and took Lilly's hand. Softly she said, "Listen Lil, I would love to be able to have a child. The thought of killing a baby just because its daddy isn't who I wanted it to be… well, I can't imagine doing something like that."

Lilly could see that her sister had more to say so she waited for Randi to finish her thoughts.

"Look, it doesn't matter who the daddy is, Lil. It's still your baby! Can you live with something like that?"

Lilly thought about Randi's words. She'd hoped to get answers from Randi today, but instead she'd only got more questions.

# CHAPTER 26
## TRADING PLACES

Lilly parked in front of Randi's shabby little rental. Randi unbuckled her seat belt and turned her upper body to face her sister. "You know I'm here for you, right, Lil?" Randi felt that her words were insignificant given the heartbreaking decision her sister was faced with. She stretched her arms out to embrace Lilly.

Lilly hugged Randi back tightly. "That means a lot to me, Randi. Thanks for listening."

"What are you going to do? Do you have any idea?" Randi didn't think she would be able to put Lilly's dilemma out of her mind. Lilly had always been the good girl of the family. And Randi had done a fine job of playing the black sheep over the last fifteen years. More than a time or two, Randi had thought that it would be nice to switch places with Lilly for a while. But Lilly's predicament wasn't giving Randi even the slightest bit of the satisfaction she'd anticipated.

Lilly shook her head slowly and answered Randi's question. "I have no idea. I keep hoping that this is all a nightmare, and I'll wake up soon."

Randi watched Lilly's car until it reached the end of her block. She genuinely hoped Lilly would be okay. She'd always imagined that Lil had the perfect life. Randi had never thought that she'd one day feel sorry for her big sister.

After digging out a new pack of cigarettes, she unlocked the front door and dropped her purse onto the floor. Tipping the pack upside down, she smacked it firmly in the palm of her hand until she was satisfied the tobacco was properly packed. Using her ring finger and thumb, she caught hold of the edge of the plastic wrapper and peeled it off the box. Next, she opened the flap and pulled the little foil top covering the cigarettes and put her nose up to them, inhaling the delicious fragrance of the unsmoked tobacco. *It's too bad they stink so much after they're lit.*

She sat down on the top step of her run-down porch and lit a cigarette. Car loads of teenagers passed by, making their way out of the nearby high school. It was a cacophony of rumbling cars and squealing kids for nearly twenty minutes every weekday afternoon after school was dismissed. Then, the street became quiet again. All the nearby mom and pop stores had closed within a few years after the bypass was constructed. School traffic was rush hour in her forgotten neighborhood.

She thought about the situation with Momma and wondered if calling her would be the right thing to do. Maybe with Daddy out of the picture, she and Momma might stand a chance at having a normal relationship.

# CHAPTER 27
## BRASS RING

Lilly switched the radio off during the drive home and thought about the things that Randi had said to her. She couldn't shake the cold dread that she felt through her entire body. *How could I have been so stupid?* She knew there wasn't going to be an easy way out of her situation.

Lilly had thought that she had life all figured out but one little slip and the gods were punishing her. She'd invested blood, sweat, and tears in moving beyond her upbringing. *Maybe Daddy was right. Maybe I'll never amount to anything.*

Marrying Gabe had seemed like catching the brass ring. He was handsome, rich, and magnetic. She'd chosen him because he was better than someone of her upbringing deserved to marry, and she knew it. And although they didn't hesitate to let her know how very lucky she was to land Gabe, she didn't need his sisters and his mother to tell her this.

Lilly had invested so much time in learning how to behave in Gabe's world that an outsider would never know that she wasn't native to it, but Lilly knew. She lived in fear of being discovered for the fraud that she was. Marrying Gabe didn't make the hollow feeling go away.

Now, thanks to her own stupidity, there was a very real chance that she was going to lose everything she'd worked so hard for. *Without Gabe, I'm nothing.*

Lilly hadn't planned on fading into someone else's life. When she was younger, Lilly had planned on being someone important all by herself. She started college at Trinity University in the fall semester of 1990 with every intention of becoming an elementary school teacher. She threw herself into her studies and loved the newfound freedom of living away from home.

Three other students shared the expenses of a small apartment with

Lilly. She didn't make much money waiting tables at a nearby steakhouse, but she didn't need much. Between the four girls, the rent was affordable. Most nights she could bring home enough throwaway food from the restaurant to feed all four of them. When there wasn't enough from the steakhouse, ramen noodles kept their bellies full.

She finished her first year in college with a 4.0 grade point average. It didn't matter that Mother and Daddy didn't notice; Lilly was proud enough for herself. She'd already learned years before to not expect approval, especially from Daddy.

Lilly met Gabe at a friend's party the summer after her freshman year. He was different than the other guys. She couldn't have put it into words at the time, but looking back, she realized that Gabe had a polished way of carrying himself. She fell hard and fast.

It didn't occur to Lilly that Gabe came from a wealthy family until he took her home to the family lake house for Thanksgiving. She'd never been around anyone with money before.

~ November 1991 ~

Gabe waited in her tiny living room while she dressed for the feast. Lilly had borrowed a black mini skirt and a button-up shirt from one of her roommates. Her tight budget didn't allow for a new outfit, but she wanted to look her best when she met his family for the first time.

"Are you ready yet? We're going to be late if you don't hurry up!" Gabe was uncharacteristically impatient.

"Give me a minute! I'm almost finished." Lilly sprayed her teased-up hair and gave her makeup another critical look. She didn't want to look too made up. She slipped on her bangle bracelets and decided she'd done enough damage.

"Well, do I look okay?" His approval mattered to her more than she cared to admit.

Gabe looked uncomfortable and didn't answer immediately. "You look beautiful, Lil."

"Don't sound so convincing!" Lilly grinned.

"It's just that…" Gabe cleared his throat. "Do you have a skirt that's a little longer?"

"Maybe, why?" Lilly figured that Gabe would like the black mini skirt. He always told her that he loved her legs, especially when they were wrapped around him.

"Mother and Daddy are a little old fashioned. Just want them to see you for the lady that you are." Gabe melted her with one of his boyish smiles.

Lilly wasn't sure what to expect as they drove down the winding lake road. Trees sheltered any real view of the lake or the houses surrounding it.

She thought that it was a cool tradition for Gabe's family to have Thanksgiving dinner at their lake cabin. Gabe had two sisters, a brother, their spouses, and nieces and nephews, so she was preparing herself for a crowded gathering.

"We're here!" Gabe announced as he stopped the car at a gate blocking the road. "I'll open the gate, and you drive through so I can close it behind us."

Lilly slid over to the driver's seat and waited for Gabe to swing the gate open all the way. *Wow, these people are really private.*

She scooted back over to the passenger side of Gabe's car once she'd navigated through the entry. While waiting for Gabe to lock up, she noticed a little cabin on the left side of the road. The cabin had a single light in one of the windows, a candle perhaps.

"I don't think anyone else is here yet, Gabe." *Or they're so old fashioned that they don't use electricity.*

"No, they're here." Gabe pointed down the road to a cluster of vehicles in front of a stone wall.

"This isn't your family's cabin?" Lilly pointed to the little cabin beside them.

"It's one of our cabins." Gabe seemed embarrassed.

The family lake house was actually a collection of five houses on Medina Lake ranging in size from the small one-room cabin with the light in the window to a formidable 5,000 square foot home with vaulted ceilings and two-story high windows. The stone wall with all the vehicles parked in front of it sheltered the largest home.

Gabe parked his car next to a well-kept older model Cadillac and turned to Lilly. "Are you ready to meet my family?"

"I can't wait!" Lilly was lying. She was slightly terrified to meet his family after seeing the collection of houses and cars. She'd felt far more ready when she thought his family might be a religious bunch that hadn't enough money to have electricity installed in their one room shack yet.

The massive stairs leading up to the main house were covered with expensive looking tiles. Stone planters adorned the railing all along the patio. Someone had taken care to place luminaria with little Texas stars on each step and around the patio. The soft candlelight was stunning. Lilly was sure she'd just stepped onto a photo shoot for Better Homes and Gardens.

Golden rays spilled out of the floor length windows and lit the entryway. Gabe squeezed her hand as if to reassure her and rang the bell. The door opened with a lavender scented whoosh to reveal a heavyset lady with perfectly coifed hair.

"Gabriel! What on earth are you doing ringing the bell like a guest?" Her smile revealed unusually white teeth for someone of her age. She stretched her plump arms out to receive a hug.

"Aunt Julia!" Clearly pleased to see Aunt Julia, Gabe embraced her warmly. "I'd love to introduce you to my friend! Aunt Julia Belle, meet Lillian Carter; Lilly, this is my dear Aunt Julia Belle Chenowyth!"

"I'm very pleased to meet you Mrs. Chenowyth." Offering her hand for a shake, Lilly hoped that she was being proper enough.

Aunt Julia waved her hand in a dismissive manner, "You must call me Aunt Julia. Mrs. Chenowyth was my mother!" She shook Lilly's hand and patted the top of it with her free hand. "Please come in and meet the rest of our clan."

So far, so good, Lilly thought. Hopefully the rest of the family would be as happy to meet her as Aunt Julia was.

Meeting Gabe's entire family proved to be relatively painless. At the time, she was still naïve enough to confuse politeness with acceptance.

"Gabe tells us that you are a student, Lillian." Gabe's mother commented during dinner between bites. Lilly didn't consider it a question but felt she should answer.

"That's right Mrs. Chenowyth; I'm going to be a teacher."

"That's so nice. An admirable profession for a young woman." Gabe's mother, the complete physical opposite of her sister-in-law, smiled and took a very small bite of her turkey.

"What does your family do Lillian? I don't believe I've met your parents before." Mr. Chenowyth had seemed keenly interested in Lilly's last name when introduced.

"Daddy is in the insurance business, and Mother is a housewife." Lilly had never given much thought to her parents' occupations before.

"Oh, does your father own an agency then?" Mr. Chenowyth raised his eyebrows slightly. He looked hopeful.

"No, he's a salesman; sells homeowner's insurance, vehicle insurance, that type of thing." Lilly fiddled with her napkin in her lap, twisting it into tight coils. She had the sinking feeling that her answer wasn't acceptable.

Mr. Chenowyth looked disappointed to hear this and resumed eating. Lilly couldn't read Gabe's expression, which made her feel even worse. She took a sip of her wine and focused on the tart fruity flavor of it.

The rest of Thanksgiving dinner was uneventful, but it was clear to Lilly that Gabe's family had no idea she and Gabe were dating.

Eventually Gabe did tell his family that Lilly was more than a friend. Gabe's family must have approved because he proposed to her in the fall of 1992. Lilly was thrilled to be the future Mrs. Chenowyth.

She announced the news to her parents, but she didn't involve them in the planning of the wedding. It was tradition for the bride's parents to pay for the ceremony; however, she knew that her parents wouldn't be able to deliver the type of wedding that the Chenowyths were accustomed to. Unbeknownst to his parents, she and Gabe paid for most of it with loans that would put them in debt for years afterward. While the loans bothered Gabe, it didn't matter to Lilly. She would've done anything to keep up appearances.

To gain her mother-in-law's approval, Lilly threw herself headfirst into all of Mrs. Chenowyth's favorite charities. In fact, she focused so much on her volunteer work that she flunked herself out of her third year of college. "No matter," she thought, "I'm not going to have to work once we're married."

Lilly had taken great pride in learning how to fit into Gabe's world. She had been certain that once she was refined enough and polished enough, she would finally be happy.

Now that she had mastered the game, Lilly realized she'd been a lot happier back when she and Gabe were living in their first apartment, struggling to pay their bills.

# CHAPTER 28
## TOO MANY CHOICES

Genevieve had used the week after leaving Randall to put her affairs in order. She'd taken a great deal of money out of their savings account and retained a divorce attorney. The attorney came highly recommended by Raine's boss. Mr. Kendall was kind enough to take the time to set up the consultation for Genevieve. She couldn't understand why Raine didn't care for Mr. Kendall.

"But Raine, he seems like such a nice man!"

"Mom, he's not nice at all!" Raine insisted. "He's an old troll!"

"Raine! That's an awful thing to say!" Genevieve scolded her. "That man went out of his way to help us!" She thought Raine sounded like a thirteen-year-old child, whining about a chore she didn't want to do.

"You mean he went out of his way to help *you*, Mom." Raine corrected her mother, rolling her eyes in an exaggerated manner. Raine sat on the sofa with her bare feet tucked underneath her.

She looked like a teenager to Genevieve. She was acting like one, too. "Well, you can think whatever you wish, Raine, but I think he's kind." She was somewhat amused by Raine's annoyance.

Genevieve also set up a checking account in her own name and bought her first cell phone during that week. She imagined that she was soaring up through the dark crushing waters of her old life toward the bright surface of her new life.

Still, Genevieve found it very strange to have so much freedom. In fact, as the weeks wore on, her newfound liberty had become downright disturbing. She wasn't accustomed to having so many options. And Genevieve knew she had irritated Raine on more than one occasion with her indecisiveness.

"Mom, just pick one already!" Raine and Genevieve stood in the tea and coffee aisle of the H-E-B market, examining the vast array of herbal teas.

"I will. There are so many different kinds, I can't decide which one I want to try first." She'd narrowed it down to three different teas.

"Get them all, Mom! Try them all! They're only two bucks a box." Raine tapped an impatient rhythm with her foot.

"I'll just get the chamomile." Genevieve put the box of tea into the cart. Once they reached the end of the aisle, she picked the box back up and went to exchange it for a mint tea.

With an exasperated smile on her face, Raine shook her head.

Genevieve's inability to make a choice wasn't limited to groceries or shopping. For the first time in forty years, Genevieve not only had choices available, she had the responsibility to choose. This fact scared the holy hell out of her.

And there were so many things for Genevieve to decide. Raine and Lilly had produced a lengthy to-do list for their mother. Each day since, Raine took time to review the list. "Mom, have you given any more thought to where you would like to live?"

"I really don't know, honey. What do you think?" Genevieve didn't have a clue about the different areas in the city.

"I gave you the apartment guide. Did you see anything you liked?"

"They all look the same to me, Raine." Genevieve busied herself scrubbing the kitchen sink.

"Okay, they might look the same, but you still need to pick one. At least go check some of them out! You won't know until you see them!" Raine snapped at her mother. She pulled a water bottle out of the refrigerator and shut the door with a slam.

"Well, for heaven's sake Raine, you don't have to be rude! I'm not going to live with you forever!" Genevieve marveled at how quickly that she'd worn out her welcome.

"Mom, I know you're not going to live with me forever. That's not my point! You aren't doing anything to put your life back together!"

"That's simply not true." Taken off guard by Raine's attack, that was the best response that she could come up with on such short notice. She felt like a small child being reprimanded by her mother.

"Really? How are you going to get around, Mom? Are you buying a car? Taking the bus? And where are you going to live? In a house? In an apartment? How are you going to pay for it? Do you even know how much money you'll be getting each month? Where is it coming from? Alimony? Welfare? Retirement funds? Have you thought about any of this?" Raine took a break from her tirade and sorted through the mail lying on the counter.

Genevieve spoke in a cold, quiet manner she normally reserved for only the worst offenses. "Thank you for being so concerned with my wellbeing Raine. I appreciate that you've taken the time to orchestrate a schedule for me since you are so experienced at managing life. I'm very sorry to inconvenience you with my little problems."

Wounded, Genevieve retreated to the guestroom. She needed to think, and Raine clearly needed a little space.

# CHAPTER 29
## IT'S ALWAYS ABOUT HER

Raine finished the scrubbing job that her mother had started moments before stomping off to the guestroom to pout. Her mother had done it again, and Raine was furious. She refuses to play any role other than the victim, Raine thought to herself. Mother used her guilt trips to give herself a free pass from all responsibility. *Must be nice to be excused from real life.*

When Raine was a child, there was no room for her own sadness. Mother's suffering was priority. Raine had been given no choice other than to feel sorry for her mother. It wasn't until she'd grown up that she understood how selfish her mother was.

One memory stood out in Raine's mind more strongly than the others. She was seven years old, it was summertime, and she was bored out of her mind. Randi was at her summer babysitting job, and Mother was busy in the garden. She was left to her own devices for the morning.

Like most kids who live out in the country, Raine discovered all sorts of creative things to do with rocks and twigs. Earlier that morning, while walking along the tree line, Raine had found a smooth, solid stick. About the same size as the baton, Lilly twirled when she was in high school, the hefty branch felt good to her hand.

Raine walked up and down their gravel driveway looking for fossils, scooting the rocks around with her new favorite stick. She got the great idea to pretend her stick was a baseball bat and some of the roundest rocks were little tiny baseballs.

She tossed rock after rock up into the air and swung at them, missing each time. Raine was about to give up and switch to a game of pretend golf when she hit a homerun. Stunned that she had actually managed to hit a rock, it took Raine a second or two to connect the shattered front window with her actions.

With a hoe still in her hand and small clumps of dirt flying off her, Mother came running around the side of the house from the garden area. She had a look of horror on her face. "Oh no! Your father is going to be furious with you!"

Raine didn't fully understand what Mother meant until that evening when Daddy arrived home.

"Come downstairs Raine, your father wants to speak with you." Mother sounded scared.

Filled with dread, Raine slowly walked down the flight of stairs to find Daddy waiting for her in the living room. Twisting her apron skirt, Mother stood near the piano with her eyes downcast. Raine's pleading gaze was lost on Mother.

"Come here." Daddy pointed to the spot right in front of him. Raine could see that he was holding her stick in his right hand.

Frightened, Raine didn't move quickly enough, and Daddy yanked her over to the exact spot that he had instructed her to stand. Even though she tried very hard not to cry, Raine couldn't stop herself. She knew from watching Randi get into trouble that crying would make Daddy even angrier.

"Are you trying to cost me more money than you already do?" Daddy's voice was calm, but Raine knew that *he* wasn't calm.

Unsure how to answer Daddy's question, Raine shook her head. Raine could tell that her response wasn't satisfactory to Daddy. His face was contorted in an expression that Raine had seen before. Panic traveled from her bare toes to the top of her head.

"Turn around and put your hands on the wall." Daddy instructed Raine.

"No, Daddy, I'm sorry!" Raine thought she might be able to reason with Daddy.

"Now!"

Trembling, Raine turned around and put her hands on the wall. She had a fleeting thought that she might get into trouble for putting her hands on the wall, too. It was against the rules to touch the walls.

The pain from the stick was searing as Daddy lashed her bottom and legs. He struck her over and over again. Raine couldn't have stopped the scream coming out of her mouth if her life depended on it. Instinctively, she put her hands behind her legs to stop the blows. This only angered Daddy more. In a desperate act to escape the pummeling, Raine dropped down into a ball. She could feel the crack of the stick on her back and head.

"No, Randall! Stop it! It's enough!" Mother shrieked at the top of her lungs in a voice that Raine would never forget. Mother was sobbing.

Daddy dropped the stick and walked out of the room. Mother picked Raine up and carried her upstairs to the bedroom. Raine had never been so frightened in her life. She was too terrified to speak. Raine never forgot that beating nor did she forget what Mother said to her afterward.

"How could you, Raine?" Raine thought she misunderstood her mother at first. She winced as Mother roughly cleaned her wounds.

"How could you do something so stupid? If anyone sees you, they'll take you away from me! You should have known better! You know how mad Daddy gets! What did you think would happen?"

On top of feeling scared of Daddy, she was afraid someone would take her away from Mother. Full of guilt and fear, Raine's heart sat heavy like a rock in her chest.

## ~ Enter Shanti ~

Raine did everything in her power to avoid another thrashing like the one she received on that summer day. She stayed out of Daddy's way and tried to be very careful not to break or dirty anything. It wasn't easy to stay out of trouble. Randi moved out of the house when Raine was eight years old, and there weren't any children living nearby.

If it weren't for her new friend Shanti, Raine would've been a very lonely little girl. Shanti played house with Raine for hours at a time. Looking for hidden treasures, they explored the fields and dirt roads. It didn't take long for Raine to realize that Mother and Daddy couldn't see Shanti.

"Go for a walk with me." Shanti sat across from Raine at the breakfast table, twirling her long, dark curls with her fingers, waiting for Raine to finish her eggs.

"I can't today, I have to go with Mother to the store." Raine didn't want to go. The store was boring because she had to stay with Mother. She wasn't even allowed to look at the small toy aisle.

"Aw, can't I go with you?" Shanti made a puppy dog face at Raine.

"I'll ask Mother, but I don't think you're gonna like it."

"Who are you talking to, Raine?" Mother was washing up the breakfast dishes and overheard their conversation.

"Shanti. She wants to go with us to the store. Can she? Please?"

"Who on earth is Shanti?" Mother looked alarmed.

Raine pointed at the spot where Shanti sat.

"Raine, you have quite the imagination." Mother shook her head and turned back around to continue washing dishes.

The nice thing about having a friend that no one else could see was that Raine didn't have to ask permission to play with her. Plus, she could go anywhere that Raine wanted her to. She even went to school with Raine. Whenever Raine had trouble reading something aloud to the class, Shanti would whisper the right words into Raine's ear.

"The brown cow grazed in the field," Shanti slowly spoke into Raine's ear. Raine repeated the sentence aloud for the class.

"That is correct, Raine. You may sit down," Raine's teacher said.

Shanti was very good at math, too. She could explain things to Raine much better than the teacher did. Shanti paid attention in class whenever Raine didn't. Raine liked school a lot better once Shanti started going with her. Shanti liked school too until parent-teacher conferences.

"Raine is bright, and of course she is always well mannered. However…" Mrs. Howard's scratchy old voice trailed off. Raine's teacher tapped her pen on the arm of her chair; something that she did when she was trying to decide what words to use next. Raine watched Mrs. Howard from the back of the classroom while pretending to be reading a book. Mrs. Howard had instructed her to sit in the reading center while she spoke with Mother.

"Your daughter is very smart, Mrs. Carter, but she doesn't pay attention in class. She seems very distracted, daydreaming almost all of the time."

"But I don't understand. Isn't Raine getting good grades?" Her mother sounded baffled. "Her last report card was good - mostly A's and B's. What seems to be the problem?"

"Frankly, Mrs. Carter, I don't know how your daughter is making the grades that she is! Unless she is cheating, and I suppose that is a possibility."

"I don't think Raine would cheat, Mrs. Howard. She's a very obedient child at home." Mother's face looked like she had just tasted something bad.

"I'd like to put Raine up in the front of the class." Mrs. Howard pointed to the little desk that was parked right in front of her own.

"I think sitting up front, away from the distractions of the other students may help Raine to concentrate. With your permission, of course." The front desk was reserved normally for troublemakers.

"If you think it will help, then by all means feel free to do so."

So Raine, and Shanti, were moved up to the front desk. Raine found that it was harder to understand Shanti with Mrs. Howard staring right at her all the time. And Shanti didn't like Mrs. Howard at all.

"I don't want to come to school with you today," Shanti pouted, her dark eyes flashing.

"Why not?"

"Mrs. Howard is mean and besides, she stares at me all the time. I don't want to be there."

"Please? I'll be really lonely without you."

"No, Raine, I'm not coming!"

"If you do, I'll let you have the big swing for the whole recess." Raine had tried to bribe Shanti.

"I'm sorry, but I don't want to be around that mean old witch! She doesn't like me at all!" Shanti was adamant.

"Don't be silly, Shanti! She can't even see you to *not* like you!" Raine could tell that this hurt Shanti's feelings. They never talked about why other people couldn't see Shanti. Raine was aware that no one else could see her friend. She had assumed that Shanti also knew that no one else could see her.

"Well, I'm not going today. I'm gonna stay here." Shanti crossed her arms in a defiant gesture. She sat in her favorite spot on Raine's bed.

"Fine." Raine shrugged her shoulders. She'd noticed that Shanti got mad a lot lately. Raine got ready for school without Shanti.

It felt strange to ride the bus by herself. Normally, she sat with Shanti. The morning went well for Raine, even though her friend wasn't there to help her with reading. After lunch, Raine was surprised to see Shanti sitting at her desk.

"What are you doing here? I thought you weren't coming today," Raine whispered in Shanti's ear.

"I heard that Mrs. Howard is going to be gone this afternoon. She got sick." Shanti had a funny little smile on her face.

Raine was about to ask Shanti where she heard that news when a pretty, young woman with long brown hair walked into the classroom.

"Hello class, my name is Beth Woods." She smiled shyly. "You may call me Ms. Woods. I'll be your substitute for the rest of the day. Mrs. Howard is ill."

Ms. Woods sat in Mrs. Howard's chair and looked over the big green lesson planner stationed in the middle of her desk. Raine studied Shanti's face. Her dark eyes were glittery. She looked like she knew a great big secret.

"Okay, class, let's begin by reviewing your math worksheet from yesterday. Hopefully you were able to finish it at home with no trouble." Ms. Woods looked up and asked, "Before we begin, does anyone have any questions?"

The rest of the afternoon went by smoothly. Raine was happy to have Ms. Woods as her teacher for the rest of the day. Ms. Woods was so nice. She wondered, if something were to happen to mean old Mrs. Howard, would Ms. Woods be her teacher all the time?

The next morning, Raine was pleasantly surprised to see Ms. Woods sitting at Mrs. Howard's desk again.

"Good morning class. I'll be your teacher for the rest of the week. Mrs. Howard is still not feeling well. Hopefully she'll be well by Monday."

Shanti smiled at Raine and said, "Don't you like her a lot better than Mrs. Howard? Wouldn't it be nice if she were your teacher all of the time?"

Raine had a weird feeling about the way Shanti was acting. But she did like Ms. Woods a lot better than Mrs. Howard.

# CHAPTER 30
## EYE DROPS

Genevieve heard the terrible news about Raine's teacher when she was in line at the bank.

"They're hoping she'll recover. I heard that her husband is the primary suspect. Such a sad thing, they've been married for over thirty years." The bank teller displayed an appropriately sad face as she relayed the newest gossip in town.

"Excuse me," Genevieve interrupted, "I couldn't help overhearing your conversation. Are you talking about Mrs. Howard, the teacher?"

"Why yes dear, you haven't heard?" The teller looked very happy to have someone fresh to share the tragic news with.

"Mrs. Howard got really sick a few days ago, vomiting and confused. They said she didn't know where she was. Happened during school. They found her on the floor in the teachers' lounge foaming at the mouth!"

"Oh how awful! Mrs. Howard is my youngest girl's teacher! She said Mrs. Howard was home sick, but I had no idea it was so bad! Do they know what caused it?"

"Oh my, yes, she was poisoned!" The bank teller pronounced the words with great flair. Genevieve thought the gabby old teller would've been a great actress.

"The doctors say it was some sort of eye drop; and of course, her husband is the primary suspect. Apparently, it can kill you if you drink enough of it. Can you imagine that?"

"No, I suppose not." Genevieve answered softly. She wondered what kind of person would poison their wife.

During dinner that evening, Genevieve asked Raine about her teacher. "Did you know that Mrs. Howard is very sick?"

"Yes, and we have a substitute named Ms. Woods. She's really nice and pretty. I like her a lot." Raine's voice was cheery.

"I was thinking that it might be nice if you made a get-well card for Mrs. Howard." Genevieve took a bite of meatloaf and watched Raine's expression. She knew that Raine didn't care for Mrs. Howard. If truth were known, Genevieve didn't like Mrs. Howard much either.

"Ms. Woods loves to read, just like me. And her favorite color is purple." Raine took a drink of her milk. "I wish she could always be my teacher."

Genevieve decided to let the subject go concerning Mrs. Howard. It was clear to her that Raine wasn't too upset about her teacher being ill.

Several days later, while cleaning the upstairs bathroom, Genevieve found something that worried her very much. She was straightening underneath the vanity when a small, white plastic bottle caught her eye. Not thinking much about it, she picked it up to toss it into the trash. She realized she was holding an empty eye drop bottle.

"Randall? Can you hear me?" When he didn't answer, she went to find him. As usual for a Saturday afternoon, he was parked in front of the television.

"Did you use the last of your eye drops?"

"I haven't used them in a long time. Why?"

"Just wondering if I needed to pick up some for you when I go to town later."

"What would make you think of that? I haven't needed eye drops for almost a year now." Randall turned his head around to look at Genevieve's face. She'd raised suspicion. Her husband could smell a lie a mile away.

"Oh, I thought you were still having allergy problems." Genevieve busied herself straightening the coffee table. "Ok, that's good. Anything else I can pick up for you?"

"Yeah, I'm almost out of beer. You can stop by the liquor store." Randall turned back to the game on television.

"Sure, honey." Genevieve sighed in relief. Randall seemed to be distracted from the eye drop question. Her thoughts turned back to the empty bottle and she couldn't help but think of poor Mrs. Howard.

Genevieve put the empty bottle deep into the burn pile out by the pond. When Mrs. Howard died several days later, Genevieve made sure to burn the trash.

# CHAPTER 31
## A REAL FRIEND

As time went by, Raine's friend Shanti came to see her less and less. Raine didn't mind so much because she'd made a friend that everyone could see. She was ten years old when she met Alisha. Winter had loosened her chilly grip on Texas, and a gentle spring breeze flowed through the open school bus windows. With no friends to talk to after school, Raine boarded the bus as soon as class was dismissed. She would lose herself in a book to pass the time and to avoid eye contact with the other students as they got on the bus. It was safer that way.

"Is this seat taken?" The new girl's entire freckled face was wearing a smile. Her hair looked like a golden-red Brillo pad in the sunlight. Her left arm was chock full of books and her right arm held a purple jacket. She was clearly the new kid everyone was talking about. The girl was a novelty because she was from the East Coast and because she was new.

It was always exciting to have a new student in their small school. The new kid's popularity status was automatically elevated, at least for a short period of time. Eventually, the temporary status of popular was adjusted to either "cool" or "not cool" based on a number of factors which often remained mysterious to the baffled new kid.

Stunned that the new kid wanted to sit next to her, Raine took a full ten seconds to give an answer. "No, it's not taken," she finally managed to squeak out. Raine moved her backpack onto her lap to make room for the new girl.

"Hi, my name's Alisha." She put her books on her lap and stuck her hand out to shake Raine's, exactly like a grownup would. Her East Coast accent was very different from Raine's Texas drawl.

"I'm Raine." She stammered and took Alisha's skinny outstretched hand. "Nice to meet you."

"Who's your teacher?" Alisha asked.

"Mrs. Turner, fourth grade. Whose class are you in?"

"Mrs. Reems. I'm in the fourth grade too!" Alisha smiled as if this were an amazing thing.

Raine didn't know what else to say to Alisha, so she began reading her book again. She didn't comprehend the printed words on the page; instead, she was thinking about the new girl and wondering if this would be the only conversation they ever had. Raine wasn't exactly popular. In fact, she was practically invisible.

"You're reading Nancy Drew! I love Nancy Drew!" Alisha sounded very pleased to meet a fellow Nancy Drew fan.

"I do, too! What's your favorite one?"

"The Bungalow Mystery." Alisha didn't hesitate for even a second before answering. "Yours?"

"The Hidden Staircase! But I really like all of them."

"Me too! What else do you like to read?"

Raine paused for a second before answering. She was nervous that Alisha would laugh at her. "The Wonderful Wizard of Oz. But there are more stories about Oz than just the one. I think they're all good."

"I do too! Most kids don't even know that the author wrote more about Oz than the one book!" Alisha wasn't laughing at Raine. She sounded as excited as Raine felt inside.

The girls became best friends, spending almost every spare moment together. Raine loved being around Alisha and her family. Luckily, Raine's mother didn't mind. Alisha's mom and dad welcomed Raine with open arms. Raine had never been more comfortable in her whole life than when she was at Alisha's house.

By the time Raine entered the fifth grade, she only saw Shanti in her dreams. And that was fine by her. Shanti wasn't very nice anymore.

# CHAPTER 32
## TEN YEARS LATER

November 2011

Genevieve heard a soft tap at the door. She figured Raine must've forgotten something. She'd left just a few moments before to run some errands. Genevieve unlatched the chain lock and opened the apartment door. Instead of Raine, her middle daughter stood before her.

"Hi Momma." Too thin and still beautiful, Miranda hadn't changed much over the last ten years. Her daughter smiled and said, "It's been a long time."

Genevieve pressed a shaking hand over her heart. She'd hoped and prayed to see Randi so many times over the last ten years. She'd agonized over what may have become of her daughter, wondered what in the world she'd done to make Randi go away. Genevieve had even practiced what she would say if she were to ever see her girl again. Now that Randi was standing before her, Genevieve couldn't remember a single thing that she'd planned to say. "Miranda, honey…"

"Can I come in Momma? I'd like to visit a little while."

"Oh, yes honey, of course. How rude of me!" Genevieve stepped back and opened the door all the way. She ushered Randi over to the living room furniture.

"Momma, I'm sorry I took so long to come see you." Perched on the edge of the sofa, Randi picked at a loose string on her silky skirt hem.

"How've you been?" Genevieve decided to play it safe with neutral conversation. She didn't want to say the wrong thing and have to wait another ten years before she saw Randi again.

"I've been okay. Just trying to make it; working when I can." Randi looked as uneasy as Genevieve felt. There was an uncomfortable silence.

"I saw Lilly last week." Randi offered.

"That's nice. Did you see the children?" *Have you ever seen her children?* Genevieve wondered once more why Randi didn't stay in touch with her family.

"No, we had lunch, just the two of us." Randi crossed her legs and rested her hands in her lap. "It was good to see her again."

They made small talk for a little while, both of them dancing around anything of substance. Genevieve studied her daughter's face and wondered why Miranda was there. She could hold a superficial conversation with the best of them, but the polite distance was beginning to suffocate her.

Genevieve leaned forward, elbows on her knees and cupped her chin in both hands. "Randi, it's been so long since we've talked; we couldn't possibly catch up on everything at one time. Is there something you wanted to talk about?"

"I don't know Momma," Randi hesitated, "I guess I needed to see you. I heard you left Daddy." The last part of her words came rushing out all at once.

"I thought that maybe I'd hear from you before now, Randi. It's been over a decade." Genevieve had spent so many tears on Randi that she had tapped out almost all her emotion where Randi was concerned.

"And, yes, I left Daddy. I couldn't live that way any longer." Genevieve felt very business-like when she said those words to her. She looked directly into Randi's eyes and tried to decide the best way to explain why she'd chosen to break free from Randall.

Randi fastened her gaze onto her folded hands. Genevieve couldn't read her expression.

"I know you were close to Daddy. You were his favorite, and you probably view him differently than the rest of the family does." Genevieve tried very hard to not belittle Randall to his favored child. It was so hard to choose the right words. Randi didn't interject, so Genevieve continued to explain.

"But Daddy was cruel to me. I lived far too long in fear. I pretended that things were okay so that you girls could have a good home." Genevieve sighed. It wasn't easy to talk to Randi about this. Even though her daughter was an adult, she felt guilty damaging her father's image.

"Daddy was good to you, Randi," she explained, "but he was abusive to Lilly and Raine." Acid tears stung Genevieve's eyes. "He was too hard on them, both physically and emotionally. I won't ever forgive myself for subjecting them to that kind of treatment."

Randi didn't say a word, didn't raise her eyes from her own lap. Genevieve could imagine how very difficult this conversation must be for Randi. She'd adored her father, and he'd treated her like she was a princess.

102

Genevieve leaned forward and covered Randi's hand with her own in a gesture of comfort. "I'm sure you don't want to hear all of this Randi, but it's true."

Randi violently pulled her hands away from Genevieve's and finally made eye contact. The red-hot fury emanating from her daughter startled Genevieve. She'd expected Randi to defend Randall, but she hadn't anticipated this much anger from her.

"Oh, come on, Randi, you couldn't have been blind! You must've seen or heard something!" Genevieve was beginning to feel some anger of her own. "How can you be so self-centered?"

# CHAPTER 33
## RANDI'S SECRET

Randi's words began as a roaring rush of anger born from the depths of her soul. Forming into molten lava, they spewed out of her mouth with the all the destructive power of a volcanic eruption.

"I couldn't have been blind? I must've seen or heard something? Me? What did I miss?" Randi thought about the last conversation she'd had with her mother.

"What I missed," she gasped for air, "was the part where my momma stopped my daddy from raping me!" Randi couldn't believe she'd attacked her mother with those horrible, ugly words. But there it was. The truth was a big, stinking, poisonous, pile of shit and it lay firmly between mother and daughter.

"You were the only blind one in that house, Momma! And we all paid for it!" Mother's horrified expression gave Randi some sort of bitter satisfaction.

"I didn't know! Why didn't you come to me? Why?" Genevieve's mouth opened and closed several more times, but no sound accompanied the motion. She cupped her eyes with her hands, as if to somehow shut out the repulsive truth.

"How could you have not seen it? I was a kid Momma! You had to have known something was wrong. You walked in on him more than once." Standing up, Randi pointed at her mother's face to emphasize her accusations.

~ Summer 1988 ~

"Shhhhh, it's Daddy." Randi was accustomed to being awakened up by his

104

whisper in her ear. She lay motionless, hoping he'd go away. But he never went away. Daddy started coming to Randi's bed within a few nights after Lilly moved to her own bedroom.

Eyes shut tightly, Randi tried to keep her breathing slow and steady. If Daddy didn't know that she was awake and aware he was touching her, she could pretend it didn't happen and it wouldn't be real. Randi was frightened of Daddy. He wasn't mean to Randi, but she saw the way he treated Lilly and Momma. She was afraid of what would happen if she told him to stop.

Sometimes he would just put his hand inside of her panties. She could feel him moving and jerking and hear his breathing become more uneven and heavier. When he was done, he would quietly slip out of her bed and leave the room. But lately, Daddy had been doing other things to Randi. The touching wasn't so bad, but she wasn't sure what to think of the other stuff.

Daddy scooted down underneath Randi's pink bedspread until he was by her feet. Randi's heart began to beat very fast. She silently prayed, "Please Our Father in Heaven, make him stop."

She could feel him slowly pull her panties down to her ankles and off one foot. He moved her legs apart very carefully. Randi pretended she was dead. She could feel something warm and wet on her privates and realized he was licking her down there. It felt nice, but she knew it wasn't a good thing.

She flinched with pain when Daddy put a finger inside of her girl parts. He'd never done that before. She could feel his scratchy fingernail and imagined that it was cutting her inside. She tried to be quiet, but a whimper escaped her. Daddy stopped moving his finger, and she could feel a lot of pressure. It felt like he was trying to break her insides open. It was so hard to be quiet.

She opened her eyes, and wet, hot tears ran down the sides of her temples into her ears and hair. Randi thought she saw someone standing at the foot of her bed. She snapped her eyes shut tightly. Daddy quickly got up and left her panties caught around one ankle. Several moments later, she could hear muffled voices arguing downstairs.

In the early morning light, Randi saw the dried spot of blood on her bed sheet. She was scared that something was wrong with her but was afraid to tell Momma. And if she told Momma what Daddy had done, something really bad might happen. Randi stripped her stained Holly Hobbie sheets off and threw them into the laundry room hamper. Momma must have not seen the blood because she didn't ask Randi about it.

Daddy's nighttime visits continued until Randi was sixteen years old. She understood long before the abuse stopped that what Daddy was doing to her was wrong. Randi didn't like what Daddy did to her, but being his special girl was better than the alternative. She knew she was going to hell because she didn't stop him.

# CHAPTER 34
## THE SLAP

Raine arrived home that afternoon to find Mother in tears. *Oh Lord, now what?* She was growing tired of her weeping. Raine had read that grief is a normal process of healing from a divorce. She wanted to be a supportive daughter, but Mother's moods were starting to piss her off. Mother needed to start rebuilding her life instead of sitting around agonizing over the past.

"What's wrong?" Raine began to put groceries away in her cramped little kitchen. There was only one row of cabinets, which were already jam-packed with dishes and dry goods. The top of her refrigerator served double duty as a place for cereal boxes and potato chip bags. The only thing that kept Raine from feeling claustrophobic was the mirrored paneling on two of the walls. Raine had thought the mirrored walls tacky at first, but she quickly learned to appreciate them.

When she didn't answer, Raine turned around. Mother sat at the breakfast bar with her head down. Her shoulders were shaking as if she were laughing hysterically. She made no sound.

"I know this is hard, but you have to move on! It's been months now since you left Daddy, and it's time to focus your energy on something besides self-pity."

Mother raised her head and in a tearstained voice asked Raine a simple question. "Did Daddy ever touch you?"

"Did Daddy ever touch me?" Puzzled, Raine repeated back the question.

"Yes, Raine, did Daddy ever touch you?" Mother blew her nose into a tissue and waited for a response.

"Do you mean touch me, as in hug me? Pat my back? Spank me? Of course, he touched me." Raine scowled. "Sometimes," she added.

"No, I mean, did he ever touch you inappropriately?" Mother seemed to have trouble forming the words.

"If you would consider a beating inappropriate, then yes, Daddy touched me… inappropriately." Raine was getting angry. She didn't care for the direction that this conversation was heading. The past was over and done with. In her opinion, dragging up the negative wasn't going to change anything for anyone.

"No, Raine, I'm not talking about a beating. I mean in a sexual way."

"God, no! I would never let him touch me like that!" Raine began to wipe invisible dirt off the countertop.

"You might not have been able to stop him." Mother examined her own fingernails carefully.

"Why would you say something like that? What on earth are you talking about?"

"Daddy did… things, disgusting things, to Randi." Mother's voice broke, and she burst into tears again.

This got Raine's full attention and she stopped her busy work to look at her mother's face. "Like what?"

"I can't say the words, it's too horrible. She blames me too. She thinks I knew about it and did nothing to stop it. This is too much! I can't believe I'm the bad guy here." Mother sobbed even harder.

"Did you know about it?" Raine could hear her own heart pounding in her ears. Turning away again from Mother, she began to wipe the front of the stainless-steel refrigerator off. She needed to find something to distract herself from the rage creeping up her throat like bile. *Demolishing a building might do the trick right now.*

"No, I didn't know about it! I would never let my child be abused like that."

"You did allow your children to be abused. You allowed Daddy to beat the hell out of me with a stick. Then you blamed it on me. What kind of mother does that?" Raine's voice was reaching an ear-splitting pitch and she didn't care one bit.

"Seriously, Raine? You're still angry after all these years? And you're mad at me? He might've been a little rough on you that time, but you broke a window. You needed to have a consequence." Mother shook her head in disbelief.

"I was so bruised that it was lucky for you it was summertime! That's not a consequence; that's brutality! Why are you sticking up for him? You've always made excuses for him, and you still are!"

"Raine, that's so unfair! You have no idea what it was like to be in my shoes!"

"In your shoes? You covered for him every time, Mother. You have no idea what it was like to be in our shoes. Did you ever once think about what we went through? Daddy terrorized us. And you allowed it!"

"I won't listen to this, Raine! You're being disrespectful, and it's uncalled for. I did the best that I could with you girls. You don't know how hard it was to be married to your father for all those years. And besides, I would have never talked to my mother the way you talk to me." Mother stood up abruptly. "I'm clearly not wanted here."

"Goddammit, Mother! Stop playing the fucking victim! My whole life I've had to listen to your self-pity. I can't carry your burden any longer. You're a train wreck!" Raine slammed her hand down on the countertop so hard she could feel the aftershocks all the way up to her shoulder.

"I'll be out by the end of the week. In the meantime, I'll be sure to stay out of your way."

"Really? Where are you going to go? To Lilly's? I'm sure she doesn't need a third child to take care of. To Randi's house? If she has a house? Thanks to you and Daddy, she's so fucked up she can't function like a normal human being! Good luck finding another person to take you in!"

Mother walked over and slapped Raine across the face so hard that Raine had to step backward to keep her balance. Stunned, Raine sank onto the nearest barstool. The mirror on the bar wall reflected a perfect scarlet hand print on Raine's left cheek. She instinctively covered her wounded cheek with her hand.

"Oh, God, Raine! I didn't mean to." She reached out to touch Raine's face as if to comfort her.

"Don't!" Raine paused and forced herself to lower her voice. She made a stopping motion with her free hand. "Don't touch me."

Raine waited for a full minute before she spoke again. "It would be best for both of us if you would find another place to stay."

# CHAPTER 35
## RECONSIDERATION

Up to this point, Genevieve had lived her entire life based on Randall's desires. She did everything she could to minimize the possibility that Randall would become angry with her. Genevieve wasn't certain that she possessed her own thoughts anymore. Unable to make a judgment on the simplest of matters, she often found herself frozen in fear of making the wrong choice.

Once again, she was frozen in her tracks. She was an intrusion in her youngest child's life. Her eldest daughter had enough people to take care of, and her middle child was, as Raine had put it, fucked up. She hadn't thought through her decision to leave Randall. Genevieve was beginning to wonder if she'd made a huge mistake. *Maybe I should've stayed. Maybe it wasn't as bad as I made it out to be. He was always a good provider; it's not like I ever went without.*

When she was a young bride, she'd told herself that submitting to her husband's every desire was the Christian thing to do. Genevieve would sit in the Wednesday night women's bible study and listen to the teachings exhorting young wives to be submissive to their husbands. The thought of her husband ruling over her, owning her body, protecting, and guiding her, excited Genevieve. She felt deliciously safe and righteous.

Her friend Carol was one of the few people that got close enough to Genevieve to challenge her perspective.

~ Fall 1972 ~

"How can you say that Genny?" Carol stopped chopping apples to watch Genevieve's expression. Kimmy entertained baby Lilly on the kitchen floor

110

while Genevieve and Carol worked on a big batch of apple butter. "How can you even think that a wife is supposed to..." she struggled to find the right words, "obey her husband, as if she were a child?"

"I have faith that the Lord will provide all that I need, as long as I follow the teachings of the Bible. It's that simple, Carol!"

"I understand that, but where do you come up with submission? A husband and wife are supposed to submit to each other. He is commanded to love you, and you are commanded to respect him. But nowhere does the Bible say he can treat you like a child!"

"According to the book of Titus, we are supposed to obey our usbands. You can't believe in the Word and choose to ignore parts of it."

"And you can't ignore the fact that he is taking advantage of your faith! The bruise on your cheek is proof of that, Genny!"

Carol eventually stopped coming around. Randall didn't like her anyway, so it was for the best. Genevieve tried to remain steadfast in her belief that if she were to be obedient to her husband she would fall under God's sweet protection.

When Genevieve's faith began to waver, she prayed fervently. Her prayers went unanswered and Genevieve eventually decided that God hated her. Submission was the only teaching that her husband revered. The man that had promised to love and cherish her until death did them part grew to loathe her more each day.

Now, feeling unwanted by her grown children and unsure of herself, Genevieve was giving serious consideration to returning home to him. She needed to think. Gray skies hinted at rain. She found her scarf and jacket and decided to go for a walk anyway.

# CHAPTER 36
## GHOST FROM THE PAST

Shanti waited until Genevieve left the apartment. She'd overheard the entire argument between Raine and her mother. It'd been a long time since Shanti had visited Raine. She could tell that Raine needed her now, and she wasn't going to let her down.

"I heard everything, Raine." Shanti knew that Raine hadn't expected to see her because Raine flinched when she heard Shanti's voice.

"What are you doing here?" Raine wiped her tears with her sleeve. She swiveled the barstool to face Shanti.

"Aren't you happy to see me? I've missed you, Raine." Shanti was hurt that Raine didn't seem excited to see her.

"It's just that I haven't seen you for ages. Where've you been?"

"I've been around." Shanti fiddled with the tattered bracelet on her left wrist. Little white alphabet beads spelled out Shanti's name. Raine had given it to her for their ninth birthday.

"Your mother is a lying bitch, Raine. You know that, don't you? She doesn't care about you. Never did."

"That's not true. Mother was afraid of Daddy. She still is."

"Now who is making excuses for whom? Your mother allowed your daddy to hurt you. I saw it with my own eyes. I was there; I know."

Raine shook her head slowly side to side. "You don't understand. Mother didn't always see what Daddy did to us."

"I wasn't going to tell you this, but you know that thing that your daddy did to Randi?"

"What about it?" Raine wiped away a stray tear from underneath her left eye.

"Well, what your daddy did to Randi, he did it to me, too."

112

"No! You're just saying that to make me feel bad, Shanti. You shut your mouth!" Shanti could see that Raine did believe her though.

"Oh, he did it to me, alright. He did it to me all the time. Your daddy touched me in my private parts. He hurt me really bad down there." Shanti pointed to her crotch. "He did it to me while you were asleep next to us, in your bed. I didn't want him to, but he did it anyway."

Raine scrunched her eyes shut and put her fingers in her ears to block out Shanti's words. "No, no no no no! I don't want to hear it! Shut up!"

Shanti waited until Raine took her fingers out of her ears and opened her eyes before she spoke again. It was hard for her to be patient but she waited. She wanted to make sure that Raine heard her. "Your daddy told me that he'd kill you if I told anyone. He didn't like you anyway. He was hoping and praying that I would tell someone so he could kill you. But I never did, not once."

"You're lying Shanti! Daddy never did that stuff to you. You're just making it up to get attention."

Shanti started to cry. "I was a little girl, Raine! It wasn't fair that I had to let your daddy do the bad stuff just to keep you safe. I was a true friend to you, Raine. I didn't tell anyone about the things that your Daddy did to me."

Raine didn't say anything. It made Shanti mad when Raine ignored her. She always cared about Raine, watching and waiting to make sure she was okay.

"Why do you think your daddy stopped hurting you after I came? Because I was sent to keep you safe. I was sent to take your punishments." The anguished look on Raine's face gave Shanti a little satisfaction. It was good to see that she had Raine's attention.

"Why are you here, Shanti? What do you want from me?"

# CHAPTER 37
## YOU NEED ME

"I don't want anything from you, Raine." Shanti's smile frightened Raine. She was very surprised to see Shanti. It'd been so long that she'd almost forgotten what Shanti looked like. In fact, Raine had almost forgotten all about Shanti.

"Why are you here?" Raine noticed that Shanti was still wearing the name bracelet she had made for her. Shanti still had the same dark curls as she did when they were children. Her face had matured a little, but she looked very much the same as she did years ago.

"You need me."

"I've been doing fine without you, Shanti. I'm good, really I am."

"Hmmm, doesn't look like it to me. Looks like you have a real problem. I think I can help you fix it." Shanti leaned back in the chair and crossed her arms. She studied Raine with liquid black eyes that appeared to be missing pupils. The effect was unnerving to Raine.

"How? There's nothing that you can do to fix the past. The damage has been done."

"I can stop him from hurting anyone ever again." Shanti leaned toward Raine and smiled. An eerie image of Shanti as a cat, tossing her prey around, flashed through Raine's mind.

"I don't know. I don't think it's a good idea." Raine avoided Shanti's piercing eyes. The less she looked at Shanti, the better.

Shanti reassured Raine, "Don't you worry about a thing. I'll take care of things, just like I always have."

Icy cold fear traveled up Raine's spine. She had figured out a long time ago that Shanti wasn't such a good friend.

Right before Shanti left, she turned and said one last thing. "Your daddy

114

never wanted you to be born. Did you know that? He wanted a boy. When he found out you were a girl, he wished you were dead. Isn't that awful?"

After Shanti was gone, Raine needed to lie down. She dreamt of darkened rooms with no doors.

# CHAPTER 38
## DETOX

After leaving Momma, Randi needed rid herself of the poison. There was only one thing that made the sick feeling go away, at least temporarily. She opened her cell phone and found his number. His phone rang at least seven times. She was about to hang up when he answered.

"It's Randi. Do you have some time for me today?"

"Sure baby, when?" The timbre of his voice instantly made her feel linked to the ground again.

"As soon as possible. I can be there in twenty minutes. Will that work?"

"Yeah, I can always make time for you. You coming by yourself?"

"It's just me. It's personal today."

Randi lit a cigarette and waited for the next bus. The bus delivered her near the Alamo Heights district ten minutes later. She walked the rest of the way from Basse Road down Jones Maltsberger toward the home on Corona Avenue. It was obvious to Randi that the streets in this old money neighborhood weren't designed to be walked on. There were no sidewalks to be found between the bus stop and her destination.

Several newer-model SUVs drove carefully around her at a greatly reduced speed, as if to say "you don't belong here and you are in the way." Randi held her head high and continued on to the spacious home on Corona Avenue. She focused on beautiful oak trees lining the street. The humidity from the impending thunderstorm enhanced the distinct fragrance of bougainvillea shrubs growing in the professionally landscaped yards.

Randi rang the bell and waited impatiently for him to open the massive wooden door. The home was one of a kind, designed in the 1940s by the famous Texas State architect Atlee B. Ayres. He'd inherited the home from his parents many years ago. Along with the house, they'd left enough money that it wasn't necessary for him to work.

His financial status allowed him to make underground films catered to a particular market. Wealthy clients, who paid handsomely to remain anonymous, commissioned his films. The films, which would sadly never be viewed by the rest of the world, were truly works of art. His specialty was erotic films in which the commissioner participated actively. It was a lucrative business to be sure, but there was a certain amount of anguish involved for him.

His art was never going to be appreciated by the masses. He understood that he was paid abundantly, not so much for his artistic creations but for his ability to be discreet. There was enough evidence in his collection of works to take down a substantial amount of those in power in San Antonio, never mind all of Texas. He had thought about this fact during his lowest moments but never seriously considered crossing that treacherous threshold. To do so would be tantamount to suicide, and he liked himself far too much to commit such an act.

Randi had worked for him on multiple occasions, starring in the lead female roles. He appreciated her natural abilities and her physical beauty. She suspected he might be in love, or at the very least infatuated with her. Randi kept him at arm's length, and he accepted this.

She was beginning to think that he might've not heard the bell when the door opened. "Darlin'! I'm so glad you called!" He pulled her into a warm embrace. He smelled like spices and whiskey. She felt better right away - she always did.

"Come in, baby doll! How are you? It's been too long. I was starting to wonder when you were going to come see Papa." His casual smile made her a little lightheaded. At six and a half feet tall, she had to look up to him. He wasn't the best looking guy she'd ever laid eyes on, but he had a rugged look that appealed to Randi.

"I've been busy." She smiled and shrugged her thin shoulders. "I've missed you, though." She started to cry.

"Aw, baby doll, don't cry." He pulled her delicate frame to him and held her close. "Shhhhh...Papa knows what you need."

Randi let him lead her to the room. She went into the bathroom to change out of her clothing. He'd taken care to leave a gown for her. It was a garment that she'd not seen before, an old-fashioned nightgown made from white cotton fabric. She took off her street clothes and slipped the soft thin gown over her head.

He was sitting in a leather chair waiting for her. Small changes had been made to the room. The camera was on a tripod, and his tools were placed carefully on a velvet covered tray by the chair. "You look exquisite baby doll. Do you mind if I film? It's for my own personal collection, of course."

It didn't matter to Randi what he would use the film for. She needed to purge. She shrugged her shoulders in indifference. "No, I don't mind."

"Come to Papa." He beckoned with both hands for her to walk over to him. This was part of the process. She waited a moment for the next part of the script.

"Come here now!" He ordered, pointing at the space in front of him. She obeyed. The plush carpet was cool and soft under her bare feet.

"You've been a bad girl today, haven't you?" He looked impatient. She stood in front of him with her hands clasped behind her back. She remained silent.

"Answer me!" He paused for a few seconds, waiting for her reply. "Have you been a bad girl today?" Enveloped fully in his role, he demanded an answer.

"No, I didn't do anything bad today." She answered in a small, helpless voice.

"You're lying to me, you little bitch! If you'd only be honest I wouldn't have to punish you like this. When will you learn to tell the truth?"

"I'm sorry! I didn't mean to!" Even though Randi knew this was an act, real tears welled up in her eyes.

"What am I supposed to do with you? How long will it take for you to learn your lessons?" His face had transformed into a mask of anger. His fingers tapped out an ominous rhythm on the leather-covered arm of the chair.

"I don't know." Tears streamed down Randi's face.

"I know." He patted his lap. "Come here." He gestured for her to lie face down across his legs. Placing herself perpendicular to his body, she got down on her knees and draped her body across his thighs. With his left forearm across her back and his left hand on her right shoulder, he pinned her to his lap. She squeezed her eyes shut and braced herself for the next part of the play.

Randi cried out in genuine pain as he spanked her with his open palm. "Five, six, seven, eight, nine, ten…." He counted out the number of swats he gave her. He paused for a few seconds then began to rub her sore bottom.

She groaned with real pleasure. He lifted her thin cotton gown up over her bottom to her waist and began to rub her bare skin. The contrast of the spanking with his caresses was cathartic. It was the only way she could rid herself of the poison inside.

He continued, alternating increasing pain with increasing pleasure, for several hours. When it was over, he was nearly as exhausted as she was. He switched off the video recorder and his role.

She slept soundly in his arms afterward, clean and pure again.

# CHAPTER 39
## SHANTI'S SOLUTION

Shanti knew exactly what she was supposed to do. It couldn't be avoided any longer. Raine's daddy had ruined everything. Raine's mother had helped him all along the way. They needed to be stopped. And, she thought, they deserved a little punishment, too.

When she left, Raine was fast asleep. It was better for Shanti if Raine slept. Then Raine couldn't interfere. She had a loose plan starting with Raine's daddy. She'd worry about Raine's mother later.

She put the key in the ignition of Raine's little Toyota. She'd watched Raine drive it enough times that she knew exactly what to do. She stopped at a hardware store along the way for supplies. She was relieved that Raine had enough cash in her purse to cover her purchases since she didn't know Raine's debit card PIN number.

It wasn't difficult to find the place. Everything looked virtually the same as it did years before. Instead of parking in the drive, Shanti hid the car along the tree line. There was a well-worn dirt path that had been used as a road of sorts through the years by farm trucks. Sheltered from the main road, high school kids also used it as a place to party.

Shanti gathered up her supplies and stuffed them into a black trash bag. She tossed the bag over her shoulder, Santa Claus style, and walked through the tree line toward the homestead area. She made her way behind the hog pen, around the backside of the barn, to the rear of the old farmhouse. Randall's car was parked in the drive in its normal spot. There were no signs of him in the yard.

The house looked empty from the back-porch window. She slowly turned the doorknob on the back door. As usual, it wasn't locked. The outdated kitchen was a wreck. Dirty dishes were piled all over the faded

119

yellow counter. The stench of unwashed dishes and trash competed with the burnt odor from a coffee maker left on and forgotten. All the liquid had steamed off, leaving only a smoldering burnt ring at the bottom of the glass carafe. The combination of smells made Shanti sick to her stomach. An empty bottle of Jack Daniel's sat between the burners on the stovetop next to a half empty plastic bottle of cheap vodka.

She could hear the faint noise of a television coming from the living room. Shanti sat her trash bag down in front of the chipped white enamel stove and picked up a cast iron pan that was sitting on the back burner. The blackened skillet had an inch of cooled bacon grease in it, but that didn't matter to her. As she walked toward the living room she could feel her shoes sticking in dried spills of something on the linoleum floor. *Probably spilled Jack and Coke.*

A freshly made drink waited on the end table by Randall's empty recliner. The ice cubes hadn't a chance to melt, so Shanti knew he couldn't be far away. She moved over to the stairway and tuned her ears to the sounds above. She couldn't hear anything other than the soft background noise of the television. She crept up the stairs, moving carefully past the smiling school pictures of Lilly, Randi, and Raine placed all along the stairway walls.

Once she reached the top, she could hear coughing coming from the bathroom. Shanti hadn't quite worked out where she would do it yet. She weighed out the ease of ambushing him as he came out of the bathroom with the difficulty of dragging him downstairs once she was finished with him. Shanti decided that she'd better get control of him now while he was still somewhat contained. She had the element of surprise, but she might lose that once he returned to his drink.

Shanti positioned herself by the bathroom door - opposite the direction Randall would need to go in order to return downstairs. She waited motionlessly, skillet against her chest, for Randall to finish his business. The putrid odor of an alcoholic's bowel movement wafted out of the bathroom even though the door was shut. Shanti felt a searing hatred for the monster behind the closed bathroom door.

The toilet flushed, and Shanti raised the skillet high above her head. Not bothering to wash his hands, Randall opened the door and walked out of the bathroom, oblivious to Shanti's presence. Shanti took one big step toward Randall and slammed the skillet down with every ounce of strength she had onto the back of Randall's head. He staggered and made an awkward motion with his arms as if to try and steady himself.

Globs of rancid bacon grease splattered all over the floral print wallpaper and Shanti's face. The feeling of nasty grease hitting her face infuriated Shanti, so she whacked Randall one more time before he went down. The second blow was even harder than the first, and it made a satisfying clanking sound against Randall's head.

Shanti ran downstairs with skillet in hand. She slammed the skillet back onto the burner, picked up the trash bag, and ran back upstairs. She was relieved to see Randall still lying motionless by the bathroom door. She checked for his pulse and was happy to find that he still had one, albeit faint. Shanti had plans for Randall, and she wanted him alive and alert for most of them.

She rummaged through the trash bag and found one of the packages of painter's drop cloth. She'd splurged on the sturdy canvas type for this part of the job. Next, she pulled out a new roll of duct tape. Shanti ripped the plastic covering off and located the edge of the tape with her fingernail. She unwound a long strip of tape and tore it off with her teeth. Seating herself on his rear end, Shanti straddled Randall's body. She pulled Randall's limp arms behind his back and began to tape his wrists together. She wasn't sure how much tape it would take to hold him so she tore off another long strip and re-enforced the restraint.

After binding his wrists, Shanti squatted at Randall's feet and pulled his legs together. She bound his ankles using twice as much duct tape as she did on his wrists. The phrase "dead weight" held new meaning for her after lifting Randall's limbs. Completely flaccid, the sheer weight of Randall's flesh made this part of her mission exhausting.

She studied Randall with her eyes while she rested for a moment. Randall didn't seem as big and frightening as he had when she was a child. Gravity and alcohol abuse had left their calling cards on Randall's face, leaving him with the deceptive appearance of a harmless old man. Shanti wasn't fooled for a moment by the old man disguise. She knew that the same beast that had cruelly abused her was still inside.

Face down with his head turned to one side; drool ran out of Randall's gaping mouth onto the sculptured blue carpet. Shanti could smell the sickly-sweet odor of liquor on his breath. She decided she'd better work fast. Even though he was bound, it'd be a lot easier to place him where she wanted him while he was still unconscious.

She unfolded the drop cloth lengthwise and placed it alongside Randall's body. She stepped over Randall to the side opposite the drop cloth. Using her legs to anchor herself, Shanti rolled Randall toward her until he was on his side. She opened the drop cloth some more, placing it where Randall had lain face down just moments before.

With a grunt, Shanti used her right foot to roll Randall onto the drop cloth back into a face down position. She repeated the process on the opposite side to ensure she had plenty of cloth all around Randall.

Shanti reached into the bag and pulled out two packages of the cheaper plastic drop cloth. She proceeded to tape the plastic film over the surrounding walls, taking extra care to cover the baseboards and exposed carpet.

She reached into the bag and pulled out a large heavy stick, much like the one Randall had beat the shit out of Raine with so many years ago. Shanti placed herself where Randall would be able to see her when he regained consciousness.

After a few minutes, Randall stirred slightly. Shanti's heart rate increased with excitement. She had waited for this moment for a long, long time. As a frightened little girl, the only thing Shanti could do was imagine making Randall pay. He was too big and too strong to contend with. Now Shanti had the upper hand and it felt even better than she'd anticipated.

His eyes fluttered open and Randall looked relaxed at first. It only took a moment for alarm to contort his features. "What in the hell?" His words were slurred, likely the result of the booze and the blows to the back of his head.

"Hello, Daddy!" Amused, Shanti smirked. "How are you feeling?"

"What in the fuck is this? What in the hell are you doing?"

"Relax, Daddy dearest, this is nothing more than a little payback for all the love you've shown your family through the years."

"Untie me! Let me loose now, you little bitch!" Randall was becoming angrier by the second.

"No." Shanti faked a pout and crossed her arms like a stubborn child refusing to obey.

"Let me up now!" Randall ordered.

"You say that as if you're still in charge." Shanti's voice was calm and mild. She smiled and watched his expression.

"Goddammit! You'll regret it if you don't let me up right now!"

"Or what? What will you do?" Shanti suppressed a laugh. "You don't get it, do you? For a change, you're not the one in control."

Randall made a futile attempt to pull loose from the sticky restraints. Shanti thought it was very entertaining to watch Randall flopping and shaking around. *Yes, this is good stuff.*

Randall settled down a bit and looked around as best as he could in his face down position. "What're you gonna' do with me? What's the plastic for?" Randall sounded as if he was trying to control his voice, but Shanti could hear the fear seeping through.

*Good, the man has enough sense to know he's in trouble.*

"Let's start with a little game that I like to call the house special." Shanti stood up and with the stick in her right hand tapped a steady rhythm onto her left palm. She swung the stick toward Randall's face and stopped just short of his pitted nose. He instinctively flinched, screwing his eyes tightly shut and pulling his lips inward as if to protect them from a blow. Shanti giggled at Randall's reaction.

"Let's see how you like being beaten with a stick, Daddy dearest!"

Randall barely had time to turn his face away before the solid stick made contact with his bruised skull. Shanti counted the blows, "one, two, three, four and five."

Randall groaned in pain. The sound of his pain combined with the hollow thump of the stick was like music to Shanti's ears. She stopped counting and continued to thrash Randall from head to toe. She was enjoying herself so much that she almost didn't hear the logical voice in her head.

*You'd better stop or you won't be able to dole out the other punishments you have planned. Remember Shanti, he needs to be alive and awake for it!*

Shanti stopped and shook Randall. He tightened his muscles in response to her touch. "Can you hear me?" Sweat dripped off Shanti's hair onto the side of Randall's face as she whispered into his ear.

He didn't respond so Shanti poked him in his ribs with the stick. Randall begged in a weak voice. "Stop, please!"

"Oh, no Daddy dearest, we're not done yet!" She rummaged around her bag and pulled out a pair of sheers, the kind that paramedics carry. She started at Randall's ankles and began to cut a straight line up his pant leg. She snipped to an even beat until she reached his waistband. She made the same cut on the other leg.

Shanti placed the scissors bag into the bag and found a pair of yellow rubber gloves and the next tool for the job. It was a window washer's squeegee with a foot-long wooden handle. For show, she presented it to Randall for him to inspect.

"See this, big man? Wonder how you'll like it?"

Through bruised, puffy eyes Randall tried to look. She made sure to hold the squeegee in front of his face long enough for him to get a good look. Incoherent sounds of protest escaped Randall's mouth.

She pulled the gloves on and stood over Randall's midsection, facing the direction of his feet and inserted the handle end of the squeegee. She violated him in the same way that he had brutalized her long ago. He writhed around, screaming in agony. Shanti didn't bother to count this time. She continued thrusting the squeegee handle violently until her arms were shaking with fatigue. By the time she was done sodomizing him, Randall had vomited and was no longer making any noise at all. She knew he was still alive because his breath gurgled through the vomit pooled in his mouth.

Shanti was exhausted and needed a break before the final phase. She peeled the gloves off and sat on the floor to gather her thoughts. The late afternoon sun cast long rays through the bathroom window out into the hallway. She figured she'd better finish up before it got too dark. Once her arms felt steady again, Shanti picked up the bloodied stick she'd beat him with and placed the smaller pointy end into Randall's open mouth. Randall gagged as she wiggled the stick all the way back to his throat. Squatting,

Shanti braced the back of Randall's head with her feet to keep him from moving away. She grasped the stick with both of her hands and rammed it as hard as she could into what she hoped was Randall's brain. It was more difficult than she'd thought it would be to force the stick in, so she pulled back out a little and shoved again. This time she felt a crunch.

Randall's legs and feet convulsed violently for what seemed like a full minute. Copious amounts of blood flowed out of Randall's mouth. Shanti put a bath towel in front of his face to sop up some of the sticky red fluid. Once Randall's body lay completely still, Shanti pulled off the rubber gloves and felt his deformed neck for a pulse. *Mission accomplished.*

Shanti had reached the part of the plan that was still a little fuzzy. She hadn't thought it through to the end. She only knew that she needed to get rid of his body and the mess.

She put the rubber gloves back on and decided to wing it. Detached, she looked over the scene that lay before her. *Just tackle one thing at a time. First things first.* She began to pull the blood-spattered plastic film off the walls. Shanti stuffed the balled-up plastic into her trash bag along with the squeegee.

She tugged on the stick that still skewered Randall's head but to no avail. It was stuck. Shanti sat on her butt and put her right foot on his forehead and her left foot on his shoulder. She gave the stick another yank while using her legs to push his head away at the same time. The stick made a horrible sucking sound as she wrenched it free. She placed the stick, covered with stringy little pieces of flesh and brain matter, into the trash bag. She was starting to feel a little queasy.

Shanti slipped off her soiled shoes and dropped them into the bag on top of the bloody stick. She wrapped the canvas loosely over the sides of Randall's body and gathered the excess up around his head. Slowly, she tugged him toward the top of the stairs. She decided to slide him down feet first and spun his carcass around on the landing until his feet were hanging off the first step.

Pulling him down the stairway was much easier than dragging him across a level floor. His head thumped onto each step keeping the descent to a manageable pace. Shanti lugged him over the thick carpet in the living room, through the tiled area in the foyer, and onto the linoleum in the kitchen. With both hands, she shoved the kitchen table and chairs toward the laundry room to make a clear pathway to the back door.

Shanti found an old rusty wheelbarrow out in the tool shed and parked it beside the back porch. She ran back into the kitchen and slipped his body across the linoleum, out onto the concrete porch. The rough concrete had the texture of sandpaper, making it impossible to slide Randall's body. She resorted to rolling his body off the porch onto the wheelbarrow below. It sounded like a big sack of potatoes when his body landed.

Huffing and puffing, Shanti wheeled Randall across the yard to the pigpen. Moving his body was a lot harder than she'd thought it would be. *God help me if I dump his ass before I get him there!*

After what felt like an eternity, Shanti made it to the pigpen. Expecting to be fed, the hogs made excited noises and gathered around the gate. *This is gonna suck.*

Shanti debated the best way to dump Randall's body. She decided to shove through the gate, wheelbarrow, body, and all. *Ready, set, go!* She dug her toes into the muck to propel the wheelbarrow as far into the herd of pigs as she could. In a single movement, Shanti tipped Randall's body onto the ground and pulled the wheelbarrow backward. Almost tripping over her own feet, she scrambled backward to yank the wheelbarrow out of the pigpen.

The darkening sky warned Shanti that time was limited. She returned the wheelbarrow to the shed and stripped her bloodstained, pig-slopped clothing off by the back porch. She threw her dirtied garments into the washing machine and went about cleaning up the house in one of Genevieve's bathrobes. She gathered up her trash bag and took it outside to the overflowing trashcan. She dumped some of the trash out and placed her bag on top. Shanti squirted lighter fluid in circular motions on top of the full can and lit a match. Soon the acrid odor of burning trash filled the air. She realized too late that her shoes were in the burning bag. *Oh well, they'd be a mess to try and clean up.*

While she waited for her clothes to dry, she showered in the upstairs bathroom. After a final walk-through, she felt satisfied that things were back in order. It was completely dark by the time she walked barefoot back to Raine's car. Worn out, she could barely keep her eyes open while driving back to the apartment.

# CHAPTER 40
## THE BIGGER MONSTER

In an attempt to stay out of Raine's way and to give herself some time to think, Genevieve walked for hours. She found a branch of the public library and stayed until closing time, using the computer to look for apartments. Everything was so expensive. The attorney had promised her she'd have enough to live on, but things were moving slowly. They'd been unable to serve Randall with the divorce petition; so, at least temporarily, everything was at a standstill.

The attorney was charging her over two hundred dollars an hour which made Genevieve hesitant to contact him unnecessarily. This added to her already indecisive state of mind. She left the library no farther along in her search for housing.

The night sky was beginning to cloud up, and the scent in the air promised rain. Genevieve made her way back to Raine's apartment barely in time to avoid a downpour. Raine was nowhere to be found.

She was peeling potatoes when Raine stormed through the front door. "Raine? Is that you?"

Raine went to her bedroom without answering. Genevieve hoped she wasn't pouting still. She covered the chopped potatoes with water and turned the burner onto low. Raine stayed in her bedroom so Genevieve went to Raine's doorway. "Raine? Are you hungry? I'm cooking."

"Sure, I could eat something. How long before it's ready?" Raine sounded sleepy.

"About half an hour," Genevieve leaned against the doorframe. "Are you feeling all right?"

"I'm tired. It's been a really long day." Raine turned onto her side and tucked her hand underneath her pillow. She closed her eyes.

"Take a little nap dear, I'll let you know when dinner is ready." She pulled the comforter up over Raine's shoulders. She noticed Raine's hair was damp. *Must've gotten caught in the storm somewhere.*

Genevieve finished up dinner and put it in the oven on low to keep it warm until Raine woke up. She dug around in Raine's desk and found a yellow legal pad. Using a pencil, Genevieve made two columns. The first column she headed with the words "On my own"; the second column was marked "Back with Randall." She proceeded to weigh out the pros and cons with each scenario.

When she was done the inequality between both tallies was profound. It was apparent to her that in one scenario she would be assured of financial security, bought and paid for with the currency of fear and shame. On the flip side, she could have independence, paid for with a different kind of fear, the fear of the unknown. The unknown was a monster in the dark that threatened to swallow her whole and spit her out. It was by far the more terrifying option of the two.

Bitter tears dripped onto her list. She'd created her own trap, strategically placing monsters on one side of her decision and demons on the other. *What a stupid old fool I am. My children resent me, my husband loathes me, and I've used up all my new beginnings.*

She looked up at the clock on the stove and decided she should wake Raine.

# CHAPTER 41
## GENNY'S DECISION

Raine watched in horror as the pigs crowded over his body. He didn't make a sound, didn't move at all, as they tore his flesh with their razor-sharp teeth. "No!" she screamed but the words were muffled. Her mouth was frozen and the only sound she managed to make didn't reach beyond her throat.

Someone else was there with her but Raine couldn't see her face. *Why isn't she helping him? My God! They're ripping him to shreds! Please! Do something!* A shovel stood propped up against the side of the fence. She thought that maybe she could frighten the pigs away with the shovel. Raine tried to run toward the gate but her legs were frozen. A horrible crunching sound emanated throughout the yard. The pigs were devouring him. The images were too much to bear so Raine slipped back into the darkness.

"Raine, honey." Mother's voice cut through woolen layers of sleep. "Wake up and have some dinner."

Raine slowly sat up in bed and rubbed her eyes. She had bizarre memories of an awful dream but she couldn't quite recall the details. *Something horrible had happened; someone had died. Yes, that was it. Someone had died in a terrible way.*

She sat on the toilet, leaving the bathroom light off, and the door open. She thought some more about the gruesome nightmare while she emptied her bladder. The dream had created a deep unease that wasn't leaving her. She could still smell the stench of his blood mixed with pig manure.

"Mother?" For a brief moment, a fear of being alone rendered Raine childlike.

"In here," Mother called from the kitchen. "I'm fixing your plate."

Two plates full of meatloaf and mashed potatoes waited on the little dinette table. "It smells delicious. What's the occasion?"

"I want to talk to you." Mother poured iced tea into two glasses and placed them on the table. "I've made a decision."

"I thought your decision was to move out. Have you found a place?" Raine didn't anticipate that Mother would look for a house today. She had expected that Mother would spend the day feeling sorry for herself instead.

"Let's eat before it gets cold." Mother motioned with her hand for Raine to sit.

Raine took a bite of meatloaf and waited for Mother to respond to her question. Instead of answering, Mother began to take small bites of her mashed potatoes. That old familiar anger began to tap on Raine's skull.

"Aren't you going to answer me?"

"What dear? What was the question?" Mother sounded very innocent as she scooped up another small portion of mashed potatoes.

"Are you being serious? You're avoiding the question, aren't you?" Raine dropped her fork onto her plate and pushed her chair back. "I'm not sure why I thought we could have a real conversation! It's always games with you!"

"I don't remember your question, Raine." Mother answered in a mild tone and continued to push her food around with her fork as if it were a detailed excavation project that needed her undivided attention.

"Did you find a place to live?"

"I've decided to go back home." Mother avoided Raine's gaze. "I think your father and I can work things out."

"You what? Are you kidding me?" When Mother didn't answer, Raine continued, "You were miserable with Daddy! He treated you like shit! You meant nothing to him! We meant nothing to him!"

"Raine, let's face it, I'm too old to start over and I've worn out my welcome with you." Mother sounded weary. "I've had my little sabbatical, now it's time to go back to the life I chose."

"You are making a huge mistake, Mother! I can't believe you've come this far only to turn back." Raine searched for the right words of inspiration but nothing seemed adequate.

"I have to be realistic. I'm in my sixties and there is nowhere to go but back." Mother took a sip of her tea and paused, lost in thought. She added, "Hopefully, your father will be glad to see me. He's too old to start over, too."

# CHAPTER 42
## SLEEPWALKING

Genevieve did hope that Randall would take her back. She'd realized how obsolete she was to the rest of the world. Her children had their own lives and she didn't see how she could fit in. Randall had been her entire world for ages.

She ignored Raine's disapproving glare and finished her dinner. Once the dishes were cleaned up, she went to the guestroom to pack. She'd ask Raine to take her back home in the morning. *No sense in waking Randall up or keeping Raine out late tonight.*

It was after midnight before Genevieve climbed into bed. As she lay there she imagined what Randall's response might be to her return. She was sure there would be a penance to pay.

After tossing and turning for what seemed like over an hour, Genevieve got up and dug around in Raine's bathroom for something that might help her fall asleep. She examined all the bottles in Raine's medicine cabinet, looking for anything that said, "May cause drowsiness". Settling on some cold medicine, Genevieve filled a small paper cup with tap water and took the capsules.

Not wanting to cast light into Raine's room, she shut the bathroom light off before opening the door. Her eyes hadn't adjusted to the darkness yet and she nearly ran into Raine. "Oh God! You scared me!"

Raine didn't say a word. Genevieve couldn't see Raine's expression in the darkness.

"Raine, honey? Are you awake?" Raine had a history of sleepwalking. Genevieve had always been a little frightened by Raine when she would sleepwalk. It was like she was someone else.

"Yes, Genny, I'm awake."

"You're sleepwalking. Let's get you back to bed." Genevieve folded her hand into the crook of Raine's arm and tried to gently lead her toward the bed.

Raine stiffened her body and refused to move. Genevieve let go of her arm and turned on the bedroom light. She thought maybe the light would help Raine wake up.

Something in her daughter's posture was off. It took her a second or two to realize that Raine was hiding something in her right hand.

"What are you doing?"

Instead of answering, Raine swung the object violently toward Genevieve's head. A rush of adrenaline gave her the agility that she needed to swerve out of the path of Raine's blow.

"What in the hell!" Genevieve screamed in a voice that sounded foreign to her own ears. Instinctively, she slapped at Raine hard enough to knock her backward several steps.

"Raine! Wake up!"

Raine rubbed her cheek with her right hand and looked confused. "What'd you do that for?"

"You tried to clobber me!" Genevieve reached out to take the object that Raine had attempted to beat her with. It was a solid wooden rolling pin. "Are you awake now?"

"Of course I'm awake!" Raine still looked baffled.

"You were sleep walking. You haven't done that for years!" Of course, she didn't know that for sure, she thought immediately. After all, it'd been years since she'd shared the same house with her daughter. *God help the man that she marries - he'd better wear a helmet.* She made sure to lock the guest room before falling asleep.

# CHAPTER 43
## RETURNING MOTHER

"Please, wait a week before going back to Daddy! At least give yourself some time to think about it!" Raine decided to plead with her mother the next morning.

Genevieve carried her bags to the front door and said, "I've thought about it and my mind is made up."

"Don't you at least want to call the house first? You haven't heard from Daddy since you left, not even once."

To Raine's relief, her mother agreed to call Daddy before they made the drive home. Mother walked away from her while she made the call, so Raine wasn't able to hear any part of the conversation. Mother returned to the living room with a puzzled expression on her face.

"He didn't answer. I guess we'll wait and I'll try him again in a little while." Genevieve pulled a novel out of one of her bags and sat down on the sofa.

"Maybe he's out feeding the pigs." Raine offered. She speculated that Daddy didn't go many places since he'd retired. Before Mother left, he probably didn't go anywhere unless they sold booze. He didn't need to because Mother ran all his errands for him. *Wonder how long it took him to find the grocery store?*

"Yeah, maybe." Mother didn't look convinced. She opened her novel and pretended to read it.

A half an hour later, Mother tried to reach Daddy on the phone again to no avail. After a few more attempts, Mother stuffed her book into her bag and said, "Let's go."

Raine shrugged her shoulders and said, "I think you're making a mistake, but it's your choice." She helped Mother carry her bags out to the car and within minutes they were on I-10, heading toward the farm.

Mother sat in silence for the duration of the drive, so Raine's thoughts had no competition. She felt sick to her stomach. On top of the sleepwalking episode last night, she knew her mother was making the worst decision possible. Mother's choice to go back to Daddy was an insult and a betrayal. She was taking his side, as if all the things that he'd done wrong didn't matter. Raine understood the concept of forgiving and forgetting, but in this case, Daddy hadn't asked for forgiveness. The old bastard probably didn't think he'd done anything wrong.

"I'm not a small child anymore. You can't expect me to just forget," Raine said to her mother's profile. She had another thing coming if she expected Raine to give her blessing to their reunion.

Raine couldn't count the number of times her mother had said the words - "Daddy's going to be different from now on." She'd had more than her fill of empty promises and the expectation that she get amnesia each time Daddy decided to quit drinking.

She cast another glance at her mother, who was sitting with her hands together in her lap, picking at her cuticles.

Raine tapped impatiently on the steering wheel. She contemplated the right words; debated whether the words were worth saying. "Can I ask you a question?"

"Of course."

"Do you ever think about what life could've been like without Daddy?" *No, that's not right – not what I wanted to say.* "Have you ever thought about what we all might have been like without Daddy?"

"Well… that's difficult to say." Mother paused for a moment then added, "I've imagined life without him, but it always seemed unrealistic."

"But did you ever think that we might've had a chance to be normal without Daddy's abuse?"

"Normal?" Mother laughed dryly. "Who's to say what normal is? The past is the past. We couldn't possibly know how our lives would be without him unless we'd taken that path."

"We didn't choose the path we took, Mother! You made that choice for us." Raine wanted to cry. It was just like Mother to diminish her feelings. Searing pain stabbed her right eye. The highway looked fuzzy and dim. She was passing out, and there didn't seem to be a way to stop it.

"Raine! Open your eyes!" Mother's voice sounded a million miles away.

# CHAPTER 44
## CLOSE CALL

Genevieve knew that Raine was upset with her, but she didn't know what to say to her. Raine drove, staring blankly ahead. Genevieve wasn't sure that she was paying attention to the traffic in front of her.

When Raine finally spoke, Genevieve tried to reassure her best that she could. But her words appeared to upset Raine even more. Suddenly, Raine's eyes closed, and she slumped over the steering wheel.

"Raine, open your eyes!" Genevieve grasped at the steering wheel, but Raine's heavy, limp body pulled the wheel to the left, causing her little car to veer off onto the edge of the dividing ditch.

"Wake up!" She slapped Raine's back hard with her left hand while steadying the wheel with her right. Raine's foot must have slipped off the accelerator because the car was slowing down. Miraculously, Genevieve remembered to turn the ignition off.

It all happened so fast that only as the car rolled to a stop in the ditch did Genevieve marvel at her own quick reaction. She realized that another vehicle had pulled up next to them.

"Is she alright? Do you need an ambulance?" The driver shouted to Genevieve through his rolled down window. "I can call nine-one-one, if you need me to."

"Yes, please!" Genevieve didn't want to dig through her purse to find the cell phone. "She just passed out!"

"No, don't." Raine startled Genevieve by sitting upright quickly.

"Honey, you passed out! Of course, we need an ambulance!" Genevieve was sure that Raine wasn't okay. "We need to get you to a hospital right away!"

"No, really, I'm fine." Raine leaned forward to tell the passerby that he could leave.

The man paused for a moment, then shrugged his shoulders. "Suit yourself. But I wouldn't drive if I were you."

"She can drive." Raine pointed to Genevieve.

Genevieve found Raine's matter of fact tone odd, given that she'd nearly crashed her car. *Must be the shock of it all.* Nonetheless, she couldn't argue Raine's logic. In less than five minutes, they were back on the highway as if nothing had happened.

# CHAPTER 45
## WHEN OPPORTUNITY KNOCKS

Shanti studied Genevieve's profile from the passenger seat of Raine's car. She didn't expect to have this opportunity so soon. Genevieve was an idiot who didn't deserve to be a mother, Shanti thought. Mothers are supposed to protect their children.

"How are you feeling, honey?" Genevieve asked her.

"I feel fine, Genny." Shanti would prefer that Genevieve not speak. When Randall spoke, Shanti got angry, but when Genny spoke Shanti felt confused.

"I still think we should go by the ER or at least call the doctor…" Genevieve's voice trailed off. Genevieve looked like she felt a little confused, too.

Shanti went back to her own thoughts. She contemplated the best method for disposing of Genevieve. Raine would be so much better off without her. She wondered if Raine would get any life insurance money from her mom's death.

The Boerne exit seemed to appear more quickly than usual. Shanti didn't have a solid plan yet. *Think, think!* She cleared the distracting thoughts that served no purpose and began to let her mind go blank. Some of her best ideas came when Shanti simply let go.

From the end of the long drive, the farm looked in order. Genevieve made a ragged gasping sound. Shanti could see that her face was crumpled up in that stupid, ugly face that people make when they are trying not to cry.

"What's wrong, Genny? Aren't you happy to be home where you belong?"

"What is wrong with you?" Genevieve turned to look Shanti directly in the eyes. "I know you aren't thrilled with me, but is the sarcasm absolutely necessary?"

Shanti smiled a little and shrugged her shoulders. She had liked Genny, loved her even, years ago. But those warm and fuzzy emotions had since faded into cold indifference. Genny might be softer than Randall, but she was every bit as much a child abuser as he was. She knew what he had done and not once did she step in to stop it. Raine might not remember things the same way, but Shanti knew. She was forced to absorb most of the pain. Her eyes were wide open.

# CHAPTER 46
## HOME SWEET HOME

As Genevieve steered Raine's car up the drive, her heart began to gallop and her mouth felt like cotton. She tried to swallow the cotton down but it wouldn't go away. *I hope he's not too angry with me.*

Not sure whether the tears were out of hope or fear, Genevieve stifled a sob and tried not to cry. It didn't help matters to have Raine calling her by her nickname. Raine addressed her this way whenever she was upset with her.

As she rounded the corner to the house, Genevieve could see that the hogs were huddled around something. Their movements were frantic somehow, as if they were all competing to eat whatever lay there between them. She parked the car and walked quickly to the pen. They'd taken down Molly, the oldest sow in the herd. It was too late; she was clearly gone. Genevieve knew that it would be dangerous to step in to stop the cannibalism.

The pigs must have been extremely hungry or they wouldn't have eaten Molly. Genevieve wondered how long it'd been since Randall fed them. Uneasy about what to expect, she made her way to the back door of the house. Before she went in, Genevieve glanced at Raine who was still sitting in the passenger seat staring into her lap.

The smell of trash hit her nose straight away. Ugh, she thought, would it have been too much trouble for him to do a little housekeeping? To her right on the stove there were partially empty bottles of liquor. Her heart sank a little. She had hoped that Randall might have sobered up during their separation. *Stupid girl, what would make you think that?*

"Randall? Are you here?" She called out lightly, as if she weren't committed to him hearing her voice. The television was on, but the volume was turned off. Randall wasn't in his normal spot in front of it.

"Randall?" She spoke a little louder this time. "I'm home. It's Genny." She took tentative steps up the staircase, careful to avoid the creaky spots. It was too quiet. Something was wrong. By the time that she reached the landing, she had almost convinced herself that she was going to find him on the floor, dead from a heart attack.

To her surprise, the floor was empty. No dead Randall - in fact everything looked very tidy and in order. She looked in the bedrooms and the bathroom, then decided she'd better check the grounds for him. As she was going downstairs, she could hear the back door open.

"Randall? Is that you?" Greeted by more silence, Genevieve's pulse quickened. The sensation that something was wrong only intensified. She stood still for a moment to listen for footsteps. No one was moving about. She pulled her phone out of her purse quietly, careful to not make a sound. She punched in nine-one-one, but didn't press send.

She went to the kitchen to investigate. Except for her footsteps on the old linoleum floors, the house was ridiculously quiet. She couldn't even hear the hum of the refrigerator. The kitchen was empty. *Maybe he went out the back door.* "Oh well," Genevieve said out loud and opened the screen door.

She shielded her eyes from the bright sun and scanned the yard for signs of Randall. As she turned toward the house again, she caught a slight movement out of the corner of her eye. It took a few moments for her to realize that Raine was standing in the laundry room, watching her through the window. *Well for heaven's sake! Why didn't she answer me?*

With her thumb still poised over the send button on her cell phone, Genevieve began to search for Randall in all the places she could think that he might be. At his age, he could be in trouble. It wasn't like him to go anywhere these days, especially without the car. Fearing that he'd been taken to the hospital, or something even worse, Genevieve finally pushed the send button on her phone.

"Nine-one-one, what is your emergency?" the pinched voice on the other end of the line asked.

Genevieve waited outside until the police arrived. She poked her head into the back door and yelled for Raine but gave up after she didn't respond.

The police did a thorough check of the farm. They found nothing. They promised to update her if they learned anything about Randall's whereabouts. With nothing else to do about the Randall situation, Genevieve took her things out of Raine's car and went inside to unpack.

"Raine? Honey? I'm going to get settled in. You don't have to stay." Raine was standing at the kitchen sink staring out the window. Presumably, she'd been watching the police. She didn't acknowledge Genevieve's presence.

"Okay, I won't." Raine's voice was monotone. When Raine turned around to face her, Genevieve felt a spark of fear. Her normally light blue eyes appeared dark and empty, as if someone had removed her irises. Genevieve took a step backward.

The corners of Raine's mouth turned up into an eerie smile. She walked past Genevieve and out the door without saying another word.

Genevieve moved over to the window in front of the kitchen sink to watch her daughter as she left. From where Genevieve stood, it looked like Raine was talking to herself. Genevieve was disturbed by Raine's behavior, but she had other things to worry about.

# CHAPTER 47
## RIGHT PLACE – WRONG TIME

Shanti had a big conversation with herself. She wanted to get rid of Raine's mother real bad. *Real bad.* In the end, she decided it wasn't the right time. *Especially with the cops around.* The last thing that she needed was the cops coming back and snooping. She'd be careful, of course, but they'd already spotted her there. Oh well, she thought, there would be another time. Patience is a virtue.

She contemplated it one last time, right before leaving. Then, Shanti talked herself out of the sweet images of bashing Genevieve's face in. *I'd like to shut you up for good, stupid bitch.*

The thing about Genevieve that she hated the most, was that innocent little victim act that she put on for everyone. Poor Genny, she's such a helpless thing. And Raine believed it. But Shanti knew better. She knew that Genny wasn't the victim. Genny had watched what Randall did to her and never once tried to stop him.

So, that made Genny just as much at fault as Randall was. And the right thing to do was to make her pay. The only thing left to do was work out the details, the "when" and the "where". The "how" was mostly already determined. It was all a matter of time and opportunity, Shanti reassured herself.

To pass the time during the drive back to San Antonio, Shanti replayed different variations in her mind. Thinking about doing away with Genevieve made Shanti aroused. She didn't normally feel carnal, neither did Raine for that matter. Serenity and a few of the others were the ones who kept those kinds of feelings. Shanti understood anger and hate. She wasn't comfortable with impure thoughts, and she felt rage at her own weakness. She knew from experience that the feeling wouldn't pass easily. Only one thing ever stopped her revolting urges - pain.

Once inside Raine's apartment, she searched for the leather bag. Sometimes Raine hid it from her. Other times, she thought that Serenity was the one who moved it from its hiding spot. It took her a half an hour to find it behind a stack of shoe boxes in the back of Raine's closet. Beautiful images of Genny's limp body and mangled face flashed through Shanti's mind. She was so aroused that her panties were soaked. She had to stop it. This wasn't meant for her - this curse that muddled her thinking.

Desperate to stop the madness, she pulled her jeans and panties off. She unzipped the leather bag and found the special strap. Made of leather, it was approximately two inches wide and riddled with metal studs. She lay spread eagle on Raine's bed and whipped herself across her bare thighs and pubic area until the sensation of pain became bigger than the craving.

# CHAPTER 48
## JACKPOT

It was like the gods had swooped down and scooped Randall up. It didn't look like he'd planned on leaving. A full glass of liquor and cola was still by his armchair with dead flies floating in it. His slippers were on the floor in front of his chair. The television was still on. A cast iron skillet that he'd probably cooked his breakfast with sat on the stove, unwashed. In the refrigerator, there was a pound of ground beef that looked like it had been there since the day Genny had left.

She was surprised to see a load of laundry in the dryer. She couldn't even imagine Randall washing laundry. *I suppose he didn't have a choice.*

It took Genevieve a little while to realize that her teacup collection was missing from the china hutch. As she looked around she could see that he had begun to remove traces of her from his life. *I wonder if he missed me at all.* She wasn't sure why this bothered her so much. After all, she thought, I'm the one who left.

Genevieve remembered that the pigs were hungry and found their feed in the barn. After she fed and watered the hogs, she started the car up to make sure the battery wasn't dead. She'd need to make a trip to the grocery store to replenish some of the supplies.

She set about cleaning up the little messes left behind by Randall and felt better having something to focus on. It was strange to be back in the house after being gone for so long. Not bad, not good, just odd.

Once she was done tidying up, she grabbed her purse, keys, and the kitchen trash to take to the burn pile. Genevieve wasn't sure that it was even legal to burn trash nowadays, but their neighbors still did it too. Seems like an earth friendly practice, she thought. *At least we're not filling up a dump.*

When she tossed the bag onto the mostly burnt pile, something bright blue caught her eye. She leaned in closer and could see what appeared to be a partially burned canvas shoe. She picked up the bag of trash from where she'd casually tossed it and placed it over the shoe.

She rolled the car windows down and enjoyed the crisp November air during her drive to town. Genevieve always loved fall and winter in the Texas Hill Country. It was cold enough to wear sweaters and bake but not too cold to grow fall vegetables.

Genevieve had started to make a mental list of the ingredients she'd need from the store when it occurred to her that she wasn't the least bit sad or worried about Randall. If pressed to describe her feelings, she'd have to say that she was relieved. She knew that she was bad for even thinking it, but she honestly hoped he never returned. Of course, she reminded herself, she wasn't that lucky. He was probably back to hanging out at bars again and just hadn't made it home yet.

Hours turned into days and days turned into weeks. And still Randall didn't return. Life went on as if he'd never existed. After the initial shock wore from Randall being gone, Genevieve felt like she'd won the lottery. She'd kept all the things that she'd wanted and lost the one thing that made her life hell.

# CHAPTER 49
## NO CHOICE

Finding the money for an abortion wouldn't be a problem for Lilly. Gabe didn't monitor her spending. He wasn't the kind of man who complained about his wife's purchases. He had no reason to because Lilly wasn't the kind of woman to blow her husband's hard-earned money on senseless things.

Pacing back and forth, Lilly had already worn a path between the patio and the shrubs. She wasn't bothering to hide her cigarette butts today. She had a decision to make, and hiding the evidence of her bad habit was the least of her worries.

Her heart ached with guilt at the very thought of getting rid of her baby. But the rest of her body froze with terror at the understanding that she would lose everything if she didn't. Even if Gabe were to be forgiving, his family wouldn't be.

Lilly dug the phone book out of her desk drawer. It didn't take long to find the number she was looking for. The appointment was made. Lilly tossed her phone onto the counter, buried her face into her hands, and cried like a little girl.

Lilly was a little surprised to see a wall of protesters already surrounding the clinic when she arrived the next morning at 8:00 am. That's dedication, she thought. Several kind-faced women wielding picket signs approached her as she walked toward the entrance.

One of the women thrust a pamphlet toward her and said, "You don't have to do this, Ma'am. There are other options for you." Lilly thought about denying the reason she was there but decided to save her breath. She took the pamphlet and pulled open the heavy glass door to the clinic.

Inside, the clinic was packed and most of the patients did not look anything like Lilly. *Maybe I should've talked to Dr. Canavan first.* Lilly had wanted to make certain there was no way for Gabe to find out. She knew that laws existed to protect patient privacy, but the family doctor was paid well by the Chenowyth family. She wasn't certain that she could trust him.

She signed in at the reception desk and looked over the waiting area to find a seat away from everyone else. There were almost no empty seats, so she settled on one next to a dark-haired girl who sat with her hands tucked under her knees. Staring at her lap, the girl looked like she'd been crying for days.

All the old tattered magazines were in use, so Lilly pulled the pamphlet out of her pocket. The front of the brochure sported a photo of a newborn baby nestled safely in its mother's arms. Inside the first line read, "You have other choices. Unwanted pregnancies occur for many reasons. Whether your unwanted pregnancy is the result of birth control failure or rape, abortion doesn't have to be your only option."

Another photo inside depicted a very young pregnant woman with an exaggerated expression of worry across her pretty features. The message continued on the next page, "You can give your baby the gift of life while blessing another family with the most precious gift of all. Consider adoption before making your decision." Phone numbers were listed along with a website.

Lilly picked up her purse and walked up to the reception desk. "I won't be needing my appointment. Can you cancel it for me?"

"Sure, no problem." The receptionist agreed. "Would you like to reschedule today?"

"No, thank you." Lilly couldn't wait to get out of that horrible place.

# CHAPTER 50
## A TANGLED WEB

Lilly waited for Gabe in their sunken formal living room. They rarely used the cave-like room except for the occasional party.

"What are you doing in here?" Gabe stood at the top of the stairs with his briefcase still in his hand.

"We need to talk." Lilly's voice began to tremble. "I have something that I need to tell you."

"Where are the children?" Gabe knew Lilly so well that it wasn't going to be easy for her to pull this off.

"Jane is keeping them for us overnight."

"Wow, it must be bad, otherwise you'd be in a negligee right now!" Gabe made a nervous joke.

Lilly took in a deep breath that turned out to be a sob. She knew that the only way to keep Gabe from seeing right through her was to believe the story she was about to tell him. Her survival in his world depended on it.

"I think you should sit down." She patted the spot next to her on the sofa.

"Did someone die?" Lilly couldn't read Gabe's face in the darkened room, but his voice gave away his unease. He sat next to her and waited for her to speak.

"No, something happened that I should've told you about." Lilly looked down at her hands. "I didn't because I didn't know how to tell you. And now..." Her voice trailed off. "I still don't know how to tell you."

"Just say it, Lil." Gabe's voice was thin and worried. He reached behind Lilly to turn on the lamp.

"I was raped." She exhaled. It was a lie, but her tears were real.

Gabe sputtered, "What? When? Where was I?" He stood up as if he

147

were going to leave then sat back down abruptly. "How long ago?"

"In August." Her voice cracked, and she felt like someone had kicked her in the stomach.

"How? Where? Did it happen in our home?" Gabe's face turned into a mask of pure anger. His reaction wasn't what Lilly had hoped for.

"No, not in our house!" Lilly felt defensive. She sniffed her tears back and explained. "I must've forgotten to lock the car when I went inside to pay for gas. It was after training class. A man got into the backseat and hid until I stopped at the grocery store." Afraid that Gabe would see that she was lying, she put her face into her hands and cried some more.

Gabe put his arm around her and pulled her head onto his chest. He waited a few minutes before asking her to tell him more.

"He held a gun to my head from the backseat and told me he'd blow my brains out." Lilly had pulled herself together enough to finish. "So, I did what he told me to." She covered her eyes with her palms and continued to cry.

"I was so scared that I wouldn't live. I just let him do it." Then she added the words that she hoped would keep Gabe from asking too many questions. "I'm so ashamed."

"Shhhhh...don't cry honey. We'll get through this together." Gabe kissed her temple tenderly. Lilly felt very guilty for what she was about to tell him next.

"No, you don't understand." She shook her head vehemently, "There's more, and it's not good."

Gabe stiffened and pulled back from her. "Then tell me. What could be worse?"

"I'm pregnant." Lilly couldn't have prepared herself for the agony on Gabe's face. "And I don't know what to do now."

"Oh my fucking God! You're pregnant?" Gabe put his hands through the sides of his hair and tugged. "You only told me about the rape because you're pregnant?"

She started to protest but Gabe stopped her. "No! I thought you were coming to me because I'm your husband and you needed comfort, but you're only telling me because you don't have a choice!" He pushed her away and got up from the couch. At the top of the stairway he turned to her and said, "I need time to think. Don't try to follow me."

Moments later, the sound of his car speeding away let her know he'd gone. Lilly felt a sick relief. At least he knows now, she thought. *But not the truth, not the whole truth.*

Gabe didn't come home that night after Lilly's confession. With the children gone and only her thoughts to keep her company, Lilly was very alone. She'd always joked about wanting a night all to herself with no children and no husband. But this, this was an awful kind of alone. She walked through the rooms of her home, taking time in each one of them. Each room was filled with twenty years' worth of memories and treasures. One of the many displays of frames held a collection of photos from their honeymoon. Another arrangement featured snapshots of happy smiles from around the Christmas tree. Caleb was barely walking in some of the photos, but he had no trouble tearing into packages from Santa.

Everywhere Lilly turned, there were advertisements of her picture-perfect life. *What's wrong with me? I should be happy. I have more than I ever wanted, and I'm miserable.*

Throughout the night, Lilly's nerves gave her a bad case of diarrhea. To make matters worse, her morning sick tummy was back with a vengeance. By the time that Gabe came home, the sun was coming up and she was a wreck. Not sure what to expect from him, Lilly waited in their bed with the covers pulled up around her neck.

"Hey," Gabe spoke softly. "How are you?" He reached toward Lilly and squeezed her hand.

Lilly cleared her throat. "I'm not good." Her hand trembled in his warm grasp. "I'm so sorry for not talking to you. I was afraid you wouldn't look at me in the same way." She hung her head down and shook it sideways. "I wanted it to go away."

Gabe rubbed her arm gently. "I'm sorry if I overreacted. I know it's not your fault." He leaned back onto his pillows and pulled Lilly onto his chest. They sat for a while holding each other. Finally, Gabe spoke.

"Do you want to abort the pregnancy?" He paused to kiss her forehead. "You shouldn't have to carry this animal's baby."

"No, I don't think I could. It's still my baby, still a human being. I'd feel too guilty."

Gabe sighed, "I was afraid you'd feel that way. An abortion would be the easiest answer, Lil. Think about it, no one would have to know."

"Look, I know what they can be like! I know they'll pretend to sympathize and support while tearing me apart at the seams behind my back." Lilly understood full well how judgmental their friends and family could be.

"Do you intend on keeping the baby?" Gabe's voice quivered. "Because I don't think I can raise the child of a man that raped my wife."

"No, I wouldn't do that to you." Lilly couldn't imagine forcing Gabe to live with her mistake.

"I've spoken with Mother and Daddy. We've made arrangements to keep this out of the public while you're…" Gabe seemed to be searching for the right words. "Until you deliver."

"You've already made arrangements? Without talking to me first?"

"You don't have the right to be angry Lil," Gabe said. "You didn't tell me about the rape and I'm your husband!"

Lilly's pride kept her from answering him for a moment. She wanted to argue with him; wanted to say that he and his parents had no right to decide her future. But the voice of wisdom in her head reminded her that her entire world was at stake. So, she agreed with him. "You're right. So now what?"

"You're going to see Dr. Canavan first to rule out any diseases and to make sure the pregnancy is healthy. I'll be going with you." Lilly understood that Gabe wasn't going for emotional support. He was going to be certain that the plan would be followed to the letter.

"Once you begin to show, you and Laney will stay at the lake house until the baby is born. As far as our friends go, they'll think you're helping out your sick aunt in Colorado."

Lilly blotted tears from her eyes with the blanket. "That's such a long time to be away from home."

Gabe continued without responding to her. "Once you're at the lake house, you won't leave until the baby is delivered. Dr. Canavan will come to you for your checkups. The staff will bring supplies and groceries to you. You'll deliver at the lake house when the time arrives. We figure you'll be confined for about four months." He added, "If you can dress in a way that hides your condition as long as possible."

"I don't know if I can stand being in one place for so long, Gabe!" Lilly felt trapped already. She tried to imagine what it would be like to not step foot into a grocery store, drive a car, or see her own home for four long months.

"What about Caleb's school? He can't miss school!"

"Lil, think about it. Caleb can't go with you. He'll notice that you are pregnant. We can't expect a six-year-old child to keep a secret, and he shouldn't have to. We don't have a choice. He can stay in school here at home. We'll hire a nanny to help out after school."

The thought of being away from Caleb made all the other stuff seem insignificant. Sniffling, Lilly nodded. "I'll think about it." She rubbed her forehead. There was so much to take in, and her head was pounding. She needed sleep.

"One last thing," Gabe finished, "arrangements will be made for the adoption by Gouldier." Abe Gouldier was the Chenowyth family attorney. He'd proven long ago that he could be trusted with their deepest secrets.

Lilly lay down on her side and pulled the comforter up over her shoulders. Gabe curled up around her, and they both slept.

On the surface, Lilly and Gabe settled back into the rhythm of their life. Gabe went to the office each day and came home for dinner each night. Lilly kept house, cared for the children, and did her volunteer work.

Underneath, both Lilly and Gabe were shaken to the core. A week passed and Gabe hadn't made love to Lilly once. She'd assumed at first that he was afraid of catching a STD, but Gabe stayed away from Lilly even after she had received a clean bill of health from Dr. Canavan.

"Goodnight; sweet dreams." Gabe said as he was turning off the light. Gabe only wished her this when he was actually going to sleep.

Lilly decided to swallow her fear of rejection and moved over to Gabe's side of the bed. She thought she felt him tense up slightly. He didn't reach for her, as he normally would have. Tentatively, Lilly began to stroke his chest and abdomen. Still, Gabe made no move to reciprocate.

Lilly caressed her way down to his waistband. Gabe's breathing became uneven, but he lay completely still. As Lilly started to play with the elastic on his briefs, Gabe grabbed her wrist.

"Don't." Only one word, but it was as sharp as a knife.

"Why not?" Lilly sat up slightly. "What's the matter?"

"Are you serious?" Gabe got out of bed and switched the lamp on. He looked like he was about to attack an intruder. "You really don't know?"

"Know what?" Her heart started to pound in her ears and her mouth was suddenly dry.

"I can't look at you! I can't touch you without thinking about what he did to you." Gabe's face was red and his fists were clenched.

"I'm still your wife, Gabe. Are we going to live this way forever?"

"I didn't say forever, Lil, but for now, I can't." Gabe pulled his sweatpants on. "I know this sounds harsh, but when I see you, I'm disgusted. I just can't get past it. You're carrying someone else's child."

Gabe slept in the guestroom after that night. Lilly's pregnancy felt like a prison sentence to her. She looked in the mirror each morning and wondered when she would be showing enough to go to the lake house. Even though it would mean more restrictions, at least she wouldn't have the pain of facing Gabe's rejection each day. And it would mean she was that much closer to the end of this nightmare.

~ A Proposition ~

Lilly scrolled down through her contact list and found Randi's number. Randi didn't answer the first time, so Lilly dialed again. She didn't want to leave a message. Lilly was about to hang up when Randi answered. She sounded sleepy even though it was almost noon.

"Can you meet me for lunch today? I know that it's last minute."

Randi cleared her throat and said, "Just a second." Lilly could hear Randi's muffled voice talking with someone.

"Yeah, sure. What time?"

"It's noon now; can you be ready by 1:00 p.m.?" Lilly added, "I really need to see you. I feel like I'm losing my mind."

"Sure. Can you come get me?" Quickly she added, "I'm not at home."

Lilly wrote down the address and was surprised to see a familiar street name, Corona Avenue. Corona Avenue was less than a mile away from her home.

While she waited for the babysitter to arrive, Lilly watered the plants. I'll have to remember to make a list of things for Gabe to do while I'm gone, she thought.

The home at the address Randi gave Lilly was a complete contrast to Randi's rental house. Stately oak trees lined the driveway to the exquisite house. Lilly dialed Randi's cell to let her know that she'd arrived. Randi's phone went to voice mail, so she left a message, "Hey Randi, it's me. I'm here."

Five minutes later Randi still hadn't come outside, so Lilly knocked on the massive front door. Thinking that she might have the wrong address, she started to go back to her car when the door opened. Before her stood a man that strongly resembled the lumberjack on a paper towel advertisement.

"You must be Lilly! Please, come in!" Smiling broadly, he extended his hand to shake Lilly's. "I'm Robert. Randi's told me so much about you! I'm pleased to finally meet you!"

"It's nice to meet you too, Robert." Lilly stepped inside the impressive foyer. "You have a lovely home."

"Thank you. It was my parents' home." Robert added, "I've been trying to convince your sister to make this place even more beautiful by moving in with me. Maybe you can persuade her to at least consider my proposition."

Enjoying the conversation, Lilly smiled. "I would have to know what your proposition is in order to convince Randi to accept it."

Robert leaned over and whispered, "I've asked Randi to marry me." He looked like an excited little kid waiting to go to the carnival.

"What did she say?"

He frowned slightly, "She'll think about it."

"I'll see what I can do." Lilly patted Robert's arm to reassure him.

"Lil! Sorry to take so long." Randi's voice floated down from the upstairs landing.

"It's okay. I was just getting acquainted with Robert."

"Would you ladies prefer to stay here for lunch? We have Madeleine here today, and she's a wonderful chef!" Robert interjected. "The two of you could have a nice private lunch on the terrace."

Randi smiled at Lilly. "Well, what do you think, sis?"

"I wouldn't want to be a bother. We can go out."

Robert quickly assured Lilly; "You won't be any trouble at all. Madeleine would rather cook than do anything else. It'll give her an excuse for not doing my laundry today."

Both Randi and Lilly laughed.

"If it's not any trouble, that sounds perfect." Lilly agreed to stay. She wasn't just being polite. Robert's home had a peaceful feeling about it.

"Great, I'll let Madeleine know. She'll be thrilled!" Robert turned his head back as he was leaving and said, "You know where to go, baby doll. I'll have Madeleine bring you ladies some drinks."

Lilly raised an eyebrow and said "Wow! He's definitely into you, Randi. What a charmer!"

Randi smiled and shrugged her shoulders. "I kind of like him, too."

"He proposed? Are you going to accept?"

"Maybe. I need to think about it." Randi led Lilly through to the terrace. It was as grand as the interior of the home. Complete with several wrought iron dining tables, settees, sheer curtains, and an outdoor fireplace, the terrace was a room in its own right.

"If you love him, what's to think about Randi? He looks like a keeper!" Lilly teased Randi a little bit. She was curious as to why Randi hadn't already accepted. Robert was wealthy, decent looking, and clearly enamored with Randi.

"I dunno; I guess I need to be sure I'm doing it for the right reasons, and I'm more than a little scared to be married to anyone."

Madeleine, who looked like a grandmother from a fairy tale, brought iced tea and a salad to start their lunch. Lilly took her first bite of salad and said, "You should marry him just to have Madeleine!"

"You're awful, Lil!" Randi laughed. "I did think about it, though! It'd be like eating at a five-star restaurant every day." She stabbed a piece of her salad with her fork and added, "One of the wrong reasons to marry him."

"What about you, Lil? How have you been? Have you decided what you're going to do?" Randi had called Lilly several times to check on her, but Lilly hadn't returned any of the calls.

"I told Gabe about the pregnancy."

"You did?" Randi raised both eyebrows and waited to hear more.

"Yes, but he doesn't know the whole truth." Lilly brought Randi up to date. When she'd finished telling her about the plans that the Chenowyths had in store for the baby, Randi looked sad.

"How do you feel about the adoption?"

"It breaks my heart to think that I'll never be in my child's life, but I couldn't expect Gabe to raise it." The familiar sting of tears blurred her vision. She'd cried so much lately that her eyes felt bruised.

"I have a question for you. Don't answer now; I haven't talked to Robert yet." Randi took Lilly's hands into her own. "Would you consider letting me adopt your baby?"

Lilly thought for a few moments before responding. She didn't want to hurt Randi with her answer. The truth of the matter was that Randi wasn't stable enough to adopt a baby. She owned nothing; couldn't hold down a steady job, and so far, hadn't managed to stay in a relationship for longer than six months. Even if Lilly wanted Randi to adopt her baby, Gabe's parents wouldn't allow it. They would be searching for parents that could pay for the expenses.

"Lilly, I know I've not been stable. I've made so many mistakes, but I've always wanted a baby. I can't get pregnant."

"I don't think Gabe's parents would go for it. They are going to be looking for someone with enough money to reimburse them for their expenses."

"So, I'll talk to Robert. He's not exactly hurting for money." Randi waved her fork in the air, pointing to their luxurious surroundings. "And besides, it's your baby. You're the one with the final say."

"It doesn't work that way in the Chenowyth family. They get their way. They have enough money to buy their way. With this situation, what they want is to make this embarrassment disappear. And if I want to keep my life as it is, I'll give them what they want." Lilly knew that her voice sounded bitter.

"Do you want to keep your life as it is? Is that what you want?"

"I'm crazy if I don't. I've got everything I've ever wanted. And it's not Gabe's fault that I'm unhappy. I need to find a way to fix me. Breaking apart my family won't fix me. It'll make matters worse."

"True. Then you will be dealing with an entirely different kind of agony." Randi finished the last of her iced tea and then refocused the conversation. "What would convince you, convince the mighty Chenowyth family to let me adopt the baby?"

"If you were to marry Robert, they'd be more likely to agree." Lilly didn't want to give Randi false hope, but she knew that Randi didn't stand a chance on her own.

"I'll talk to Robert tonight." Randi looked optimistic.

"One more thing, once I go to the lake house, I won't be able to leave. Do you think there is any way that you can stay for a while with me? No one else can know I'm there except for staff. I'm gonna be so lonely." If someone had told Lilly six months ago that she would be hoping to spend time with Randi, she wouldn't have believed it.

"I'm sure I can find some time in my busy schedule." Randi said with a smirk. Lilly smiled back. They both knew that Randi wasn't the type to keep a regular schedule.

Lilly left Robert's house feeling a little lighter. The small chance that her sister and Robert could adopt her baby injected hope into her sad heart.

# CHAPTER 51
## WEDDING BELLS

Randi waited until dinner that night to talk to Robert about the baby.

"How was your visit with your sister?" Robert looked ridiculously big sitting at the small patio table. As usual, Randi had chosen to dine outside. Something about the massive formal dining room and all its carved wood furniture intimidated her.

"It was really nice." Randi drank a sip of her wine. "Thank you for offering lunch to her."

"My pleasure, baby doll." Robert nodded agreeably.

"Robert? I have something to ask you." Randi took a deep breath. "And it's big."

Robert teased, "Sure you can invite your sister for lunch again."

"Thanks, but it's a lot bigger than that."

Randi's expression must have conveyed her seriousness because Robert's smile faded. "What then? If you're going to ask me to give you more time to decide, then the answer is yes. You know that I'll give you all the time you need - as long as your answer is yes."

"Actually, I wanted to say yes but with a contingency." Randi knew she shouldn't have said it that way. *How romantic of me.*

"I want you to know that my answer is yes, no matter what. I will marry you." She paused for a second or two before going on. "Remember me telling you that Lilly is pregnant?"

"Of course. Did she decide what she was going to do about it?" Robert hadn't given his opinion about Lilly's situation. Randi couldn't even imagine Robert passing judgement on another human being. She supposed that his line of work had taught him to be non-judgmental.

"Her in-laws have decided for her." Randi brought him up to date with all the details.

"Wow, a closed adoption. Has to be tough for her." Robert looked empathetic. "How's she handling it?"

"She's falling apart, but she doesn't want to put Gabe through any more than he's already gone through." Randi chewed her bottom lip, a habit of hers when she was nervous.

"That's a tough choice." Robert speared a piece of steak with his fork and stuffed it into his mouth. "So, how does this affect your answer to my proposal?"

"It doesn't, other than I'd like to adopt her baby. I thought you should know going into it." Randi kept her eyes fixed on his.

"Ah, Randi, I don't know." Robert shook his head. "I'd love to have children with you, but I'd hoped they'd be ours."

"Robert, I don't think I can. I had chlamydia when I was younger. The doctor said my fallopian tubes are scarred up; that I probably won't ever be able to conceive." A sinking sensation stabbed at Randi's heart. She wondered if this was going to be a deal-breaker. She and Robert hadn't talked about having children. Let's face it, she thought, we don't exactly have a normal relationship. *Do porn producers and adult film actresses even think about having kids?*

Robert stared blankly toward the pool. Randi waited quietly for a response. Robert began to say something and then stopped.

A flash of adrenaline made Randi's heart feel like it was thumping out of her chest. "If having your own baby is that important, then maybe I'm not the one for you! I've spent my whole life alone, so don't think I'm gonna' fall apart now!"

Robert looked surprised by Randi's outburst but still said nothing.

Randi threw her napkin onto the table and stood up to leave. "Goddammit Robert! I don't need this shit!"

"Okay, I'll do it." Robert's voice was serious, but he had an expression of amusement on his face. "You are incredibly cute when you're angry."

"You will? You mean it?" Randi felt foolish. She sat down and smiled slightly. "I guess I just acted like a dumbass."

"I've been chasing you for years, baby doll. Did you really think a little thing like that would get rid of me? Please!" He waved his hand as if to dismiss this little thing called infertility. Robert grinned from ear to ear.

"I'm sorry, I should have told you before now. I didn't think it would matter."

"It doesn't matter."

"I didn't think I'd ever have the chance to have a family with someone." Randi knew she should be happy, but that old familiar anxiety washed over her. She was always waiting for the other shoe to drop.

# CHAPTER 52
## DENIED

Lilly was glad that Randi and Robert didn't wait long to marry. She knew it would be pointless to propose her idea to Mr. Chenowyth before then. In early January, she'd scheduled an appointment with her father-in-law's secretary - unbeknownst to Gabe.

"What brings you here Lilly?" Mr. Chenowyth was his normal, cordial self. He gestured for her to sit in one of his expensive leather chairs. Somewhat relieved, Lilly sat. She hadn't known what to expect. It was the first time she'd seen either one of Gabe's parents since the announcement of her pregnancy.

"I wanted to talk to you about the…" Lilly cleared her throat. Her voice seemed to have disappeared. "Uh, about the adoption."

Mr. Chenowyth rested his manicured hands on the polished oak desk and listened patiently as Lilly told him about her sister's desire to adopt the baby. To his credit, he allowed her to plead her case before politely shooting her down. "Mr. Gouldier will handle the adoption, dear. It's our wishes that we have no further contact with the child after the birth. I know it might seem difficult, but trust me, it'll be better that way."

When Lilly didn't respond, Mr. Chenowyth added, "We wouldn't want anything to jeopardize the Chenowyth family reputation. I'm sure you can understand the need for discretion."

Lilly nodded weakly and sat for a moment to gather herself before standing. An expression of distaste clouded his distinguished features as he cast a glance at her belly. Lilly was far enough along that it was quite obvious she was pregnant. She rearranged her voluminous jacket to conceal the bump before leaving his office. The family wouldn't want any of the office staff gossiping about her.

Lilly waited until she was safely in her car before allowing herself to cry. She dug around in her purse and found a package of tissues to blow her nose with. I'd better let Randi know, she thought.

Randi answered her phone in the middle of the first ring. Breathless she said, "Tell me the answer is yes!"

"I'm sorry Randi; I can't." Lilly played with the design on the steering wheel, tracing it with her fingernail. "They don't want any possibility of me having contact with the baby in the future."

"But why? That's crazy!"

"They don't want their precious family name tarnished." She'd been defeated. She was a prisoner, a bird in a golden cage.

# CHAPTER 53
## EXACTION

He waited in the designated meeting place. He knew that the old man wouldn't want him to come to his office. That was just fine by him. Secrecy was a condition that had served him well in his line of work.

The old man was prompt. Chenowyth had chosen a public park where no one would recognize him. He didn't frequent public places, especially not public places with children.

He delayed rolling his tinted window down for a few moments after Chenowyth parked. The director inside of him knew that timing was so important for creating a mood. And the mood that he wished to create for the old man was one of anxiety.

Instead, the old man's expression was one of annoyance. No matter, he thought. That would change in short order. Chenowyth was still clueless as to the reason for the meeting. He couldn't possibly be aware of Robert's connection to his own precious family. Robert took a deep drag from his cigarette and decided that he was very much going to enjoy the old man's reaction at the moment that he put two and two together. He wished he'd thought to bring a hidden camera just to be able to watch it again and again.

Chenowyth was a piece of shit wrapped up in million dollar bills. Everyone was so blinded by his money that they ignored the stench surrounding him. It wasn't the money that made the old man so revolting. Nor was it his perverted desires. Robert had dealt with lots of rich old deviants over the years. Wealthy perverts were the lifeblood of Robert's business. In Robert's book, what made Chenowyth a worthless human being was his cruel disregard for anyone other than himself.

Robert didn't say anything to the old man. *He who speaks first, loses.*

"Well?" Chenowyth demanded Robert to answer. "What's this about?"

159

"You have something I want, Mr. Chenowyth," Robert offered. "And I have something that you don't want."

"If this is about the commission, we've resolved that issue a long time ago." Mr. Chenowyth spoke firmly but quietly. "You know the ramifications of releasing such a thing."

Children squealing and playing off in the distance filled the silence as Robert thought how to word his response. He studied Chenowyth's face. *The man hasn't aged a bit over the last two decades. How is that possible?*

"Ah, but I should've released it twenty years ago. I was too concerned about my own ass to do anything other than keep your morbid little secret." Robert smiled and added, "I've grown balls and a brain since then, Mr. Chenowyth."

The old man's face turned an interesting shade of red. "You'd better think long and hard before making such a drastic move. You're not going to squeeze any more money out of me this time."

"As I recall, you offered the money in exchange for my silence. And to sweeten the deal, you threatened my life if I didn't comply." Robert felt surprisingly calm, joyful even, while reminding Mr. Chenowyth of the terms of their previous business agreement. "Don't worry. I'm not looking for money. I've got plenty of my own."

"Well, what then?" Shaking, Chenowyth was visibly angry.

"You have control over a situation that I'd like to take over for you."

"If you think you are qualified to take over anything for me, then you are mistaken!"

"Relax. It's something you don't really care about." Robert wondered what the old man thought he was going to ask for. If he had the day free, he'd toy with Chenowyth some more. "You have an arrival due in the family. Yes?"

"Wha...what? What are you referring to?"

"A child." Robert gestured toward the children running around on the playground. "A baby is due to arrive soon in the Chenowyth clan."

"How in the hell do you know that?"

"I am married to a woman who wishes to adopt your family's unwanted child."

"Lillian's sister? Never. We want no contact with the child's adoptive parents. It's unacceptable." Mr. Chenowyth looked shell-shocked.

"I think you'd better consider the path of acceptance, Mr. Chenowyth." Robert smiled. "If you don't, you'll have to consider the path of prison time. What will your loved ones think?"

"You wouldn't." Even though he spoke the words, the old man didn't seem so sure of himself now.

"I would." Robert continued, "You should know that if I were to..., shall we say, expire before my time, the film will be released automatically."

Mr. Chenowyth said nothing. Robert finished with his conditions. "We would be happy to keep the adoption out of the dirty paws of the press, of course. However, the child would be allowed to know Lillian as Aunt Lillian. We will pay for all expenses, as well."

Robert gave Mr. Chenowyth only twenty-four hours to make his decision.

# CHAPTER 54
## ANSWERED PRAYERS

Lilly felt like she'd just fallen asleep. "Lil, wake up. We need to talk!" Gabe's voice cut through her dream. She hated being woke up from a dead sleep. She felt chilled and sweaty at the same time.

"I don't know how in the hell you managed to convince my dad, but he's agreed to let your sister, of all people, adopt that baby!"

His words began to sink into Lilly's groggy brain. "Wait, I didn't convince him. He told me absolutely not!"

"When did you talk to him about it, Lil?"

Lilly's heart sank. She'd already broken Gabe's trust and now this. "The other day I went to his office. Randi wants a baby so badly, and it seems like a shame to give this baby to a stranger."

"You've got to be joking, Lil! Your sister? Could you pick a bigger flake to adopt this baby?" Gabe scratched his head in disbelief.

"I think she's finally getting her life together, Gabe." Lilly picked at her fingernail nervously. "And Robert seems to be good for her."

Gabe snorted. "Do you know what he does for a living?"

"He's an heir, I think." Lilly hadn't thought to ask. She knew that he had a lot of money. Truth be told, she didn't care what he did for a living, if he was good for Randi.

"You might want to find out before you hand your baby over to him." Gabe left the room before Lilly could respond.

Blown away by Gabe's announcement, Lilly dialed Randi's number to find out if it was true.

"I don't know what you said to convince him, Lil. Whatever it was, thank you a million times over! We just got the phone call from Mr. Chenowyth himself." Randi had never sounded more excited.

"I'm not sure that you should be thanking me. I didn't say anything more. He was completely against it when I left his office." Lilly thought that it didn't matter why he changed his mind. She was simply thankful that he had.

"When will you leave for the lake house?" Randi asked.

"Within the next few weeks." Lilly examined her expanding profile in the full-length mirror. She was obviously pregnant looking. "Are you still planning on going with me?"

"Yes, as long as you don't mind Robert visiting from time to time. We are still newlyweds after all." Randi had a smile in her voice. Lilly wasn't used to Randi sounding so happy.

# CHAPTER 55
## IT HAPPENED TO ME TOO

### March 2012

The months of confinement were passing slowly for Lilly. Rather than feeling trapped by her seclusion, she tried to view it as a break from her day to day life. But the truth of the matter was that she was stuck. A few of her acquaintances had phoned to check on her and her made-up ailing aunt, but for the most part, no one appeared to notice that she wasn't in San Antonio.

Robert brought Randi out to Medina every Monday morning and picked her up every Friday afternoon to take her to their home in San Antonio. Gabe arrived every Friday morning to see Laney but was gone by early afternoon. Weekends were long and lonely for Laney and her. She was convinced that until she'd given birth, she would continue to be invisible to Gabe. Their marriage was in trouble, and she didn't have any idea how to make it better. Just like Margaret Mitchell's character, Scarlett O'Hara, in 'Gone With the Wind', Lilly's motto had become, "I'll think about it tomorrow."

She hoped that once the baby was born, their life would take on some resemblance of normalcy, but for now, it was too much to hope for. While she didn't think Gabe would divorce her, Lilly didn't know if he would ever feel truly married to her again. Trust had been broken, and to make the matter worse for Gabe, a reminder of that horrible life changing event would be present in their lives as Lilly's niece or nephew.

It was early Monday morning, and Lilly could see Robert's car making its way down the long driveway. She was surprised at how much she'd come to look forward to Randi's arrivals. So many years had passed that they were not a part of each other's lives at all.

"Honey, I'm home!" Randi poked her head in the door and announced herself.

"I'm in the kitchen dear!" The sisters found themselves being playful for the first time in their relationship. Laughter and goofing around wasn't safe growing up – just another opportunity for Daddy to misunderstand their intentions. And Mother never joked. She'd been too worried and sad all the time to be silly.

"How's our baby doing?" Randi inquired, gently rubbing Lillian's ever expanding belly.

"Baby It is doing fine!" The girls had decided to call the baby by "It" since they didn't want to know the gender before birth. Everyone else was appalled by this temporary name. But the girls thought it was hilarious. It was fun to be on the same side for a change.

"Have breakfast with me on the dock." Laney was still sleeping, and it was the perfect time of the day to visit without distractions.

Over coffee and bagels, the sisters caught each other up. "Have you heard from Mother lately?" Lilly knew that she should check on her mom more often, but it felt like the same conversation every time.

"No," Randi shook her head. "Not for a while. Last time we talked, she told me that she was pretty sure that Daddy was taken by aliens." Randi laughed a little.

"Was she serious?" Lilly never knew with Mother. She wouldn't blame her if she'd lost her mind. *Who wouldn't after living with Daddy all of those years.*

"I don't think so, but I guess that explanation is as good as any." Randi turned her gaze out to the shimmering lake. They sipped on their coffee, each lost in their own thoughts for a few minutes.

"Can I ask you something?" Randi hesitated before continuing. "Did Daddy ever touch you?"

Lilly's hands began to tremble slightly. *Calm down. You don't have to tell anybody anything. No one knows.* "Why are you asking me this?" She tried to think about the sounds of the lake.

"I'm guessing Momma told you about what Daddy did when I was a kid." Randi sounded like she was about to cry. "I've always wondered… why me?" Big tears began to slide down Randi's cheeks. "I mean, why me? What did I do to make him hate me so much?" She waved her hands in a gesture of despair.

Lilly had avoided this subject like a plague. To talk about it would make it real. She looked at her sister's tear stained face and felt guilty. She knew what it felt like to think that she was alone, to feel dirty and flawed.

"Randi, it wasn't just you. Why do you think I couldn't wait to leave?" Lilly recalled the feeling of relief when she drove away from home for the last time. She'd hoped to never think about those times again.

Remembering made her feel unclean and broken.

After finding out that Daddy had done the same thing to Randi, Lilly was ashamed. *I should have stopped him.* She hadn't once thought that he might touch Randi or Raine. It had never occurred to her that telling someone about the abuse could have been a good thing. The realization that she had failed to protect her sister added to Lilly's mound of guilt.

"Oh God! Do you think he hurt Raine too?"

Randi just shrugged her shoulders. She looked like she was still trying to process Lilly's admission.

# CHAPTER 56
## JUSTICE TRAIN

Randi wasn't sure what the emotion could be described as. She was relieved in a way because this meant Daddy didn't only hate her. But it didn't make it any easier. Her logical side might understand that her father was wrong, but the mean voice in her head still said she was trash.

She'd decided to quit smoking for the baby, but if any occasion called for a cigarette, this was it. Randi excused herself and went to get a cigarette from her emergency stash. Instead of going back out to the dock where Lilly still sat, she found a spot in front where she could smoke in private.

She supposed that there wasn't anything to do about Daddy. It was ancient history, except that he was still out there somewhere and getting away with everything. And then there was Momma. *She knew more than she let on, and she never tried to stop him.*

Randi wanted some sort of retribution. It was a small thing somehow when she'd thought that Daddy had only abused her. But to find out that it happened to Lilly changed everything. No man should be allowed to do what Daddy did to his children.

She squashed out her cigarette in a planter and pulled her phone out. Maybe the answers weren't apparent to her, but Robert would know what to do.

Robert pulled into the drive an hour later. Randi didn't even wait for him to park the car all the way before leaning in the window for a kiss. "Hi handsome!"

"Whoa you crazy broad! Let me put the car in park first!" Grinning from ear to ear, Robert's eyes sparkled. He swung open the door and swooped her up in a big bear hug.

No matter what was going on around them, Randi always felt safe in

Robert's arms. She put her face into his neck and held on a little longer, breathing in his scent.

"What's this about, baby doll? I left as soon as you called." When she didn't answer, he gently unwound her arms and turned her chin up so he could see her eyes.

Randi told him about the conversations between herself and Lil.

"Have you thought about suing him?"

"I didn't know if that was possible. I'm not sure where to start." Randi turned her palms upward in a gesture of helplessness.

Robert held out his hand for her. "Come on. Let's walk down to the lake." They found a spot near the edge of the water. They poked around in the rocks and shells while they talked.

"You said sue him, but shouldn't it be something that he goes to jail for?" Randi asked. "I mean, it's not like he destroyed my car. He destroyed my childhood."

"He should do time." Robert added, "Or, as I've said before, he should have to be alone in a room with me for one hour."

"So, what would be the point of me suing him? Why not let the police and criminal system do their job?" Randi skipped a rock out onto the glassy water.

"Because prosecutors aren't likely to take this one on."

"But what he did to me, to us, was horrible! How could they not do something?"

Robert shook his head, "Don't take it personally, baby girl. It's just been too long. The DA looks for cases that they think they can prove beyond a shadow of a doubt. They'll see your case as too old – and not enough evidence."

"What would be the point of taking him to court then? It's not like I can throw him in prison in civil court."

"No, but you can hurt him so bad, he'll wish he was in prison." Robert smiled. "Plus, he won't have a free attorney, like he would in a criminal case. He'll either have to cough up the money or represent himself. That alone will feel like punishment, if your dad is anything like you've described him."

Randi tried to imagine what her father's reaction would be to finding out he was being sued by his children. "He probably won't respond to the lawsuit," she said. "He's arrogant enough to think that he doesn't have to answer to anyone."

Robert chuckled. "He might find himself in jail, after all!"

By the time that Robert left that night, Randi knew what she wanted to do. He promised to get in touch with an attorney.

# CHAPTER 57
## LILLY CLIMBS ON BOARD

The sisters stayed in their own spaces for most of the next day. Lilly puttered around in the massive kitchen while Randi lounged on the deck with a mystery novel. Cooking soothed her, and she couldn't seem to eat enough with this pregnancy. Lilly replayed the previous day's conversation about Daddy in her head. She supposed Randi was doing the same.

The day inched along slowly. Six o'clock in the evening meant a precious phone call from Caleb. Most days that was her high point. On this day, the phone call was the only thing that she had to look forward to.

She'd already changed in to her pajamas by the time Caleb called her. "Baby, how was your day? I miss you so much!" Lilly forced herself to use a cheerful tone, but the tears were seeping through.

"Momma, are you ever coming home? It's been too many days for me." Caleb sounded a little tearful too. She could hear the background noise of a television show that he liked to watch. Gabe was talking to someone else, presumably the nanny.

"Oh honey, I'll be home before you know it." She hated lying to him. She held onto the hope that in time, he wouldn't remember these months away from his mother. Since the day of his birth, he'd only been apart from her for less than a week total.

"Momma please! Can't you tell your aunt to let you come home? Doesn't she know that you have a little boy?"

Lilly soothed her son as best she could and sang his favorite song. Then she put Laney on the phone to let her babble at her brother. The huge knot in her throat made it almost impossible to speak to Gabe after the children were done talking.

"Gabe, I can't stand this anymore!" Her words came out in big hiccups.

"Please! Can't you bring him to me? Just for the weekend? This is too hard for him and me!" She didn't want to beg him this way, but her heart was shattered.

Gabe maintained his composure and tried to reassure her that this was their only option. Lilly cried herself to sleep for the third night in a row. Sometime in the night, she had another gut-wrenching dream.

In the dream, she had returned home and was waiting for Caleb to get out of school. The overcast sky was promising a storm, and the wind was picking up. Her car was parked in the pick-up lane where all the teachers were leading their students out to be released to their parents. She waited and waited, but Caleb's teacher never walked out. All the other cars began to drive away. There were no children left to pick up.

"Excuse me," she rolled her window down to ask the remaining attendant, "Have you seen Caleb Chenowyth?"

When she looked more closely at the attendant, Lilly realized it was Gabe's mother. She simply pointed to the school parking lot. Lilly could barely see the back of Caleb's head and his backpack. He was climbing into a Lexus that looked exactly like her own.

The attendant, who looked like her mother-in-law, said to Lilly, "He's with his mother."

"But I am his mother!" Lilly protested. A gust of cold rain blew into her car window, drenching her and making her hair stick to the sides of her face.

"No dear," Mrs. Chenowyth shook her head. "His real mother would never leave him."

Lilly's pillow was soaked with sweat and tears when she awoke. She lay in the darkness for some time, trying to fall back asleep. The alarm clock read after midnight. Lilly finally heaved her tired, pregnant body out of bed and put her robe on.

Silvery light from the moon flooded the entire house through the two story tall windows. She didn't bother to turn on any lamps. In her heart, she felt like going on a hunger strike, but the baby made it impossible to go for more than four hours without wanting to eat something. She rummaged around in the refrigerator and found a cup of yogurt. As quietly as possible, she took a spoon out of the dishwasher and went out onto the deck to eat her yogurt.

Something about the moonlight's cool glow gave Lilly a sense of tranquility. A bullfrog off in the distance croaked a lonely sound. The nighttime revealed an entirely different world. A world in which things and money and appearances didn't matter. Every creature was doing what they were designed to do, with no thought as to what the other creatures might think about it. *How silly we are. Always worried about how things might appear to others. Bullfrogs must know the secret. They aren't sad or happy – they just are.*

In her distracted state, Lilly hadn't noticed Randi standing beside her. "Couldn't sleep?" Randi asked.

"No, you either?" Lilly patted the seat next to her, motioning for Randi to sit next to her on the glider.

"We need to decide what to do about Daddy," Randi said. "He's out there roaming around and completely getting away with everything."

"What can we do?" This was a genuine question. Lilly had the notion that the past should remain where it belonged. "We don't ever have to see Daddy again. And I don't know what we could do anyway."

"We could take him to court."

Lilly immediately didn't like the idea. "Seriously? Isn't it a little too late for that? It happened years ago."

"No, it's not too late," Randi said. "I read that the statute of limitations is something like thirty years after the victim turns eighteen years old."

"Well, I can see you've been doing your research." Lilly chuckled a little. "But have you really thought about what it would be like to drag up the past? To pay for attorneys with no guarantee of winning anything?" She added, "I'm assuming it would be a civil case, not a criminal case."

"It should be a criminal case, but I don't know if a prosecutor would want to touch it with a ten-foot pole." Randi shrugged.

"I don't know. I'd need to think about it." To Lilly, it sounded like a bad idea. She thought of the bad publicity, the money for attorneys, and the agony of reliving those days.

"At this point, my first thought is to say no way." Lilly went on to explain. "The energy that it would take to do something like this seems like it's not worth it. I want to move on. I've had enough drama for a lifetime already."

"Yeah, I get that Lil. But what Daddy did was wrong. He shouldn't get away with it. I think by not prosecuting him, we are basically excusing him from his actions."

"Let me think for a day or so." Lilly was too spent to even talk about it at that moment. Already drained from her situation, the thought of suing their father was too much. Less than two days ago, she hadn't told a single soul about what Daddy did to her.

Randi nodded in agreement. The sisters glided back and forth together without talking for a few moments.

Lilly broke the stillness. "Do you remember our secret fort out behind the tree line?"

"Yeah, I do." Randi smiled wistfully. "What about it?"

"Nothing really. I was just thinking about how safe it felt to be there." Unbeknownst to Mother or Daddy, they had built it the year Lilly turned twelve, with scraps of lumber from a torn-down chicken coop. Whenever Mother and Daddy would fight, the girls would go there to escape the toxic cloud hanging over the entire house.

"I loved that fort, but I don't think I've felt safe anywhere, ever," Randi said.

"I think I know what you mean. I act like I've got it together on the outside, but inside I'm always waiting for something bad to happen." Lilly paused, searching for the right words. "I've always thought that if I could stay on top of the day, if I could keep my house clean, if I could look good enough, then the monsters would stay in the dungeon where I'd locked them. The monsters are still there though, right where I left them - just growling and threatening to break out."

Randi put her hand over Lilly's, and they rocked in the dark for a while longer.

~ A Clarifying Moment ~

By late March, Lilly realized she hadn't heard from her mother for over a month. It wasn't unusual to go for weeks without talking to Mother - they hadn't exactly been close for the past twenty years. But with Daddy still presumably missing, she'd expected to at least get a phone call from time to time.

She waited until Laney was taking her nap to call her mom. She was surprised when Mother, sounding out of breath, answered after just one ring.

"Any news from Daddy?" Lilly doodled on the message pad near the phone. She never thought about what she was sketching during phone conversations. It was just something that she did to pass the time, an outlet for her nervous energy.

"No dear, not a word," Mother said. "I check weekly with the police and the hospitals. But nothing yet."

"Well, I suppose you'll hear something eventually." *Neither one of us are too broken up over the matter,* Lilly thought.

"How are you and the children?" Mother asked. Lilly wasn't sure that Mother actually cared, but she updated her anyway with everything except the baby. Telling the lie about being raped to yet one more person would make her feel like she was committing an even bigger sin. *No matter, it's not like I'm going to see her any time soon.*

"Have you heard how Randi and her new husband are doing?"

"Good, I think." Lilly wondered if she should tell Mother that Randi was going to adopt a baby. She quickly decided against it. Better to let Randi tell Mother.

Lilly went back and forth in her mind before asking her mother the question. It was the kind of question she wasn't sure that she wanted the answer to. It would have been preferable to do it in person but it would be months before Lilly could stand in front of her mother to ask it.

"Did you know what Daddy was doing to Randi?" Lilly had the urge to fill up the silence after the question with more words but forced herself to wait for Mother's answer. Her hand continued to sketch lacey patterns.

Mother was quiet for so long that Lilly thought she'd hung up. "Mother? Are you there?"

"Yes, I'm here. I'm not sure how to answer that."

"It's a simple question. Did you know that Daddy was…abusing her?"

Mother stammered, "It's not that simple, Lillian. I wondered at times, but your Daddy wasn't the kind of man that you just accuse of something without proof. I was scared of him, honestly I was."

Then Mother uttered the words that Lilly would never forget, no matter how hard she might try. "And besides, between you and me, I think Randi encouraged your father's attention."

"Oh my God! How can you say that about a child? She was a kid!" Lilly's blood had turned to an icy liquid in her veins. She slammed the phone receiver down before her mother could respond.

Lilly paced the sunny kitchen several times, to try to catch her breath and calm her pounding heart. In one of her rapid turns around the center island, she caught her pinky toe and jammed it hard. All of the rage and hurt from inside swelled up and exploded into uncontrollable weeping. She was sitting on the floor, barefooted and in her nightgown, when Randi rushed to the kitchen to see what all the fuss was about.

"Shhhhh, it's okay!" Randi wrapped her arms around Lilly's shuddering back. "What's the matter? Are you having contractions?"

"No! I'm done with Mother, and I'm done with Daddy." Lilly didn't want to hurt Randi with Mother's words, so she didn't elaborate. "As soon as this baby is born, we are getting an attorney and taking both of them to court!"

Randi didn't ask Lilly anything more. Instead, she gently rubbed her sister's back and sat with her on the cold tiled floor, rocking her back and forth.

# CHAPTER 58
## WHAT ANY MOTHER WOULD HAVE DONE

Genevieve sat at her kitchen table for a good while after Lilly hung up on her. She sipped on her lukewarm coffee and thought about all her suspicions so many years ago. Randall and Miranda had a relationship that she wasn't a part of. It had never occurred to her to step in between them. She knew that incest was wrong. *The word itself makes me sick.* But she didn't know that anything was going on for certain.

Genny didn't feel like she had the right to interrupt their time together. And things were a little calmer for her during those years. His attention to Randi meant that he didn't seem as irritated with Genny. So, she did what she supposed anyone would do in her shoes. She just looked the other way.

But now, her girls were telling her that she'd gotten it all wrong. That somehow she should have known what Randall was doing to Randi during their private time together. As if it were somehow all her fault. *The nerve of these girls!*

One memory kept poking at Genny. Randall was three sheets to the wind by four o'clock on a Saturday afternoon. He was in a boisterous mood, but at least he was happy. From experience, Genny knew that it could go either way. She'd much rather have a happy, obnoxious drunk than a mean, paranoid one.

"Dance with me, Genny!" Randall liked to turn the record player up loud when he was drinking. Genny had never been very comfortable dancing, especially not with Randall. He was abrupt and careless when he was drunk. She didn't like being yanked around.

"Okay." She agreed because if she didn't, he'd make a big deal about how she wasn't any fun. Eventually he'd get mad, and the whole night would be ruined.

After dragging Genny around the living room a time or two, he motioned for fifteen-year-old Miranda to join him. Relieved, Genny ignored the uneasy look on Randi's face. She left the two of them to go make herself a drink. Genevieve had decided earlier in that year, if she couldn't convince Randall to stop drinking, then she might as well join him. It made the evenings a little more relaxing, and his moods didn't stress her out as much as before.

She filled her glass with ice cubes and slowly poured the whiskey over them. Genny thought about going outside for some fresh air but thought better of it. She went upstairs to check on five-year-old Raine, who was still playing with her dollhouse. By the time she walked back into the living room, the song had changed to a slow dance. She had expected that Randall would insist on another dance from her.

Instead, Randall and Miranda swayed in one spot. Their bodies close, Randall had one hand cupped around Miranda's right butt cheek and was running his other hand up the length of her back. Genny felt betrayed and hurt. To avoid the awkward humiliation, she went upstairs and started a bath. She'd soaked in the tub until the water turned cold. By the time she went back downstairs, the music had stopped. Randall and Miranda were nowhere to be found.

Only now, did it occur to Genny that Miranda was a child at the time. *What am I supposed to do about it now? What's done is done.* She couldn't bear to think about it for another moment, so she picked up her knitting project.

# CHAPTER 59
## RAINE IN THE LOOP

Raine hadn't talked to anyone in the family since Mother moved back in with Daddy. She'd had enough of them to last her a while. An invitation to Randi's wedding had arrived in the mail, but she decided at the last minute not to go. It seemed like too much pretending. At a wedding, everyone expected you to smile and say nice things to the newlywed couple. Raine didn't feel like being a fake.

Shanti had only been around a few times since Mother left. And that was a good thing. Raine was frightened by Shanti. She was just so intense sometimes.

It was still dark outside when her phone rang. Mother was probably trying to reach her again. Raine had ignored all her previous calls. Instead it was Randi.

"Listen, I know it's early. Can we talk for a minute? I was hoping to catch you before you started your day."

"Yeah, sure. What's up?" Raine turned on the bedside lamp and reached for her water bottle. Waking up with a dry throat was a nasty side effect of the sleeping pills she'd been taking lately.

"Lilly and I have been talking about Daddy and..." Randi stopped speaking for a moment. "You know, about what he did to me."

Raine didn't know how to respond. She'd only heard from Mother and Shanti about what Daddy did to Randi. Not wanting to make any assumptions, she finally asked, "What do you mean?"

"I know Momma must've said something to you. She was a mess the day I told her. You know - about Daddy touching me in a sexual way."

"What about it?" Raine realized she must've sounded abrupt and tried to soften her question by adding, "I mean, it's terrible, but why are you calling me about it now?"

"Did Daddy ever touch you in that way?"

"No, absolutely not!" She was beginning to feel agitated. This was exactly how the conversation started with Mother on that day. *What in the hell is wrong with these people? Thinking they know something.*

"Daddy did the same thing to Lillian." Randi was making a rhythmic noise that Raine could hear through the phone. She could picture her sister tapping a pen or something.

"So what if he did? What are we going to do? Have a group therapy session? That'll fix everything, right? I know that I must sound like a sarcastic ass to you. But I really don't have any desire to drudge up more of the past." She'd had her fill of whining about the past from Mother last fall.

"Actually, we're going to sue him." This was the last thing that Raine expected Randi to say.

"What Daddy did was wrong. He shouldn't be allowed to get away with it." Randi continued. "I don't know if it'll be a civil matter or a criminal one because of all the time that has passed, but I intend on finding out. I just wanted you to know. I thought you might want to help us."

"Okay, I get that you want Daddy punished. He was a horrible father, but do you think that you'll win anything? It's been years since all that happened." Raine pushed the comforter off her legs and went into the kitchen to start some coffee. It was almost time to jump into the shower.

"I don't know. Honestly, I don't care. I think it's more about not accepting what he did – about telling him that it's not okay."

"Is Daddy back yet?" Raine hadn't spoken to Mother to find out. "Because I have the feeling he's not coming back. Ever."

What Raine didn't say to Randi was that she was almost certain Daddy would never come back. Shanti had told her so. She'd begged to know where Daddy was, but Shanti had refused to tell her that much. She'd only gloated over the fact that she knew something that Raine didn't. At his age, she couldn't picture him running off with another woman. And besides, she wondered, what woman would want to be with him anyway?

"Not that I'm aware of. And Momma doesn't seem too worried about him."

"Do you blame her?" Raine asked. "I wouldn't care either if I were in her shoes. In fact, I'd be hoping he didn't. Have you told Mother about your plans to sue?"

"No, not yet. Lilly and I haven't gotten that far." Randi paused and then said, "I'm not sure we should tell Momma. She's been on Daddy's side for so long, I don't think she'll be okay with it. I expect her to cover for him."

"I agree. He's treated her like crap for years, and yet she always defends him."

Later, while she was taking a shower, she thought about the magnitude of what her older sisters were getting ready to do. It sounded like a big shit-storm to her.

# CHAPTER 60
## BROKEN FOUNDATIONS

It was late April. The baby was due to arrive soon. Lilly wasn't holding up well, mostly because she'd not seen Caleb for months. She felt like she was nearing a nervous breakdown, so Dr. Canavan prescribed something for sleep. Nights were hell for her. Torturous thoughts kept her from getting the sleep that she so desperately needed. To make matters even worse, Gabe wasn't speaking much at all. She had crazy thoughts that he might be involved with the nanny. In a small moment of stupidity, during their last phone conversation, she'd asked about the young woman.

"Gabe, what's she like?"

"What's *who* like?" He already sounded irritated with her, but she ignored the warning signs and continued.

"The nanny! Is she pretty?" Lilly already knew the answer. She'd found the girl's profile on Facebook. Completely opposite of Lilly, the nanny looked like she was barely twenty. Photo after photo displayed the smiling nanny in carefree poses, mostly wearing fitted blouses and shorts that revealed her long tan legs. The girl didn't appear to be a tramp. She looked like the kind of girl a man would fall in love with.

"I guess she's attractive. I hadn't noticed. Why?" Lilly could almost hear his hairs stand on end through the phone.

"No reason."

"Oh, come on, Lil! I know this is hard for you, but don't start imagining things. She's practically a kid." Lilly didn't feel reassured by his words.

She tried to think about anything other than her husband having an affair with their young nanny. It was a strange place for Lilly to be in. She'd always trusted Gabe before. *Ah, but we've never been apart for so long, especially while I'm knocked up with someone else's kid.* She hated that pessimistic voice in her head.

It was a marvel really; how calm Gabe had managed to stay during the entire circumstance. She supposed that it had something to do with his upbringing. All that training to keep up appearances must come in handy during a time like this, she thought. Or perhaps he's getting his revenge by having an affair. Her dirty little secret only fueled the notion that Gabe might be cheating on her. *After all, if I did it - who's to say that he wouldn't?*

Lilly didn't like to think about her affair. She wished that she could wave a magic wand and erase that part of her life, erase this baby and go back to the way things were. Everything was different now. The colors of the sky were even changed. She'd poisoned everything around her. Her only lifeline was constructed of pure hope - hope that eventually life would feel normal again.

Every morning while eating breakfast, Laney watched her educational programs in the living room. It gave Lilly a little break from entertaining her. At the same time, Lilly watched self-help videos on YouTube. *Maybe it will help me figure out why I was so fucked up in the first place,* she thought.

And in a sense, the videos did help. Perhaps they had a placebo effect. Either way, they gave her something to focus on other than her little boy whom she hadn't seen for months and the unborn baby inside of her that was separating her from life as she'd known it.

Randi rolled her eyes every time she caught Lilly watching the videos. "Watching that mumbo jumbo crap again?" she asked with a smirk. Randi poured herself a cup of coffee and sat down at the breakfast bar with Lilly.

Lilly paused her laptop and said, "Easy now! You might want to give a listen from time to time."

"I tried all that for a while. Even went to group therapy for a little bit. Talk about bullshit!" Randi stirred her coffee slowly, watching the ribbons of creamer swirl around in her cup.

"Yeah?"

"Oh, most definitely! The last group I went to actually convinced me to tell Momma about what Daddy did. Said it would help heal my inner child. God, was that a disaster! Momma shut me down before I could tell her. I didn't have the guts to finish. I just quit talking to Momma after that." Randi continued to stir her coffee even though the creamer was completely mixed in.

Lilly didn't know what to say, so she waited.

"The worst part was that I couldn't stand to be in the group after that. Everyone knew and I hated their pity. So, I stopped going, stopped talking and started drinking. It was kind of like, you know, what was the use? Too much to fix and I didn't have the energy. Momma didn't want to hear it. Still doesn't."

"That's true." Lilly hadn't understood how absent her mother was until this past year. She'd always blamed everything on Daddy. It was easy to make him to be the bad guy. Definitely, he was the worst, but for all those years, Mother helped him. *Enabled him. Yes, that is the right word.*

Randi finally looked up from her coffee cup. "Do you think we'll ever move past all of this? Because I don't know how to pull it out of my life. I think that it's so much a part of me now, like tree roots grown into a foundation, that if I pull it all out, the foundation will crumble. You know?"

"And yet the tree roots are breaking the foundation already," Lilly added to Randi's thought. She sat for a while, soaking up Randi's words. She envied people with normal problems – things like broken furnaces and broken cars.

# CHAPTER 61
## UNTO THE SWINE

There was still no sign of Randall. With each passing week Genny became more agitated. Not because she was worried about him or missed him. Rather she didn't like the uneasy feeling of wondering when he might pop back into her life. Although he wasn't there, he wasn't gone either. Genny didn't dare to rearrange a single thing from the way that Randall liked it.

If she knew that he was not returning in fact, then she would be free to change the furniture around. And she wouldn't feel like she had to keep his favorite things in the pantry. But as the situation stood, it was best to act as if Randall could return at any moment.

She was also careful to take the time to dress nicely and to fix her hair each morning. When he returned, she wanted to look pretty as possible. Maybe then he'd be a little more forgiving of her for leaving him months before.

Spring had arrived full force, and the bulbs were blooming in the front bed. It was warm enough that she opened the windows to air the house out. Genny always loved the clean smell of spring air. It reminded her of childhood when everything was simple.

She started her morning routine of dusting furniture and washing windows. The chores helped to take her mind off the underlying tension of wondering when Randall would return. She hated that he took up so much of her thoughts.

After finishing the house work, Genny put on her muck boots and went to the pigs. It was past time to clean out their pens. Normally Randall's job, she'd not thought much about it.

She counted heads in the yard and then gated the pigs off from the interior of the barn. The shovel and wheelbarrow were right where they should be, so she began to scoop up the matted straw and toss it into the wheelbarrow. Genny reminded herself to be careful with the twisting motion. She'd thrown her back out several summers ago, while digging a new garden bed. It wouldn't take much abuse to injure it again.

The first section didn't take very long, so Genny paused to take a little break. After drinking some water, she put her gloves back on and shoved the wheelbarrow out into the yard. It took a lot of huffing and puffing to push it over the damp ground, but she finally managed to make her way out to the compost pile.

Boy, I'm out of shape, she thought as she lifted the wheelbarrow handles to dump it. When she pulled the empty cart away from the straw, something gold and shiny caught her eye. Embedded in a clump of straw and muck was what appeared to be a piece of metal. Curious, Genny squatted down to get a closer look. She realized that it looked like part of a watch band sticking out.

Not wanting to get her gloves any dirtier than necessary, Genny looked around for something to dig the metal out with. She found two sticks and began to scrape the muck away from the metal. It didn't take very many swipes to realize that the chunk of metal was Randall's watch. It was the watch that he'd won for making salesman of the year. For years, he'd brag to anyone that would listen about how he'd earned that stupid watch. Of course, he didn't go on to tell them that he came in almost dead last every year after.

Genny sprinted up to the house and called the police. "I need an officer out here right away. My husband's been missing for months and I just found his wrist watch. He never took it off." The dispatcher didn't view this as an emergency, and instead, reassured her that she'd send someone out as soon as possible. The cops must've been bored out of their minds because less than fifteen minutes later a cruiser rolled up the drive to Genny's property.

"Ma'am can you show us where you found the watch?" The officer looked like he wasn't old enough to shave. She wondered if the force had taken to hiring Boy Scouts.

"Sure, right this way." She led them to the hog pen.

Both officers stood in the clean section and swept the area with their eyes. "Aren't you going to look around for clues?" Genny asked.

"Well, ma'am, it's a little difficult to know what we're looking for. The watch could've fallen off, or he could have taken it off..." Genny interrupted him before the officer finished his sentence.

"No," she shook her head emphatically. "Randall never took the watch off. If it's in the pig pen, then you need to search the whole thing. Something happened to him in here."

"Excuse us for a moment." The officers went back to their car and appeared to be discussing the situation. One of the officers spoke on his radio. After a few minutes, they returned to Genny.

"Okay, we're just gonna take a look around, at this point. If we find anything suspicious, then we'll contact our CSI unit." Genny had the notion that they had agreed to humor her and weren't expecting to find a thing. She didn't care what they thought so long as they looked.

"I'll just go wash up while you boys look around." Her heart was banging all around in her chest. Something had happened to Randall in that barn.

Less than ten minutes later, one of the officers yelled for the other to come see something. Genny forced herself to wait for a while before going down to the barn. She didn't want to be annoying. When she couldn't stand it any longer, Genny poked her head in. She'd expected to see them digging through straw but instead one officer was on his radio and the other was photographing something.

"Ma'am, I'm going to have to ask you to wait outside."

"But why? What is it?" Genny reluctantly went outside the barn after the officers asked again for her to leave. She knew they'd found something. She supposed they were trying to keep it from her until they had more help. *That, or I'm a suspect.*

She'd not thought before about being a suspect over Randall's disappearance. But why not? After all, they hadn't been on the best terms. Fear clawed at her insides. It took a great deal of effort to calm herself down.

She sat on the porch waiting and praying, but her prayers felt wrong. Praying for one's husband to be dead rather than the opposite was probably unacceptable to the Lord, she thought. So, she called Raine instead. Raine would know what she should do. The call went to Raine's voicemail, so Genny tried Lilly's number. This time she left a message.

"It's Mother, call me if you can. The police are here now, and it's about Daddy."

Another cruiser arrived followed by an unmarked suburban. The events of the day started to feel surreal. She checked her phone every few minutes thinking that she might've missed one of the girls returning her call. One of the officers that had just arrived walked up to Genny's porch to introduce himself.

"Good afternoon, ma'am. I'm Detective Langdon." He pulled out a card and handed it to Genny before continuing. "Officer Drake has told me that your husband has been missing for some time now. Is this correct?"

Genny repeated to Detective Langdon everything that she'd already told the cops before. She even explained that she'd intended on leaving Randall but had decided to come home only to discover him missing. She felt sure they already had her statement on record, and this detective was just trying to trip her up. Sweat dripped down the sides of Genny's ribs. She hoped like hell that she didn't look as nervous as she felt. He jotted notes as rapidly as his hand would allow, which didn't make her feel any better.

Detective Langdon listened patiently to her responses, asked a few more questions and scribbled some more notes.

"Can you at least tell me what they've found, Detective?" Genny thought she had the right to know that much, especially since it was on her property.

Detective Langdon cleared his throat before speaking. "It seems the officers have found what appears to be human remains. More specifically what looks to be a human skull."

"Do you think it's Randall? When will we know? Will we be able to find out what happened?" Genny had a million questions.

"They'll finish combing the pig pen and then the rest of your property. If the remains are identified as your husband's and nothing leads us to believe otherwise, then we will likely rule this as an accidental death."

Genevieve didn't need to have it spelled out for her. She'd seen what the pigs had done to poor Molly.

The investigation lasted throughout the remainder of the afternoon and in to the early evening. They found several other large bones, all appearing to be human.

"We'd like to try to make a match with your husband's dental records. We can go through the process for permission with the court system, which will take some time. Or if you would be willing to sign the release form, we can probably get results much sooner." Detective Langdon held out a clip board with a simple form for Genevieve.

She signed the form. *I have nothing to hide.*

# CHAPTER 62
## DADDY IS DEAD

The lake house felt like a prison on some days and like a retreat on others. Normally, at this time of day, Lilly would be rushing around to get Caleb off to school and planning their evening meal. Her life had been full of things to do, but she wasn't sure that all the busy work had been that important in the grand scheme of her life. The sun was just beginning to rise, and the clean fragrance of morning air began to fill the house. She wondered if the city had the same air. *Maybe I was just too busy to notice it,* she thought.

Laney was sitting on the expensive tapestry rug with her toys around her. She'd become fascinated with a simple set of nesting cups and was attempting to stack them up with her little dimpled hands.

Lilly sipped on her decaf coffee while watching her daughter play. When Laney tipped her head down, her soft baby curls barely touched the nape of her neck. Lilly sat down behind her daughter and began to kiss the back of her soft neck and silky ringlets. Laney was so lost in her play that she didn't protest as Lilly breathed in her child's delicious scent.

She wondered if she'd ever slowed down enough to enjoy Caleb in this same way. When Lilly recalled Caleb's baby and toddler years, she only remembered feeling like a manager. Certainly, she loved him - his care had been her top priority. She questioned whether she'd ever relished Caleb the way that she did Laney.

For the first time since finding out that she was pregnant with an unwanted child, Lilly found herself imagining what the baby would look like. She hadn't pictured anything with this baby. To protect her cover, she'd come to think of this baby as the product of a rape. *Only it wasn't rape, was it?* The little voice in her head taunted her. Lilly tried to muffle that voice as much as possible because it reminded her of the horrible person she'd become.

She took another drink of her coffee and gazed at the rays of sun shining in through the long bare windows. Little particles of dust floated about. Caught in the light of the sun, the dust looked like little flecks of glitter. Little floating diamonds, she mused. Lilly couldn't help but compare herself to the dust – all sparkly and pretty in the light but in reality, just a piece of dirt.

The day passed with nothing to make it memorable until the end. "Randi, wake up!" Lilly shook her sister gently. She turned the bedside lamp on. Randi had been asleep for several hours. Lilly, as usual, couldn't sleep when she was supposed to. Randi moaned an unintelligible protest and turned over.

"What do you want?" She grumbled at Lilly after a few more shakes.

"Mother left a message. Something about the police and Daddy."

"Well, why don't you call her back?" Randi pulled the fluffy comforter over her face to block the lamplight.

"It's kind of late, but I guess if the police are involved, she's probably not sleeping anyway." Lilly dialed Mother's number. She put her phone on speaker so Randi could hear too.

"Hello?" Mother answered, and Randi pulled the covers off her face. Lilly put her finger up to her lips as if to shush Randi. She didn't want to explain why she and Randi were together in the middle of the night.

"It's Lilly. I just got your message. What's this about Daddy and the police? Did they find him?" Lilly half expected Mother to say that Daddy was in jail for driving drunk.

Mother quietly said, "Probably. We'll know more after they look at Daddy's dental records."

Randi sat up in bed and made an exaggerated puzzled expression. She mouthed the words, "What did they find?"

Lilly repeated Randi's question aloud to their mother. *Spit it out already!*

"They found a skull and some large bones that they think are human." Mother went on to explain the rest.

Lilly could imagine a lot of different ways for Daddy to die – car wreck, drowning in his own vomit, liver failure, or even cancer, but being eaten by pigs was one that she'd not thought of yet. Odd, she thought, it seems fitting.

"I was hoping you could make a trip out to the house this next week," Mother said. "If it is Daddy, I'll need someone to go with me to make arrangements."

Lilly looked down at her big belly. She couldn't go, but she wasn't about to tell Mother the reason. "Have you thought about asking Raine or Randi? I'm pretty busy this week."

"No, Raine isn't returning any of my calls. I think she's a little pissed off at me."

Lilly laughed. It was funny to hear Mother say the word "pissed". "What makes you say that?"

"Let's just say that I overstayed my welcome with her. And then there is the part where I went back to your dad."

"What about Randi?" Lilly winked at Randi.

Randi glared at her sister.

"Well, not only is Randi a newlywed, she doesn't want much to do with me. And after everything that Daddy did..." Mother's voice trailed off.

"Let me talk to Randi and Raine." Lilly had to avoid being seen by anyone in her condition. The whole point of going out to the lake house was to keep her pregnancy a secret. She wasn't about to blow her cover to help plan her asshole of a father's funeral. She'd sacrificed too much already.

"I have no intentions of helping Momma with Daddy's funeral," Randi said to Lilly after the call ended. "I'm not sure that I want to be around her, and honestly I'm having a hard time with how nice you were to her. You were ready to sue her just days ago."

"I know, I know. I'm so confused." Lilly tried to explain. "On one hand, I know that she didn't really try to protect us. She screwed up big-time, but on the flip side, she is our mother. And Daddy's death, if it is Daddy, is kind of a big thing."

"Exactly. She didn't protect us, and I think that she knew," Randi added, "at least about me." She laid back down and pulled the comforter up under her chin.

"I think she was scared. Daddy is scary. I was terrified to cross him."

"But she was the adult, Lil. Can you even imagine letting someone do that to one of your kids?"

# CHAPTER 63
## RANDALL'S SECRET BOX

Genevieve had expected that the forensic results would be available within a week, but April turned into May and still she'd heard nothing. She knew in her gut that the bones belonged to Randall, but she didn't feel that she could plan a funeral until his death was confirmed.

Although Genevieve didn't feel comfortable planning a funeral, she started to look for life insurance policies and bank papers. Randall hadn't shared much with her in the way of finances, so Genevieve didn't know what she would find.

On Randall's keychain, she found the key to his little safe. She'd discovered the safe tucked in the very back of his closet one day when she was in a mood to organize. Genevieve had never let on that she was aware of the box because he would have likely moved it. It took her months to have enough time alone with his keys to figure out which one belonged to the safe.

Randall had gone out to the barn to clean the pig sty. Normally he carried his keys on him, but on that day, he'd left them sitting on his dresser. Genevieve kept one eye on the barn, which she could see from the bedroom window, and one eye on the things in his safe. Her heart beat a crazy rhythm from the adrenaline rush. She felt like she was a spy on a secret mission.

There were some documents from Mutual of Omaha, their birth certificates and a small key. Maybe to a safe deposit box or a post office box, she guessed. She didn't get the chance to examine the Mutual of Omaha papers because she could see Randall walking towards the house.

She barely got the safe put back in its hiding place before Randall made it to the upstairs bathroom. There was never another opportunity after that to look in the safe.

Now she could look at the safe and its contents for as long as she wanted. She found it in the same spot that she'd left it years ago. The Mutual of Omaha policy was life insurance in the amount of $100,000. It was payable upon death to Genevieve. *At least he did one thing right.* It wouldn't be enough to blow money whenever she wanted, but it would be sufficient to live modestly. The house was paid for.

The small key was still in the safe, as well. Turning the key slightly to inspect it, she could see a number. There wasn't a bank name on the key. Since there was only a handful of banks and one post office in Boerne, it shouldn't be too difficult to figure out what the key belonged to, she thought.

Her birth certificate was folded up inside of an envelope along with Randall's. She thought about Randall as a baby and felt sad that he turned out so mean. Every time that she'd started to hate him, she'd imagine him as a sweet little baby and wonder what had happened to cause him to turn into the monster that he was. She didn't want to believe that people were just born bad.

Later that afternoon, Genevieve drove into town to see if she could figure out what the small key opened. She started with the post office but that wasn't it. Next, she went to their bank.

"How may I help you?" The pretty young teller smiled.

"I'd like to find out if this belongs to my husband's safe deposit box." She held out the key for the teller to see.

"What is your husband's name, ma'am?"

Genevieve gave the teller Randall's full name and waited while the girl looked on her computer.

"Yes ma'am, he does have a safe deposit box. But he's the only one with access. He'll need to come in to open it."

"Oh dear, that may not be possible." Genevieve went on to explain, "He has been missing for some time. It's possible that he has passed away. Can't I just sign a form or something?"

The young clerk arranged her face into a sympathetic expression. "No ma'am I'm sorry. We must have a death certificate to release the box, that is, only if he named you as beneficiary to the box."

The teller clicked around on her computer keyboard for a few moments and then said, "I'm so sorry Mrs. Carter. Mr. Carter didn't list you as beneficiary. In fact, he didn't list anyone."

"Do you mean to tell me that I can't get the contents of my own husband's things without him designating me?"

The girl looked unsure of herself. "Let me get my manager."

Genevieve absentmindedly picked at a sticker on the bank counter while she waited for the manager. After a few minutes, the teller came back with a relieved look on her face.

"I was wrong, Mrs. Carter. You can get your husband's safe deposit box. We'll just need a copy of his death certificate."

Genevieve had hoped to see the contents of the box that day. Disappointed, she took the key back from the girl's outstretched hand and thanked her for her help.

# CHAPTER 64
# THE BIRTH

The month of April came and went. Randi stayed with Lilly around the clock beginning the first week of May. She didn't want to miss a moment of the birth. Dr. Canavan increased his visits to a weekly frequency.

"Well, little lady, I'd say you are ready to have this baby any day now." Dr. Canavan pulled his examination gloves off and tossed them into the trash can by the bed.

Lilly pushed the sheet back down to her feet and sat up with Randi's help. A contraction triggered by the cervical exam took her breath away for a moment.

"You're dilated to three centimeters and thirty percent effaced," Dr. Canavan said with a smile. "So, that means that you'd better call me as soon as you start having regular contractions five minutes apart or less."

Dr. Canavan had been reluctant to agree to the home birth. It was against his protocol. His malpractice insurance agent would have heart failure if she knew that the birth was a planned one. They had agreed that the official story would be that Lilly's labor had progressed so rapidly that the home birth was unavoidable.

Lilly hoped the birth would be easy and uneventful. Dr. Canavan had warned Lilly that the birth would have to be natural. Should something go wrong, it would be impossible to convince anyone that the home birth wasn't planned in advance if Lilly had an epidural for pain.

Lilly tried to prepare herself for a natural birth. The truth was that she was scared shitless. She'd had the works with Caleb and Laney. The thought of pushing a human being out of her vagina, while unmedicated, terrified her.

Dr. Canavan had no sooner driven away when Lilly had another strong contraction. And after that one, yet another.

"Randi? I think you'd better get Dr. Canavan on the phone." Lilly panted through another big contraction.

Randi called Dr. Canavan and then Robert.

"It's time!" Lilly could hear Randi yelling into the phone. She smiled through the pain. Randi's excitement to become a mother was obvious.

"Do you want me to call Gabe?"

"No, just let Maria know that she needs to keep Laney away." Lilly knew that Gabe would come if she asked him to. She didn't think that she could stand for him to watch her birth a child that wasn't his.

Randi shrugged her shoulders and went about clearing some space for Dr. Canavan's table and supplies. She fussed over Lilly multiple times, offered to bring her tea, fluffed her pillows, and even rubbed her back during the worst contractions.

By the time that Dr. Canavan arrived, Lilly's contractions were less than two minutes apart.

"Let's see how you're progressing." Dr. Canavan helped Lilly to lie back.

Her womb contracted once more as Dr. Canavan checked her cervix. She tried to remember her Lamaze breathing, but the best that she could do was to pant.

"Looks like I made it back just in time. You've gone from three centimeters to nine!" Dr. Canavan set up his delivery table. He sounded pleased with her.

"Ooh! I feel like I need to push already!" She didn't go through this part with Caleb and Laney. She'd been blocked and had gone through their births passively, taking direction from the nurse and the doctor on when and how to push. This was completely different. She was in charge. Her body was telling her when it was time to push. Unable to stop herself, she bore down with the next contraction.

"Don't push yet!" Dr. Canavan said. "Let's check you again."

Randi breathed with Lilly to help her suppress the urge to bare down. It was almost impossible to not push. The contraction subsided for a moment, and Dr. Canavan checked her cervix once more. Almost immediately, her uterus balled up into another contraction. She could feel the flood of warm amniotic fluid pool all around her bottom.

Dr. Canavan chuckled and said, "Feel free to push with this contraction! Your baby is crowning!"

Randi squealed with excitement and kissed Lilly on her forehead. Neither of them had noticed that Robert had arrived until he stood next to Lilly on the side opposite of Randi.

Dr. Canavan put Robert to work immediately, instructing him to support Lilly's left leg and help hold her up into a sitting position. Lilly had a fleeting memory of Gabe holding her in much the same way and stifled a sob.

"With the next contraction, take a deep breath, hold it, and push with all of your strength," Dr. Canavan added, "just like you are having a bowel movement."

The next contraction came quickly, and Lilly felt a sweet release while pushing. After the contraction subsided, her body felt as if it were being split in half. She cried out in pain.

"The head is delivered, Lilly! The next contraction we'll deliver the shoulders." Dr. Canavan supported the baby's head with the palm of his hand.

Randi began to cry. Lilly hoped they were tears of joy. She couldn't see anything. In Caleb and Laney's birthing suite, there had been a mirror placed at her feet so that she could see their births. It didn't matter; she wasn't sure that she would have been able to focus on a mirror with this birth anyway. She was down in the trenches with this one.

Delivering the shoulders was the most painful part of the entire birth, but as she felt the baby's torso and legs slip out of her, the relief was profound and immediate.

"Oh, thank God!" Lilly exclaimed.

Randi and Robert simultaneously yelled, "It's a boy!"

"Would you like to cut the cord?" Dr. Canavan held the umbilical cord scissors out to Robert and Randi. Randi deferred to Robert.

"Hell yes!" Robert took the scissors and carefully cut the tied-off cord. He beamed from ear to ear and gave each of the girls a big kiss. Robert was acting like a proud papa. She'd been worried up until this moment that he'd agreed to the adoption to appease Randi. Clearly, he was excited for his own reasons.

Once the afterbirth had been delivered and Lilly was cleaned up, she sat up on the edge of the bed. Randi and Robert were holding their new baby boy. My new baby boy, Lilly thought briefly.

"Would you like to hold him?" Randi was flushed from the excitement. She had never looked happier than she did at that very moment.

Lilly nodded because she didn't trust her voice yet. She'd been unprepared for the emotions stabbing her right through her heart. No longer was this child a concept or a burden. He was her baby. Every bit as much hers as Caleb and Laney.

Randi carefully brought the swaddled infant to Lilly. Familiar sensations washed over her as she cradled his soft little body in her arms. He was beautiful. She studied his perfect features and gently traced her finger over his tiny little hand. His downy head smelled just like her other babies. She kissed the top of his head, feeling his soft spot with her lips. So vulnerable and precious, Lilly thought.

As if he knew she was his mother, he began to route around and make little hungry sounds. She felt a letdown response in her ripened breasts. She knew that her real milk hadn't come in yet, but she would have colostrum for him. Without even thinking to ask Randi and Robert, she readjusted her robe and offered her breast to her hungry infant. Immediately, he latched his hungry little mouth to her nipple and began to suckle. The stimulation from his nursing caused her uterus to tighten with an after-pain.

"Lil?" Randi delicately asked, "Do you think that's wise? Don't we want to get him used to the bottle?"

The sisters hadn't discussed the possibility of Lilly breastfeeding the newborn. Nursing the baby even for a moment hadn't been on Lilly's radar. She hadn't imagined the birth, or anything afterward. She'd only thought about the baby's birth as a release from her prison sentence.

Now, she didn't know. Lilly didn't say it to Randi at that moment, but she wasn't sure that she could let her newborn baby go.

"I don't know, Randi. But the colostrum is good for him. It'll make him healthier." Even to Lilly's own ears, the excuse sounded weak.

"Okay." Randi looked at Robert and shrugged her shoulders. "I guess we can give him his first bottle in a little while."

"Tell you what, sis, let me and Randi go dig around in the kitchen for something to eat while you have a little time with Robert Jr."

Lilly gazed up at Robert's sympathetic face. He feels sorry for me, she thought. "Thank you," she mumbled to him and looked back down at her baby's face.

"We'll just be in the kitchen if you need anything," Randi reassured her as she walked out of the bedroom.

Lilly could hear the sounds of Laney playing with Maria in the bedroom above her. She imagined what it would be like for Laney to have her baby brother to play with. Repressed tears stung her eyes, like sharp little needles. She stifled a sob and placed her baby on the bed. She shut the door a little more forcefully than she'd intended to and then locked it.

Randi and Robert were knocking on the door before Lilly had the chance to settle back into bed with her baby. *Robert Jr.? Really?* She thought about what she might have named him but couldn't think of anything.

"Lilly! Come on, open the door please!" Randi's voice was muffled by the door, but Lilly could hear the fear. She didn't respond. She held her baby up to her other breast, but he didn't latch on. Typical of a newborn baby, he was sleepy from the birth. So, she held him against her bare breast. She could feel his delicate sweet breaths as they escaped from his tiny little nostrils. He was perfect in every way. She searched for signs that he might look like his father. All that she could see was herself. Maybe, she thought, Gabe would be convinced to let her keep him once he saw how much the baby looked like her.

"Mrs. Chenowyth, open the door please." Dr. Canavan pleaded at the door. "We still need to complete the baby's examination." He knocked loudly when Lilly didn't answer.

They seemed to give up after a few minutes of trying to convince her to open the door. Lilly knew that she couldn't keep them out forever. She just needed to figure out what she was going to say to all of them.

# CHAPTER 65
## A TURN OF EVENTS

"What in the hell do we do?" Robert asked in disbelief. Dr. Canavan, Randi and Robert had taken their conversation out to the deck to have a little privacy from the maid.

"Has she said anything up to this point that would lead you to believe she's suicidal?" Dr. Canavan asked Randi.

"I don't think she's a danger to the baby or herself, but I don't know what she's doing." Randi really wasn't sure that she believed her own words. Lilly's actions were the farthest thing away from what Randi had imagined would happen after the birth of little Robert Jr. Up until that moment, Lilly had seemed completely unattached to the baby.

"I think that I should call her husband." Dr. Canavan pulled out his cell phone and began to search for Gabe's number. After a brief conversation with Gabe, Dr. Canavan informed them that he was on his way.

"Against my better judgement, I'm not calling EMS or the police," Dr. Canavan explained. "But if this were anyone other than Mrs. Chenowyth, they would already be here." Randi suspected that he was covering his own ass just as much or more as he was Lilly's.

Randi didn't know what else to do, so she carried a kitchen chair into the hallway and placed it outside of the bedroom where Lilly was holed up. There were no noises coming from inside the room, and Randi fought off horrible images of her sister and the baby bleeding to death. They're just sleeping, Randi told herself. She sat in the chair, praying and waiting for Gabe to arrive.

After what seemed like an eternity, Gabe appeared. He and Randi had never been close. They'd only been around each other a handful of times, so Randi was surprised by the warm hug that Gabe gave her.

"How are you?" Randi was taken off guard by the caring look in Gabe's intense blue eyes.

He really is very handsome, Randi thought. No wonder Lilly doesn't want to lose him – good looking and rich.

"I'm worried. It's been over two hours since she locked the door." Randi started to cry. Gabe's unexpected kindness cut right through the wall she'd put up around herself.

"Lilly? Honey, are you okay?" Gabe knocked softly and waited for a few seconds. When Lilly didn't respond, he pulled a set of keys out of his pocket and rotated through the ring to find the right one. Within seconds the door was open.

Gabe motioned for Randi to come in with him. Dr. Canavan and Robert waited outside the door. The cool room was darkened by the closed blinds. Both Lilly and the baby were lying in bed. She gave a silent prayer of thanks as she stood next to her sleeping sister and her baby. My baby, she corrected herself.

Lilly lay on her side with little Robert protectively encircled. They must have fallen asleep while nursing, Randi thought, because Lilly's left breast was exposed and the baby's face was just an inch away.

"Lil, are you okay?" Gabe gently stroked Lilly's back and shoulder.

"Hmmm?" Lilly responded sleepily. She kept her eyes closed for a few seconds. "When did you get here?"

Randi decided to give them some privacy. Dr. Canavan and Robert were waiting in the kitchen. Robert had a beer in his hand.

"Do you want one? Take the edge off?" Robert offered.

"No thanks." Randi didn't want to be off her game during this time. She was worried about Lilly and the baby.

"Well, what do you think is going to happen now?" Robert wasn't one to beat around the bush. Although his direct way of speaking made him seem ill-mannered at times, Randi appreciated knowing where he stood.

"I don't know. During the entire pregnancy, she seemed really disconnected from the baby. I wasn't expecting this."

"Could be a little post-partum depression." Dr. Canavan offered a medical possibility for the turn of events. "And if she hasn't dealt with the circumstances under which the baby was conceived…"

Randi knew that rape wasn't a factor in Lilly's behavior because she knew the truth. She was afraid that Lilly wouldn't be able to give up Robert Jr. after all. I should've known this was too good to be true, Randi silently scolded herself. She felt foolish for thinking that she would ever be a mother.

# CHAPTER 66
## LET THE PIECES FALL

"Why didn't you have someone call me when you went into labor?" Gabe didn't sound angry.

"I don't know. I guess I felt like it would be too painful for you." Lilly repositioned the pillows so she could lean back against the headboard. She picked up her sleeping baby and cuddled him. Drained, emotionally and physically, Lilly didn't try to elaborate.

"I...I don't know whether I wanted to be there with you. Honestly, I don't, but I thought you would've at least let me know." Gabe sounded exhausted too.

"When you first told me that you couldn't abort the baby, I was so angry with you." He sighed. "But I get it. It's still a child, an innocent human being." He rubbed the back of his neck like he always did when he had a headache.

"It's not just any child. Don't you get that part?" Lilly's voice cracked from the strain of trying to not cry. "He's my child. Laney and Caleb's little brother. He needs me."

"I just don't know if I can ever look at him and not think about what his father, that monster, did to you!" Gabe almost never cried, but his tears were streaming down his cheeks.

"So where do we go from here?" she asked. "I love you more than you can imagine, I do. But giving my baby away to someone else feels so wrong. It's devastating. I don't think I can do it."

Gabe put his arms around Lilly. His shoulders shook as he wept without making a sound. She could feel his hot tears when he rested his face in the curve of her neck. Minutes passed while Gabe held her in his desperate embrace. Fear and sadness wracked her entire body. She was afraid to ask

Gabe what his embrace meant for them. Instead, she just let him hold her.

After some time had passed, the baby began to stir and make little hungry noises. Gabe sighed and pulled away from Lilly. She readjusted the baby and opened her robe. The baby latched on instantly and drank like he was starving.

Lilly expected Gabe to leave the room. Instead, he stayed with her. The room was dark enough that she couldn't read his expression. She wanted to ask him what he was thinking about, but she didn't. Mother had always said, "Don't ask a question that you don't want the answer to". Lilly thought that was a strange thing for someone to say. At that moment, she finally understood what her mother had meant.

"Do you need anything?" Gabe stood up.

"Just a diaper and wipes. You can ask Randi; she knows where they are." Poor Randi, she thought. She wasn't sure how to tell Randi, if she hadn't figured it out already.

Gabe kissed Lilly on her forehead and said, "I'll check in on you later."

"I love you," she called to his back.

"You, too." He didn't turn around.

Several minutes passed before Randi knocked on the door frame. She had a handful of diapers and a box of baby wipes. She stood awkwardly near the bed, as if she were afraid to invade Lilly's space. Lilly gestured for her to sit on the bed.

"Randi, I don't know where to start." Lilly dreaded the conversation that she was about to have. She felt like the world's biggest asshole. Not only was this the woman who had given her a way out of her dilemma with absolutely no negativity, this was her little sister. Randi had rearranged her entire life, entered a marriage even, in order to adopt Lilly's baby.

"Just say it, Lil." Randi's voice was strained and thin.

"It has absolutely nothing to do with you, but I don't think I can give my baby up." The lump in her throat almost prevented her from speaking.

"This is the last thing that I expected," she continued, "but I will never be okay if I just give him away." She wiped away the tears flooding down her face with the back of her robe sleeve. "I'm so sorry."

"Please, please rethink this!" Randi begged. Pain distorted her pretty face. "I promise we'll take very good care of him!"

"I know that you would. That's what makes this decision so hard!" Lilly reached out with her free hand to touch Randi's shoulder, but Randi shrugged her away.

"I can't believe that you are doing this to me. You know how much I've wanted this baby! Everything that Robert and I went through to be acceptable to the Chenowyths, getting married so quickly, the baby equipment, the nursery, all that should count for something!"

"You have to know that I appreciate everything you have done for me,

Randi." Lilly knew that her words meant nothing to her sister at that moment. She was very certain that she'd destroyed anything that she had with Randi, and she couldn't even begin to think about the likelihood that she'd lost Gabe, too.

"I just don't feel like I have a choice. Not giving up this baby is the worst thing that I could do for my marriage. Don't you understand how much I'm losing by keeping him? I can't live with the adoption. I can't." Lilly pleaded with her sister for understanding.

"I can't force you, but I hope you know how many lives you are going to devastate with this decision." Randi walked out before Lilly could say anything more.

Lilly sat in the darkened room trying to think of some way to put together the box of mismatched jigsaw puzzle pieces that was her life.

# CHAPTER 67
## THE INTERROGATION

It was mid-May before Genevieve heard from the police department. That morning was exceptionally hot, even by San Antonio standards. She'd hoped to hold off on using air conditioning for at least another week or two. It seemed like once she turned on the A/C for the season, it didn't get shut off until October.

Maybe I'm just getting too old to tolerate the heat, she thought as she fanned her face with a magazine. Reluctantly, she flipped the thermostat to the cool setting and began to go around the house, shutting windows. She was just closing the last of the windows in the upstairs bedrooms when she heard the crunching sound of tires coming down the driveway.

She was a little surprised to see a police cruiser. So much time had passed that she figured she'd just get a phone call with the forensic results. As quickly as her old legs would carry her, Genevieve ran downstairs.

She opened the front door just as the officer was ringing the bell. "Do you have anything yet?"

"Could you come down to the station with us, Ma'am?" The officer's stoic expression gave no indication of the results.

"Just a moment while I grab my purse." Genevieve forced herself to remain calm on the outside.

On the drive into town, Genevieve cycled through a range of emotions from composed to frantic. She made polite small talk with the officer to disguise her fear. She'd never been asked to come down to the station, so she was sure they were going to interrogate her. Or at least that's what they did in the movies, she thought.

Thankfully, the drive into town didn't take long. She felt self-conscious. It was unnerving to ride in the back of a police car through town. She wondered how she would explain herself if someone she knew were to see her in the cruiser. *I probably look like I've been arrested,* she worried.

Once at the station, the baby-faced officer escorted Genevieve into a small room. "Can I get you anything, Ma'am? Coffee or a soda?"

"No, thank you." Genevieve's stomach was too upset to drink anything. "Can you tell me how long this might take? I think I left my oven on."

"Someone will be right in with you, Ma'am." With a polite nod, the officer was gone.

Genevieve looked around the small area and thought that it was a poor excuse for an interrogation room. There was no one-way window, and the door was propped open by a chair holding a box of brochures. A small refrigerator stood in the corner with a microwave stacked on top of it. As she looked around, she wondered if this might be a break room instead.

She was resisting the urge to look inside of the mini-fridge when the detective who had searched her place entered the room.

"Good morning, Mrs. Carter." He extended his right hand to her for a shake. "How've you been?

"Fine, thank you." *Just cut to the chase,* Genevieve thought.

"I'll get right to the point. We got the results back and it appears that the dental records of your husband match the remains found on your property."

Her anxiety over being questioned repressed any happiness that she might've felt over the news that Randall was indeed gone. She waited for the questioning to begin. She'd watched enough crime investigation shows to know that she shouldn't volunteer any information.

"Would you like to speak with our chaplain or would you like me to contact your spiritual advisor?" The detective had a sympathetic expression on his face as he waited for her to answer.

She was so focused on the interrogation that it took her a full ten seconds to realize that she wasn't being questioned at all. They were simply following some rule or law about delivering the bad news to the families of the deceased.

Relief flooded through her body from the top of her head to the bottoms of her soles. "No, thank you. So, what is the next step?"

"I'll just need you to sign this form." He scooted a clipboard in front of her. "Decide which funeral home you would like to handle your husband's remains and let them know. They'll make arrangements to transport from the morgue. Then, you can consult with them regarding the service that you might like for your husband."

"Thank you, Detective." She handed the clipboard back to him and smiled.

"I'm so sorry for your loss, Mrs. Carter."

*Don't be sorry; I'm not.* She politely accepted his condolence with a small nod.

While she waited for the young officer to take her back home, she constructed a mental checklist of things to do now that Randall was officially dead. The first item on her list was to get a death certificate to the bank. She wanted to know what Randall had thought so valuable that it deserved a safe deposit box.

# CHAPTER 68
## GLIMMER OF HOPE

Several months had passed since the birth of Aiden (formerly known as Robert Jr.). Gabe hadn't filed for divorce, but he'd moved out within days after Aiden's birth. Lilly questioned herself about the wisdom of not hiring an attorney, but she reasoned that since she did not want a divorce, there was no real cause to do so - at least not yet.

Gabe was polite to Lilly, but he'd refused all her attempts to talk about reconciliation. It was difficult to get used to being treated like a stranger by her own husband, but by far the hardest part for Lilly was that she had no idea where his head was at. She didn't have the slightest clue whether he intended on staying in the marriage or not. She understood now what it meant to walk on faith.

Everything in her head told her to protect herself - to file for divorce first, while she still had access to their bank accounts. Lilly knew that she was leaving herself wide open. With his family's money and a top-notch attorney on speed dial, she wouldn't stand a chance in hell should Gabe decide to end their marriage. She'd even spoken with the lawyer that Mother had used when she'd left Daddy. But every time she thought about divorcing Gabe, it felt wrong to her, much the same way that giving up Aiden for adoption had felt wrong.

So, she prayed. A lot. Sometimes her prayers were to bring Gabe back to her, but mostly her prayers were for a peaceful heart.

Sometime during the middle of May, Mother had announced that the remains found in the pig pen were indeed their father's. Mother had him cremated and had promised a funeral service at some point in the future. So far, nothing had been arranged, but that was okay with Lilly. She had no pleasant memories of her father to share, and she'd said her goodbyes to him many years before.

Randi hadn't returned any of Lilly's phone calls. Although it hurt, she didn't blame her sister. *I probably wouldn't want to talk to me either,* she thought. And because she didn't want to deal with questions about Aiden, Lilly avoided her friends. Without Gabe, Randi, or her friends, she was lonely.

To keep her sanity, Lilly filled their days with summer activities. Caleb was enrolled in swimming lessons at the country club; Laney took toddler ballet each week, and Aiden was enrolled in a yoga class with Lilly, designed especially for mothers of newborn babies.

There were only two weeks left until the start of school season. The children were up earlier than normal because they were going to go shopping for school supplies. Laney was sitting on her knees at the table, eating cereal. Caleb had already finished his breakfast and had gone upstairs to change out of his pajamas. Lilly was nursing Aiden while she read emails on her laptop.

Lilly began the tedious process of deleting the spam emails that flooded her inbox on a daily basis. Mostly ads from different stores and websites, she considered mass deleting them all at once. She scrolled down the page to be sure that she wouldn't accidently trash something important. She clicked the "select all" button and deleted the first fifty emails. The second page loaded and an email from Gabe caught her eye.

Her anxiety level went up immediately. *Why would Gabe send me an email?* She opened the message and had to re-read the first few lines several times. She wasn't able to fully comprehend the words at first. The formal sounding email was a stark contrast to Gabe's sweet notes of the past.

"Dear Lil,

I apologize for my distance over the last year. I can't really wrap my head around what we've become. I feel guilty because I know that the pregnancy wasn't your fault. I don't know how to live with a constant reminder. I don't want to be away from you, but being with you is painful.

I have one last hope that we might find a way to work through these problems. There is a marriage retreat for couples facing infidelity issues. I realize that you were not unfaithful, but I'm battling some of the same demons as someone who has been cheated on. Could you consider doing this with me? It's a week long and no children are allowed. Mother has offered to watch all three children for us.

Please let me know if you are open to going with me. The deadline for registration is August 15th.

Gabe"

Aiden had fallen asleep while nursing and a little bit of milk drooled out of the corner of his mouth. She gently wiped his mouth and put him up over her shoulder. As she carried Aiden to his bassinette, he burped softly in his sleep. Lilly smiled as she laid him down. Whatever might happen with Gabe, she had no regrets over keeping Aiden.

She used Aiden's early naptime to dress for the day. Leaving the bathroom door open so she would be able to hear the children, Lilly turned on the shower. She studied her body as she undressed. The past few months had taken their toll on her weight. Her ribs and her hip bones protruded out slightly, making her almost look anorexic.

The only reason I have breasts at all is because I'm nursing, she thought. Heartbreak, coupled with the extra calories needed to breastfeed Aiden, had caused Lilly to drop twenty pounds below her pre-pregnancy weight. Dr. Canavan warned her at her last checkup to eat more, but she couldn't seem to muster up an appetite.

Hot jets of water massaged the sore muscles that no one was there to rub. Since Gabe had pulled away from her, she wasn't missing sex so much as she missed his comforting touch. The children were affectionate but in a needy sort of way. She gave and they took. That was the way it should be between mother and child. But the touch of a man was entirely different. Now that she no longer had Gabe's affection, she realized how much she needed it. It had been nearly a year since Gabe had made love to her. She couldn't remember the last time he'd just held her.

She tried to masturbate when the children were sleeping, but the pleasure was short lived and only left her fantasizing about the rest of it: the kisses, the cuddles and the small reassuring touches. The lack of physical affection left her raw and on the edge of tears most of the time.

Rarely did she allow herself to wonder what Gabe was doing to fulfill the same needs. It was too painful. Lilly was almost certain that Gabe had taken a lover after so much time had passed. She had strayed while they were still in the same bed. How could she expect Gabe to stay faithful after a year apart? Conjured up images of the nanny's young, tan legs wrapped around her husband burned like a branding iron in Lilly's mind. Desperate for some sort of proof that her suspicions weren't valid, Lilly had stalked both the nanny and Gabe's Facebook accounts looking for signs that they were involved with each other. It was an obsessive activity that gave her no relief. She was constantly looking for proof of something that she hoped to never find.

After she'd ran the hot water tank empty, Lilly wiped the glass shower doors clean with a squeegee. She dried the steamy vanity mirror with a hand towel and began to put face cream on, some new stuff with Retinol or something like that. The stress of the past year and sleepless nights had ganged up on her face. Little lines were creeping out from the edges, so she'd caved in and bought something labeled "age defying". A year or so ago, buying skin care to prevent aging would have shaken her to the core. Now, she just hoped like hell that it worked.

Gabe's email bounced around in Lilly's brain all the while. Something felt off about his request, but it was the only step Gabe had made toward a reconciliation so far. She finished dressing and decided that she would call him. Maybe he'd answer this time.

# CHAPTER 69
## TANKED

The day that Robert Jr. was born was the best day of Randi's life and the worst day of her life. She'd wasted a lot of time the following weeks feeling sorry for herself.

"Randi, come to bed."

Completely disoriented, Randi opened her eyes to see Robert's face peering down at her. It took her several moments to realize that she'd fallen asleep, passed out rather, on a chaise lounge. Randi had decided to throw herself a big pity party out by the pool, number of guests invited – just one. On the menu was Randi's new favorite food group, alcohol.

"What time is it?" She honestly had no idea. It could've been six in the morning just as easily as it might've been eight in the evening.

"It's nine thirty…at night." He held his hand out to help her up.

Her world spun around two or three times before finally picking a position. Threatening payback for the diet of vodka, her stomach churned. Robert handed her four ibuprofens, opened a bottle of water and put it in front of her. His expression was an even mix of concern and irritation.

"I'm sorry, I've done it again." Randi massaged the back of her neck. "I should've eaten first."

"Maybe, or perhaps you should drink less."

Robert's honesty was one of the things that Randi appreciated about him. She tried to remember this. She wanted to make excuses, but the nausea motivated her to keep her mouth shut. She let him walk her into the house. Each step intensified the pounding in her skull, and she wasn't sure that she was going to make it to the toilet in time to puke. Randi was too miserable to complain.

"Why are you doing this to yourself?" Robert asked her later while they were lying in bed. After vomiting, showering, and re-medicating herself, she was just starting to feel like she might live.

She mulled around her response for a bit. This wasn't her first go-round with excessive drinking, sometimes for months at a time. She'd managed to escape the official diagnosis of alcoholism, likely because she didn't own a car. If she had, she would have been forced into treatment from the DUI that surely would've occurred by now.

"I don't know." And honestly, she didn't know. Destroying her liver wasn't going to change Lilly's mind about the adoption. The whole baby fiasco might've triggered Randi to drink, but she continued for reasons that she couldn't explain.

"Do you want to know what I think?" His question was rhetorical because he didn't wait for her to answer.

"You're taking Lilly's decision to keep the baby and making it your fault somehow."

"Brilliant! Of course it's my fault!" Tears dripped down the sides of her temple into her hair. She rubbed at her face with the sheet.

"I screwed up my entire life. Don't you get it? I've polluted my body, fucked total strangers and done things for money that no decent woman would. I don't deserve to have a baby!" She sat up and put her bare feet onto the plush carpet. She put her elbows onto her knees and cradled her head in her hands.

Robert tried to sooth her by rubbing his hand across her back, much like one would a small child. To her relief, he didn't scold her. She needed sympathy, not an argument.

"The worst part is how foolish I must've looked to everyone, the whore trying to play Mrs. Cleaver." Bitterness seeped through her words.

"I need a smoke." Robert usually smoked only when he wanted to solve a problem.

Randi followed him out the French doors leading to the balcony. She didn't bother to put on a robe. Trees on their property created a safe-haven that shielded them from nosey neighbors. Robert offered her a cigarette, and they sat, smoking in silence. She knew that cigarettes were bad for her, but smoking with Robert felt therapeutic.

After more than half of his cigarette was gone, Robert spoke. "I understand that losing the baby was a big blow. It was to me, too. But drinking yourself to death isn't going to change anything. After Lilly pulled her shit, I wanted to suggest that we start looking for another baby to adopt."

Leaning forward in his chair, he cupped her bare knee with his hand. "But you started getting plastered every day, and I thought, who wants to raise a baby with a drunk?"

Randi took a few more drags off her cigarette and let the words sink in.

"I love you baby doll, really I do. But if you are going to spend your days laying around, tanked-up, then I think I'll pass. I didn't sign up for this." Robert stood up, kissed the top of Randi's head and went inside.

She lit another cigarette and thought about what Robert had said. She was too hungover to feel the agony in its full force. But she'd gotten the message loud and clear. Shape up or ship out.

# CHAPTER 70
## THE TRUTH HURTS

Gabe answered her call on the second ring. She'd expected to get his voice mail and was so stunned to hear his voice that she didn't say anything.

"Hello?" Gabe repeated himself.

"I got your email." Her heart beat loudly enough that she wondered if he could hear it through the phone. She'd rehearsed what she would say to him, but now that she had him on the phone, she couldn't remember.

"What do you think about my proposal?" Gabe sounded like he was speaking to a client, and her heart sank.

She forced herself to sound less desperate than she felt. "I think it's a really good idea. I'm happy that you thought of it."

"Actually, it was my mother's idea," Gabe admitted. "My family isn't big on divorce. The only other person in my family that has ever been divorced is Uncle Pete, and he had no children with the woman."

Lilly didn't know what to say. The little glimmer of hope that Gabe might still love her was just shot down by this bit of information. Gabe was being forced by his mother to try to make his marriage work. And not because Mrs. Chenowyth loved Lilly so much that she couldn't bear to see them part. Per usual, Gabe's mother was much more concerned about appearances and the damage that a divorce would do to their precious family reputation.

"So, you're only doing this because of your mother?"

Gabe didn't answer right away. Lilly sat on the bed that they had shared for years and waited for him to give her a drop of reassurance.

"Yeah, I guess so. I know it's wrong of me, but I can't look at you in the same way that I used to." Gabe's voice broke, giving away the first indication in ages that he felt anything at all.

"I think we're trying to cross a bridge that's been blown up. Maybe it's low of me, but I don't think that I can ever feel the same way again about you. Don't get me wrong; I care about you. You're the mother of my children. But in love with you? If we're being honest here, I don't think I can ever be in love with you again. And even though I'm Aiden's father by law because we're married, I can't be a daddy to that child."

The rush of information was more than Lilly expected and definitely not what she wanted to hear. She looked at their engagement and wedding photos displayed on the wall directly above their bed. All of that love just wasted, she thought bitterly.

"What's the point then? I'm not going to spend a week away from the children if you aren't even open to making this work! I don't want to get my hopes up only to be let down. I'm not a fool, Gabe!"

"Because if you don't go with me, I'll have you served with papers."

Fear shot through Lilly's body. "What papers? You're going to file for divorce? You can't do that!"

Her reaction was purely emotional, and she knew it. Of course he could file for divorce. She was astonished that he hadn't yet. It'd been months since Aiden's birth and even longer since they'd shared a bed or even a kiss.

"Mother is hoping that I won't, but if you don't go with me to this thing, she'll give her blessing for the divorce. My parents hate the thought of it, but they aren't stuck in the dark ages. They don't want me to spend the rest of my life in misery."

That's why Gabe sent the email, Lilly thought. He was documenting his attempt at marital counseling to appease his mother.

"Okay," she agreed, "I'll go. I don't want to jump through hoops to pacify your mom, but I also don't want a divorce. If there's any chance at all that we can make it work, then that's what I want to do."

Lilly needed to buy some time. She didn't want a divorce, but she would be damned if she stayed in a loveless relationship. Her heart couldn't take much more. Now she knew. Gabe didn't love her, and his family viewed her as if she were property to be managed.

As soon as they hung up, Lilly found the attorney's number and set up an appointment to sign the divorce petition she'd had drawn up weeks before.

# CHAPTER 71
## A NEW DAY

After Robert's little talk, Randi stopped drinking cold turkey. Fortunately, she didn't suffer much with physical side effects, mostly just emotional cravings. Robert was patient with her during the process, and like a wise man, he stayed out of her way when she was irritable.

He was working on a new project, so that helped to give them some distance. The film was being shot at their home, but they rarely ran into each other. She stayed in their bedroom and study most of the time, and Robert filmed downstairs in his studio. She didn't ask who had commissioned the film and Robert didn't offer.

The first few days of sobriety were spent sleeping and eating. Getting plastered on that level had taken a lot of dedication and hard work. With all the power drinking, she hadn't much time for decent food or good sleep, and she was starved for both. Madelaine doted on her, like one would a sick child.

Once she began to feel human again, Randi started to get bored. The reoccurring idea that she had something that she was supposed to be doing gnawed at the edges of her waking thoughts.

One morning, out of sheer frustration, Randi picked up a half-used spiral notebook, opened it to the first empty sheet and wrote, "What am I missing?"

She laughed at herself and half-jokingly scribbled, "A sense of purpose."

Randi continued for at least half an hour, conversing with herself on paper. She stopped and re-read her words. Not bad, she thought. She'd always enjoyed writing down her thoughts; somehow the process soothed her. At one point, she'd even started writing a novel, but after a few thousand words she'd lost steam, and the story line fizzled. So, like all the other things that Randi had started and not finished, the novel was stuffed into her vast vault of failures.

Anxious to keep going, Randi opened the laptop that Robert had given to her for Christmas. She created a blank document and began to transfer her handwritten words. As she typed, new thoughts, along with better ways to word the old thoughts, materialized into strings of sentences. The sentences intertwined into beautifully constructed paragraphs.

It was well after three o'clock in the afternoon before Randi ran out of words. She showered and then dressed in something other than pajamas for the first time in days. All the while she was putting on makeup, new verses ticked in her head. She paused long enough to scratch some of the more impressive ones into the spiral notebook.

"Well, look who's alive!" Robert leaned his head into the bathroom.

"I am!" Randi grinned at Robert's reflection in the mirror and continued to straighten her long blonde hair.

"What's the occasion?"

"I'm not sure that I want to tell you. I'm scared I'll jinx myself."

"Oh, come on; you aren't superstitious, are you?" Robert cocked his head sideways and smiled back at her.

"Maybe…," She turned around to look at Robert directly. "I've been writing again. Words just keep popping into my brain. Honestly, it feels like someone else is telling me what to write."

She shook her head in disbelief. "I'm really excited. I just don't know how long this streak will last. I'm afraid to show it to anyone yet."

"I'm happy for you, baby doll! How about taking a break and having some dinner with me? We'll go out for a change."

Randi wrapped her arms around Robert's neck and kissed him squarely on the mouth. It'd been a long time since they'd done anything together outside of sleep. "I need to apologize. I've been a royal shit. I don't know why you're still with me."

He sighed and chuckled. "If you don't know that by now, then you haven't been paying attention."

Robert pulled her body closer and began to kiss her neck, tracing little circles with his tongue. It'd been so long since they'd made love that her body's response was intense and immediate.

"I guess dinner will have to wait," she whispered as he carried her to their bed.

# CHAPTER 72
## RANDALL'S LITTLE BOX OF HORRORS

Genevieve anxiously waited for the mail to arrive each day. Without Randall's death certificate, she couldn't cash out the life insurance policy. But more importantly, she couldn't open the safe deposit box.

The certificates finally came in mid-August. The funeral home had suggested that she order several certified copies just in case she needed extra. The insurance policy should've been priority, but she was dying to find out what had been so important to Randall that he'd locked it up in a safe deposit box.

Less than twenty minutes after the mail was delivered, Genny walked through the bank doors. She went straight to the young teller that had helped her before.

"Excuse me. I was next," a voice behind her interrupted.

"I'm sorry," she apologized and backed away from the counter. Her cheeks and ears flushed with embarrassment as she sat in one of the chairs and tried to hide her impatience. Thankfully, the man in front of her didn't take long to finish his business.

"How may I help you?" The teller greeted her with a smile.

"I was here before to open my husband's safe deposit box, and I have the death certificate now."

An expression of confusion colored the girl's face, and Genevieve realized that she must have looked too happy to be a grieving widow. She didn't want people to think that she was happy about her husband's death. The last thing she needed was for the townspeople to gossip about how she'd killed her husband. Although she wasn't sad that Randall was gone, she certainly didn't do anything to cause his demise.

The young lady took the copy of the certificate from Genny's hand.

"Thank you, please give me a moment to pull up the information."

She excused herself for a moment and returned with a form. "I'll just need your signature here and here," she pointed with her pen.

After Genny signed the property release form, the teller led her into the vault. The room was full of ceiling to floor locked compartments. Genny wondered about the secret things stored in all those tiny lockers.

"It's number three sixteen." The girl pointed in the direction of Randall's box. "I'll give you some privacy."

Genny had visualized this moment for weeks. Now that she was all alone with the box, she was a little afraid. She paused for a few moments before putting the key into the lock. The locker contained a smaller box, which she pulled out and sat onto the table in the middle of the room. She'd already decided that she wouldn't examine the contents at the bank. She didn't want to get emotional around complete strangers.

She unzipped the small duffel bag that she'd brought and placed the contents of the box into it.

The drive home felt much longer than normal. Once inside, she unzipped the duffel bag and placed the stack of documents on the kitchen table.

The first scrap of paper appeared to be a date or perhaps a combination for a lock. It read 10-26-79. Genny tried to remember that day, but she couldn't think of anything special that had happened on October 26th of 1979. She placed the slip of paper to the left of the stack.

The next item in the pile was a sealed envelope, the kind of envelope that a greeting card might have come in. Whatever was inside the envelope was stiff, but not evenly shaped like one would expect a card to be. She slid her finger under the seal to open the envelope. The sharp edge gave her a papercut, and she instinctively put her finger into her mouth.

With her other hand, she dumped the contents of the envelope. Several upside-down Polaroid pictures slid out onto the table. She turned the first picture over and gasped. She didn't recognize the girl, at least not at first glance. Genny guessed that she was somewhere between ten to thirteen years old. Her eyes were closed, but she didn't have the expression of sleep. The child was partially nude, her small budding breasts exposed.

In the next photo was the same child, completely nude with her legs spread open. With her jaw slack in the picture, Genny knew that she must've been passed out. Underneath the girl's body was a patchwork crochet quilt, in a style common to the 1970s.

Something about the way that the young girl's face was positioned in the third photo gave Genny the feeling that she had seen the child before. The harder that she tried to place the child's face, the less Genny could recall. So, she went back to the task of looking through one disgusting, horrifying photograph after another.

She didn't have the first clue about what to do with Randall's box of horrendous treasures. Even worse, she had no idea how Randall had gotten the pictures. Had he been the pervert behind the camera? At best, Randall was into child pornography; but quite possibly he was a pedophile. *You already know that he's a pedophile! He did things to your Miranda!*

It was all more than Genevieve could take. She'd planned on sorting the contents of Randall's box, but in the end, everything belonged in one pile. She needed some time to figure out how to handle her discovery. The photos had been sitting in a box for decades. Genny reasoned that one more day or two wasn't going to change anything, and the children in the photos had probably been long grown. Doing anything about it would just bring up bad memories for them. If she could even do anything about it.

It was beginning to get dark outside. She hadn't eaten dinner, but after looking through those atrocious pictures, she wasn't hungry anyway. She filled up her tea kettle with cold water from the tap and put it on the back burner. The sound of the gas flame reminded her of Grandma's kitchen many years ago. She put a bag of Earl Grey tea in her favorite mug and waited for the water to boil.

What she wouldn't give to go back in time and spend the evening with her grandmother. Genny had stayed with her grandmother a great deal when she was growing up. Her parents had been young and self-involved. They'd pawned Genny off on Grandma at every opportunity. Genny didn't mind because her home was a battlefield, especially when her daddy was drunk. Grandma's house was peaceful.

And now, Genny was a grandmother. Having grandchildren was nothing like she'd imagined. Lilly rarely brought the grandbabies around. In fact, she'd had another child and didn't even bother to tell Genny until after the baby was born. Lilly's inconsiderate behavior flabbergasted Genny.

The other two showed no signs of wanting to have children, not that it mattered. Raine rarely came around, and Miranda hadn't stepped foot on the farm in over a decade. Her life was a gigantic disappointment, and she had a hard time understanding how the girls could ignore her after all that she'd sacrificed for them.

The shrill whistle of the tea kettle scared the hell out of her. She laughed at herself. It was humorous, she thought, that after all the fear Randall had inflicted on her for the past forty years, a little thing like a tea kettle whistle could make her jump.

She turned off the burner and carefully poured the boiling water into her mug. She placed the cup on the table next to the pile from the safe deposit box. *I should put it away before someone sees it.* Very funny since no one comes over anymore, she mused.

Still, she had the urge to hide the photos, so she found an empty Tupperware container and placed them into it. *I'll decide what to do about it tomorrow.*

In her dream that night, Genevieve was back in the attic room that Grandma had fixed up just for her. Bright yellow walls made the space feel like the sun was always shining. Grandma had sewn a calico bedspread out of pink, yellow and white fabrics. White lace curtains moved with the spring breeze coming in through the dormer windows. The comforting sounds of Grandma banging around in the kitchen below blended with birds singing their morning serenade.

She stretched from her toes to her fingertips and tried to remember what day it was. It must be Saturday, she thought. It seemed too late to be a school day. Grandma would've woken her up by now. Genny pushed the covers back and sat up. She noticed that there were pictures taped all around the bureau mirror. Puzzled because she didn't remember seeing them before, Genny got out of bed and walked over to the mirror to see the pictures more closely.

Shocked, she stared at the horrible images. Each photograph was of a different girl in varying stages of undress. None of the girls looked any older than thirteen. Someone had scratched their eyes out. *Why would anyone want to do that to them?*

She pulled one of the middle pictures off the mirror frame and examined it more closely. She recognized the girl. *Where do I know her from?* She turned the Polaroid over. On the back, there was a word scratched into the small white frame area. It was the girl's name – *Raine.*

Genny could hear someone coming up the stairs. She began to frantically rip all the vulgar photographs off the mirror. They were disgusting, and she had to get rid of them. Someone might find out what she had done. Wait a minute, she thought, did I do this?

Someone was knocking at the bedroom door. She tried to go faster, but there were so many pictures on the dresser. Every time she took one down, another appeared in its place.

The knocking continued, and she realized that she was in her own bed. Beads of sweat covered her forehead. The dream had been so vivid that she wasn't completely sure that she was awake.

"Just a minute." She called out even though the person at the door couldn't possibly hear her. She put her bathrobe over her nightgown and ran a brush through her messy hair. She didn't mind the silver color of her hair, but the texture had changed as she'd gotten older. *I look a lot like Medusa.*

She didn't recognize the man on her front porch at first, so she hesitated to answer the door. Genny was used to being more afraid of the man inside her home than anything the world could offer up. Now that Randall was gone, it took a lot of thinking through things to preserve her safety.

"Can I help you?" she asked the man through the screen door.

"Yes ma'am, I'm with the electric company. We're going to replace your meter. I wanted to let you know that I'm here and to make sure that any dogs are restrained."

"I don't have any dogs. Feel free to do whatever you need. Is there going to be a charge for this?"

"No ma'am, just a routine replacement. We'll install new meters for everyone eventually."

Genny watched the young man walk back to his truck. Had Randall been alive, the electrician would have been given the third degree. Randall was suspicious of everyone. He always told her that she was too naïve, but Genny knew that Randall was paranoid. She didn't know if he was born that way or the excessive drinking made him skeptical of everyone. In the end, it didn't matter why. The effect was the same. And now he was gone, she reminded herself.

Once her morning pot of coffee was brewing, her thoughts turned back to the photos from Randall's safe deposit box. *I should tell someone.* She wondered who she would tell and what good would come from it. Most of the cops on the police force probably weren't even born yet when those pictures were taken, she mused.

It didn't take very long for Genevieve to decide that reporting this to the police would create more issues than not. After all, she reasoned, those poor girls in the photographs had been through enough already. If she were to tell someone, then they would have to relive it all over again. Yes, she was sure that NOT telling was the right thing to do, all the way around.

Still, Genevieve felt the need to run her decision by someone else. Even though Raine was the youngest of her girls, she seemed to be the one that Genny could count on the most.

# CHAPTER 73
## STILL COVERING FOR HIM

At some point in May, Mother had left her the message confirming that the bones found in the pig pen were her father's. Raine was on break when she listened to Mother's voice mail. One of the girls from the typing pool noticed Raine's expression and asked if she was okay.

"Yeah, I'm fine. My dad went missing several months ago. That was my mom letting me know that they found his remains."

"Oh my God! I'm so sorry!" The poor girl looked uncomfortable.

"It's okay, we weren't close." And Raine meant what she said. She didn't feel much of anything when she thought about her father. Her sisters and her mother seemed to get all worked up about Daddy but not Raine. She figured that she was just able to let things go more easily than everyone else.

"Are you close to your mom?"

"Not really. I mean, I see her from time to time, but we don't talk much." Raine focused on her sandwich and prayed the girl would shut up.

"Oh, I see." Looking dejected by the dead-end conversation, the girl went back to her salad and magazine.

Raine was glad the girl had given up. She wasn't big on small talk, and the questioning was making her uncomfortable. Maybe it was weird, she thought, that she wasn't that connected to anyone in her family. It was easier that way. Her mom was always so helpless and needy, and Lilly was on another planet with all of her perfection. And Randi, well, she was a drunken slut, a big flake. Raine didn't enjoy being around any of them.

It was August before Raine heard from her mother again. The mid-morning Texas sun baked on Raine's sleeping head. She'd been drifting in and out of sleep for several hours when the phone rang. She fumbled around on her side table until she located her phone. Irritated that Mother seemed to always manage to call when she was sleeping, she answered curtly.

"Raine? Did I wake you?"

"What do you need?"

"I can call back if this is a bad time."

"For heaven's sake! Just tell me why you called!"

Mother sniffled and paused in her infuriating way. Raine could almost see her pouting through the phone.

"I wondered if you could come out to the house this weekend. Either today or tomorrow would be fine. I have something that I want you to see."

Raine rolled over and sighed. "Can't you just tell me what it is?"

"No honey, you need to see it. And besides, I don't want to discuss it over the phone."

As usual, Mother was making a big deal out of something little, but she agreed to drive out to the farm to appease her. She hated going to the farm.

She forced herself out of bed and dressed for the day. Oh well, she thought, it's not like I had anything better to do. From the time that Mother called until she put her key into the ignition, less than an hour had passed. As she was leaving, she noticed that the apartment complex pool was full of people enjoying the sun. Even though it was just barely 10:00 am, the city streets were already bustling with people running their errands and doing whatever normal folks did on the weekend. It seemed as if everyone in the world had something exciting to do, except for Raine. She was stuck in a rut.

She plugged her mp3 player into her radio and found her favorite playlist. Classic rock always seemed to help the drive to Boerne pass quickly. She pulled her car out onto the highway, and her thoughts turned back to her empty life.

She was starting to think that she would never find someone to settle down and have a family with. The whole dating game seemed like too much effort. Raine had never felt comfortable talking to men, and flirting was like a foreign language. When conversation between the girls in the office would turn to guys, Raine never joined in. She'd never even been kissed.

It wasn't that she hadn't tried. Her friend, Noelle, had set her up with two different guys, but both dates had gone about as poorly as possible. The first date was an exercise in humiliation which ended with Raine sneaking out of the restaurant after excusing herself to use the ladies room. The second date wasn't officially a date because he never showed. She figured that being stood up was some sort of karmic payback for the first date in which she left the poor guy waiting for her, holding the bill. Noelle hadn't offered to introduce her to anyone since then.

When she was fresh out of high school, Raine assumed that she'd find a guy (or he would find her), fall in love, and live happily ever after. Now, seven years later, Raine was having trouble picturing anything different than the life of solitude that she'd somehow settled into. *Oh God, I'm going to end up just like my mother, only forty years sooner! Maybe I should just move in with her, and we can be alone together.*

As she pulled her car into the drive, she could see that Mother had been hanging clothes out on the line. It was so much faster to use the dryer, but she refused to use it whenever the temperature outside was above sixty degrees. Raine couldn't stand the smell of line dried clothing. As a kid, she was amused by the laundry detergent commercials that boasted of a scent that was as fresh as the great outdoors. She didn't know about the rest of the world, but at the Carter house, the great outdoors smelled like pig shit.

Raine tried the knob on the front door, but it was locked, so she rang the bell. Mother didn't take long to answer. She greeted Raine with a hug and ushered her into the kitchen.

"I want to show you something, but I need a promise that you won't talk to anyone else about it." Mother had an uneasy expression on her face, and Raine gathered that whatever she was about to see wasn't a good thing.

"How can I promise you something like that without knowing what it is?" Raine didn't really plan on blowing the secret, but she felt the need to point out that Mother's request was a little unrealistic.

Mother seemed to earnestly contemplate what Raine had said. "Okay, you have a point. But I think once I show you, you'll understand why."

Raine shrugged her shoulders and said, "let's see it."

One of Mother's old rectangular Tupperware containers sat on the kitchen table. Her hands shook a little as she peeled back the lid. She handed a small stack of photographs to Raine.

Raine dropped the first disgusting photograph as if it were a hot coal. "What in the hell?"

"I know. It's bad. They're all bad. And I don't know what to do with them!" Mother shook her head as if she were in disbelief of something.

"Where did you find them?" Raine couldn't imagine what her mom was doing with something so horrible, not to mention illegal.

Mother went on to explain everything to Raine. When she'd finished, she asked Raine, "What do you think I should do?"

"I can't believe you're asking me what to do with them! Isn't it obvious?"

"Well, don't you think that reporting this now would be painful for everyone?"

"Are you seriously protecting Daddy? He's dead and gone! And you still want to keep his secrets?" Raine was furious. It was more of the same.

"It's not like that! I'm only thinking of those poor girls. It's been so long, and I can't help but think that it'll cause more harm than good."

Raine looked away from the shocking photographs spread out on the kitchen table. She recognized one of the girls, a neighbor kid around her sister Randi's age. She wondered how many secrets this old house kept. The sound of her own heartbeat pounded against her eardrums, and the lights seemed to dim. She had to get away or she was going to be sick.

# CHAPTER 74
## THE END FOR GENNY

Momma's body lay on the kitchen floor for a week before it was discovered by, ironically enough, Randall's life insurance agent. The poor lady had made an appointment with Momma just before her demise to discuss policy payout options.

Randi was knee deep in her writing when the doorbell interrupted her train of thought. Annoyed when the doorbell rang again, she saved her progress and closed her laptop. Expecting to see a girl scout or the like, her heart sank when instead two Boerne police officers were standing on the porch. This can't be good, she thought. They wouldn't drive all the way into San Antonio for something small.

The officers either downplayed the condition in which Momma's body was found, or Randi was in too much shock to grasp it. Either way, she got a clearer picture that night while watching the evening news.

"And today, an elderly woman's body was discovered at a residence outside of Boerne. She appears to have been brutally murdered. While the police declined to reveal details, we were told that photographs were stapled to the woman's body, in the shape of a cross. We were not told what the photographs were of, nor did the Boerne police indicate what the significance of the cross may have been. They are investigating this homicide as a hate crime. There are no known suspects at this time. Police are cautioning everyone in, and around, the Boerne area to exercise extra caution until a suspect has been apprehended. The victim's name is not being released until all members of her immediate family have been notified." The blonde anchorwoman then segued into the weather forecast. Robert and Randi stared at each other in stunned silence.

"Holy shit!" Robert spoke first.

"Oh my God! What kind of crazy shit is that?" The newscaster's version of the story was far different than the one the police had delivered hours before to Randi.

"They must've not been able to reach one of your sisters yet. Or they would've given your mother's name, right?"

"It would have to be Raine. The cops told me that Lilly had identified Momma's body. I can't imagine that they're holding up for a cousin or something." Randi hadn't attempted to call either one of her sisters yet. Since the birth of Robert Jr., or whatever Lilly was calling him, Randi hadn't talked to Lilly. And Raine had never answered Randi's calls before, so she didn't see the point in trying now.

"If it's okay with you, baby doll, I'll try to reach your sisters now." Robert waited for a moment and then took Randi's lack of response as permission.

Randi sat on their large leather sofa with her legs curled underneath her and listened to Robert phoning her sisters. She didn't tell him often enough how much she appreciated him. He protected her and made her feel loved in a way that no one before had. Robert had become her rock over the past year.

Robert walked back and forth as he spoke on the phone. She couldn't tell from his end of the conversation whether he was talking with Raine or Lilly. The anchor's recanting of how Momma's body was found replayed over and over in Randi's head. It occurred to Randi that she didn't really know how Momma had died. The police had said that she was murdered, the newscaster had said that it was brutal, but no one had told her exactly how Momma's life ended.

While Robert visited on the phone, he made himself a drink. He pointed to the glass and then to Randi, as if to ask her if she wanted one. She shook her head "no". Since her binge earlier in the summer, she'd stayed clean. But Robert never treated her as if she were grounded from the stuff and she appreciated that. If any occasion ever called for a drink, having one's mother murdered qualified in first place. For some reason, alcohol didn't sound appealing to Randi.

"Okay, thank you. You too. Hang in there, love." Robert finished his conversation and hung up the phone.

"Was that Lil?" Randi asked.

"Yeah. And wow!" Robert gave an exaggerated look of shock. "Lilly said it was bad."

"Did they tell her how Momma died?"

"No, they didn't. They are investigating it as a homicide because of the way her body was found, but the actual autopsy is scheduled for tomorrow morning." Robert shook his head in disbelief.

"I just can't imagine who would do something like that to an old woman."

"Like what? What did Lilly tell you?" Randi was beginning to feel like the little kid that was left out of the conversation.

"Oh honey, I think she needs to be the one to tell you. But I will say that whoever did this to your mother was a very angry man."

# CHAPTER 75
## LILLY AND THE MORGUE

Lilly took Robert's call. When she saw Randi's number pop up on her caller id, she'd hoped it would be her sister. She'd been sitting in the dark while the baby slept. She and Gabe were supposed to have left for their marriage retreat earlier that afternoon.

She'd just zipped up her suitcase when the Boerne police knocked on her door that morning. Gabe's mother had already picked up the children, so it only took her a few minutes to be ready to leave for the medical examiner's office. Although Mother had been found in Boerne, her body was brought to San Antonio. She was told that Kendall County didn't have a coroner to perform the autopsy.

She marveled at how calm she was able to remain during the process. Lilly supposed that she was in shock. It's not every day, after all, that a girl gets called upon to identify her mother's body.

"I want to prepare you," the attendant warned her. "She may not be recognizable as you are used to seeing her. She's been gone for approximately a week. And beyond the trauma that her body suffered, the natural process of decomposition will have affected her appearance."

Lilly nodded but didn't speak. Although she could smell some type of air freshener, the odor of rotting flesh was overpowering. She didn't trust her stomach enough to talk.

Just like in the movies, Mother was laid out on a gurney with a sheet of sorts over her entire body. No amount of caution could have prepared her for the grotesque look of her mother's body. Her skin was blackened in spots, with large blistery looking areas. Mother's eyes, flattened and glazed over, were wide open. Her expression was one of horror, as if she'd witnessed the most terrifying thing imaginable. All around Mother's mouth was what appeared to be dried, blackened blood. Starting at the top of Mother's forehead were evenly spaced puncture marks in a pattern of a cross that extended down to her mid sternum and across her upper chest. And her hands, the same hands that had prepared Lilly's meals and soothed her fevers, were gnarled and mottled.

Lilly gasped and felt faint. The attendant held out a basin; Lilly presumed in case she vomited. She looked away and then turned back.

"It's her. It's my mother."

Lilly allowed the officers to drive her home. She immediately took a shower, hot as she could stand, but she couldn't wash the smell of death away. The putrid stench was embedded into her sinuses.

As she was still drying off, Gabe arrived to pick her up for their trip. From the time that the officers had arrived until that moment, Lilly hadn't told another soul that her mother was dead. Telling someone, even Gabe, felt odd.

"Ready to go?" Gabe had the same detached look on his face that he'd worn for nearly a year. She noticed that he'd changed his hair a bit.

Lilly had built this moment up for weeks, planning on looking as beautiful as possible. She'd hoped to make him remember why he'd fallen in love with her in the first place. Now, after identifying her mother's decomposing dead body, none of that seemed very important.

"Yeah, about that. I don't think I'm up for this retreat." Lilly greeted Gabe at the door in a bathrobe and no make-up. She paused, trying to decide how to deliver the news.

Instantly, Gabe's face changed from disconnected to pissed-off. "You could've given me some type of notice! What in the hell are you thinking? I've already paid for it!"

"I just got back from identifying my mother's body." A small part of Lilly enjoyed Gabe's look of regret for his outburst just seconds before.

"My God! What happened? Did she have a heart attack?"

"No. It seems that she was murdered." Lilly finished tying the belt on her bathrobe and gestured for Gabe to come inside. She walked back up to their bedroom to finish dressing. Gabe waited in the living room.

She dug out some old yoga pants from her bottom drawer and found a tank top. Not bothering to apply deodorant or perfume, Lilly dressed quickly and draped a damp towel around her shoulders to catch any drips from her wet hair. She grabbed her cell phone off the bathroom counter and went back downstairs to where Gabe was waiting.

As she was coming down the stairway, she brought Gabe up to speed. "An autopsy still has to be completed. And after that, they'll likely know how she was killed. But at this point, the thing leading them to believe that she didn't die of natural causes was the condition she was found in."

"Have you told my mother?"

"No, Gabe. I came home to wash the smell of my mother's body off me."

"I didn't mean it that way, Lil." Gabe's voice was soft, apologetic even. He pulled out his cell phone and began to dial a number. "I'll let her know. I'm sure she'll be happy to keep the kids overnight."

"No," Lilly interrupted, "I want them home tonight. I was just getting ready to call her myself." The only thing that comforted Lilly was the thought of her babies, home with her. At that moment, not even Gabe could've made her feel better.

He raised an eyebrow and said, "Okay, I'll go get them."

"I'll go with you."

Riding next to Gabe for the first time in months felt strangely normal to Lilly. His Suburban smelled the same as always, like leather and his aftershave. She wondered how many other women had sat in her seat over the past few months.

The children were just having dinner with their Grandma. Gabe whispered an explanation into his mother's ear as to why they were there. Lilly forced herself to calm down and waited patiently for them to finish eating.

Mrs. Chenowyth made a small gesture to Lilly to follow her into the kitchen. "Oh my dear! Gabe just told me about your mother! I'm so sorry to hear the terrible news! Are you sure that you wouldn't like to leave the children overnight? It's so much to take in."

Lilly shook her head. "Thank you, but no. I'll take them home. Honestly, they are the only thing that feels right in my life at this moment."

Thankfully, her mother-in-law didn't argue. She simply patted Lilly's shoulder in a reassuring manner. The lump in Lilly's throat doubled in size. She'd been on guard for so long where the Chenowyths were concerned, that her gesture of kindness knocked Lilly off balance.

For the first time in ages, Gabe tucked his own children into bed. Lilly sat in their darkened bedroom, nursed Aiden to sleep, and thought about all the things that had led up to this life that she no longer recognized.

Eventually Gabe came up to the bedroom. "Are you awake?" he whispered.

"I am."

"They're asleep now. Are you sure that you don't want me to stay?"

"Thanks, but that's not necessary." Lilly would have given anything a week or two ago to have Gabe spend the night at their home. But she knew that he would just be staying out of sympathy, and she didn't want his pity.

"Okay, well I'm ten minutes away if you need anything." Gabe stunned her by kissing her on the forehead.

# CHAPTER 76
# BAD NEWS FOR RAINE

Raine was putting together sets of proposals in the copy room when the police arrived.

"Uh, Raine?" the normally bubbly receptionist looked scared as she peaked her head into the doorway. "You have visitors." She mouthed the words in a whisper, "It's the police!"

"Okay, I'll be right there." Raine did her best to appear unconcerned, but her insides were squirming. She tried to guess what the cops could be wanting with her. As far as she knew, she hadn't done anything wrong. She forced herself to stack the unbound proposals neatly on the worktable. Then she walked to the reception area with very shaky legs.

"I'm Raine Carter. What can I help you with?" She could hear the tremor in her own voice.

"Is there some place private we can talk ma'am?"

"Yes, the conference room should be empty." She pointed toward the door.

"After you, ma'am."

Raine felt relieved that they hadn't slapped the handcuffs onto her wrists yet. She closed the door after both cops were in the small conference room.

"Ma'am, we sent officers to your residence yesterday to inform you. Apparently, you weren't home. We apologize for delivering this news to your place of work. Your mother was found deceased in her home yesterday morning." The young officer's brown eyes were sympathetic. She imagined that he'd not had to deliver this kind of news before. He looked as if he were barely old enough to be out of high school.

"Do you need me to do anything?" she asked and then added, "Do my sisters know yet?"

The officer looked through some papers attached to the clipboard in his hand for a few seconds before answering. "Yes ma'am, your sister Lillian identified the body, and your other sister Miranda, I believe, was notified yesterday at her place of residence."

She nodded and quietly said, "Okay. So, what do I do now?"

"There is nothing that you need to do. The body is at the county medical examiner's office, awaiting autopsy. You'll probably want to consult with your sisters to decide which funeral home your mother's body will be released to. Since your mother's death is still being investigated, you'll want to make yourself available for questioning."

Now, she understood why both Lilly and Randi had tried to reach her last night. Raine's boss looked horrified when she delivered the news. He made a feeble attempt to offer his condolences and told her to go take care of whatever she needed to do. Not sure what she should be doing, Raine went home.

She had trouble staying awake during the drive home. Lately her head felt foggier than normal. Probably all the extra stress at work, she reasoned. Her producer had taken on another large account, which virtually doubled her workload. It was maddening to Raine that the office had no intentions of hiring additional help.

After changing into her sweats, Raine crawled into bed. She decided that a little nap might help refocus her mind. As she dozed off, she tried to remember the day that she'd last seen Mother. She could recall driving out to the farm. *Mother wanted to show me something. But what was it?* She thought maybe it was an insurance paper or something about Daddy. It must have not been that important, she decided, because she couldn't remember looking at anything.

She had known for some time that her memory wasn't great. Even when she was a child, she would sometimes forget things, like taking a test or writing a paper. It was embarrassing. She'd learned to converse in a vague way to cover up whenever she couldn't remember something. Raine's forgetfulness made her feel hesitant to get close to anyone.

Dreaming was a strange affair for Raine, and this afternoon was no different. She awoke from her nap with the sensation that she'd been somewhere else. It took her a few minutes to wake up completely. She looked at her cell phone to check the time. It read 3:15 pm. She'd slept for several hours. There was a notification that Lilly had just called and she guessed the ringing had woken her up.

Lilly answered her return call on the first ring. "Did you hear about Mother?"

"Yeah, a few hours ago."

"Can you meet me at the funeral home? Randi and I have an appointment at five o'clock today. The autopsy should be done by tomorrow and they need to know what we want for her service."

"I can. I'll be there soon."

As she drove to the mortuary, she thought about how peculiar death was. *One minute you are here, and the next, you are not.* And now they had two deaths in the family within months of each other. Daddy's death hadn't really upset her, but Mother's was different. Although she'd not always felt close to her mother, at least Mother had been there through the years. Raine was suddenly anchorless.

Both Lilly and Randi were sitting inside of Lilly's car, which was parked in the mortuary lot. Raine parked her little car next to Lilly's. Overwhelming dread made her feel weak. The thought of planning a funeral sounded worse than just about anything else she could think of. She took some very deep breaths before opening her door. Randi opened the passenger door of Lilly's car and gave Raine an uncharacteristic hug. Her eyes were puffy from crying and Raine felt uncomfortable immediately. Dealing with the details of burying their mother sounded like torture enough, never mind having to be subjected to waterworks from her sisters. She wished she were anyplace but there.

# CHAPTER 77
## DID YOU SEE THOSE MARKS?

Being the oldest of the three, Lilly naturally took charge. She was the first to walk through the white painted double doors of the funeral home. Inside, presumably to minimize sound, the floors were covered with plush carpet. Several offices were located to the left of the entryway. To the right was a conference room. A tasteful yet outdated golden plaque indicated that the chapel was straight ahead. The chapel doors were open, so Lilly assumed that there was no funeral in progress.

After a few moments, a middle-aged man with a genuine comb-over hair style came out to greet them. "Are you here for Genevieve Carter?"

"Yes, thank you." Neither Randi nor Raine responded, so Lilly answered.

"We'll just go into here." He pointed toward the conference room.

Inside the room was a rather large table with enough space for at least eight people.

"Please sit, wherever you'd like." He gestured to the chairs and waited for the girls to sit.

The next hour and a half was spent going over the arrangements. Lilly was slightly put off when he pulled out a large binder with poems to choose from for the funeral program. It seemed so impersonal, picking a poem that a ton of other people had used previously. She'd never really thought about it much before. She'd just assumed that the poem was chosen because it was the deceased person's favorite. But now, when faced with planning her own mother's funeral, it occurred to her that she had no idea of her own mother's favorite poem, author, or even musician.

After some deliberation and without much help from Randi or Raine, she chose the poem by Mary Frye, "Do Not Stand at My Grave and Weep".

Next, they moved onto the flower arrangement and then on to the casket. The funeral was set for a week away to allow for any out of town family to have adequate time to make travel arrangements. By the time that the service was arranged, Lilly had an enormous headache and her breasts were leaking with a long overdue feeding for Aiden.

She pressed her wrists into her breasts to stop the let-down reflex and winced at the stinging sensation. The ticking clock over the doorway told her that they'd been in the room for over two hours.

"I need to go soon. Is there anything else that we need to take care of?" Lilly rubbed the back of her neck to try to alleviate the ache in her head.

"No, just the payment arrangements."

Lilly and Randi had already agreed to split the cost of mother's funeral, but neither was prepared for the final number. Even without a graveside service, Genevieve's modest funeral came to over seven thousand dollars.

Raine nervously played with her collar while Randi and Lilly wrote out checks. Lilly planned to reassure her that they didn't expect anything from her. She was at a different time in her life, and Lilly knew that Raine likely didn't have more than a dime or two saved.

While Raine was fiddling with her collar, Lilly noticed deep scratches on her chest. Her hair stood on end. She'd seen scratches like those on Raine's chest once before – on a crime documentary. She almost nudged Randi's thigh to get her to look at Raine's chest but decided to wait.

The sun was setting by the time they walked out of the funeral home. Lilly wanted to stall Randi without making it obvious to their little sister. She quickly texted Randi, "Please don't say anything, but wait until Raine is gone. We need to talk."

"What's this about?" Randi asked as Raine drove away.

"Did you see her chest?"

"No, why?"

"My God! It looked like someone clawed the shit out of her!"

"Do you think she's being abused?" Randi looked confused.

"No, clawed up like someone fought her off of them!" Frowning, Lilly added, "like maybe Mother?"

"You can't be serious!"

"I don't know. You've seen her when she loses her temper. True, she was just a kid, but it was scary. Don't you remember when she hurt that boy on the bus? It was a big deal. She broke his thumbs and his right wrist! All the stupid boy did was make fun of her."

"Yeah, I'd forgotten about that. I guess because I was in high school, and it seemed like baby problems."

"I still remember it. Mother called me to come talk to the police with her. The only reason she wasn't charged with anything is that she was seven or eight years old."

"Okay but seriously? Are you saying that you think she could've done something to Momma?" Randi shook her head violently.

"I'm saying that those scratches aren't from her cat."

"What are you thinking that we should do? I mean, are you suggesting that we turn her in?" Randi was beginning to sound angry.

"I don't know. Maybe?" Lilly chewed on her bottom lip and thought about their options. "I'm guessing that we're going to all be questioned whenever the autopsy is done. At least that's how it always seems to be in the movies."

"Yeah, I suppose so." Randi agreed. "Can we sleep on it and decide tomorrow? I don't know about you, but I'm exhausted."

The sisters parted ways for the evening with the plan to finish the discussion the next day. Lilly had decided before she left the parking lot that no matter what Randi believed, talking to the police would be the only right thing to do. And God forbid that Raine did have something to do with Mother's death. If that were the case, she thought, then Raine would need far more than legal help.

# CHAPTER 78
# THE SNITCH

The investigators didn't waste much time before interviewing all three sisters. Randi thought that she was probably the first to talk with the police because the detective arrived on her doorstep early the next morning.

She had prepared herself to be asked a series of questions, things like, "Where were you the day that your mother was murdered?" and "When is the last time that you spoke with your mother?" but the interview was more of a conversation.

"How are you holding up since your mother passed?" The detective looked more like a grandmother than an officer of the law. Her kind face gave Randi a sense of safety and comfort.

"I'm in shock, I guess." Randi toyed with the strings to her robe. She hadn't really soaked it all in, that her mother was gone.

"Were you able to make arrangements for your mother's funeral yet?"

"Yeah, I think my older sister did most of the arranging. But we got it taken care of yesterday."

"I know this is a tough question to answer, but can you think of anyone that might have been angry with your mother?"

Ah, Randi thought, here comes the hard questions. "No. Well, I guess not, at least not angry enough to harm her."

"Was she in a dispute with someone?"

"No, but she'd left our father last year and then decided to go back to him. None of us were very happy about that."

The detective had a confused expression. "I'm sorry, but isn't your father deceased?"

"Yes, now he is, but he wasn't when she went back to him. Or at least she didn't know that he was dead when she decided to go back to him."

Randi stopped because she knew that she probably wasn't making much sense.

"So, let me see if I understand. Your mother left your father but then decided to go back to him? And when she returned, he was dead?"

"Yes, only she didn't know that he was dead. She just thought that he was missing." Randi took a deep breath and finished explaining. "After a few months, she found some stuff in the pig pen. Turns out that Daddy was eaten by the pigs."

"That sounds terrible!" The seasoned grandma detective looked truly horrified. She must have not been with the Boerne police when Randall's body was discovered.

"Honestly, Daddy wasn't a very nice man. We weren't close. I wouldn't wish that kind of death on anyone, but I won't miss him." Randi immediately regretted telling the detective that. She worried that the woman would think she had something to do with Mother's death.

"I'm sorry to hear that." The woman paused for a moment and looked over the paper in her hand. "So, back to your mother. Are you aware of anyone that was angry with your mother or in a dispute with her recently?

Randi shrugged her shoulders in an indecisive fashion. "No, I don't think so. We were all a little unhappy with her. She didn't pay attention to the things that had gone on with us as children. Daddy was a bully and Momma just kind of looked the other way. We weren't close, but I wouldn't say that we wished her harm."

Randi hated talking about everything. She wasn't comfortable discussing this with a stranger. And she wasn't sure how much she should divulge to the woman. Maybe better to skim the surface of all the things that had happened in her childhood, she thought. Her mind kept creeping back to Raine and the scratch marks on her chest. She didn't want to create more problems for them.

"Okay, thank you. If you think of anything else or if there is anything that we can do for you, feel free to call me." The detective pulled a business card out and handed it to Randi.

"I do have one other thing," Randi said, hesitant to finish.

The detective waited, her expression patient.

"Yesterday, when we were in the mortuary, we noticed some scratches on our little sister's chest." Randi's words felt traitorous. "I don't know what they could be from but they were really deep and all over. It looked like she'd been in a fight."

The detective thanked her and left. Randi assumed that she would be going to Lilly or Raine's house next. She had a fleeting thought to call Raine and warn her little sister.

# CHAPTER 79
# GOODBYE RAINE

Raine was getting ready to leave for work. She didn't plan on staying all day, just long enough to wrap up some loose ends. She felt vulnerable when she left things unfinished on her desk. Mother's funeral wasn't scheduled until nearly a week away, and someone would have to take over her clients until she got back.

She opened the door to find two police officers on her step. The older of the pair, a grandmotherly type, introduced herself as the detective investigating her mother's death. She asked Raine if she had a few moments.

"Sure, only a few minutes. I'm late for work." She was irritated by the intrusion, but she'd been forewarned to be available for questioning.

"How are you holding up?" The older detective's concern seemed real which made Raine feel a little less annoyed.

"I'm okay. It's a lot all at once."

"Do you know of anyone that would want to hurt your mother?"

"Not really. She didn't have friends, but I don't think that she had enemies either. I don't know what she did with her time after Daddy was gone. But, no, I don't think anyone would want to kill her." Except Shanti, she thought.

"Do you recall the last time that you saw your mother?"

"Uh, yeah, it was a week or so ago, I think. On a Saturday, I guess." Raine tried to remember the exact day.

"Where did you see her at?" The younger detective was writing furiously in his notebook.

"Well...she asked me to come look at something at the farm. So, I drove out to see her."

"What was it that she wanted to show you?"

"I think it was some insurance documents." The foggy feeling was settling in again. "But it wasn't that important. Mother always made a big deal out of everything."

"And that was a week ago?"

"Yeah, it would have been on Saturday, a little over a week ago."

"Did your mother indicate if she had anything planned after your visit?"

"No, I don't remember her saying anything." Unease settled in her gut. No matter how hard Raine tried, she couldn't remember most of her last visit to the farm. She had experienced some pretty big lapses of time before but none this pronounced.

"I noticed that you have some marks on your chest. How did you get those?"

Raine put her right hand to her chest. She'd noticed the scratches but didn't put much thought as to how they got there.

"I don't know. I really don't." Raine was beginning to feel frightened.

"Ms. Carter, would you please come with us? We'd like to continue this conversation down at the station." The detective and the officer exchanged the kind of look that meant something. Raine began to feel distant, as if her ears were stuffed with cotton, and her eyes were covered with a thick membrane.

"Shhh…" Shanti whispered in Raine's ear. "You can sleep, I'll go."

# CHAPTER 80
## ONE PLUS ONE EQUALS THREE

Christmas was just a few weeks away and Randi was beginning to adjust to the new norm of her life. Mother had been buried for almost three months, and Raine was going to be tried for her murder. DNA scraped from under Mother's nails matched Raine's.

Randi was heartbroken but worked very hard to distance herself. There wasn't anything that she could do for Raine. Although she believed Raine's defense of insanity, Randi couldn't allow herself to get too caught up in everything. The more that she thought about her family and their history, the worse she felt. Sometimes, she wished she could erase all the dark parts of her past. Writing about it was the only thing that helped. It was the most productive thing that she'd done in all her thirty-seven years.

Several days after Raine was arrested for murder, Randi and Lilly buried their mother. The service was a small, sad affair. Randi only recognized one of the neighbor kids from down the road, but everyone else looked like they were part of the do-gooders from the church that her mother hadn't attended in years.

Mother's death made all the pain over Robert Jr., now known as Aiden, seem insignificant. Randi no longer begrudged Lilly for choosing to keep the baby. The longer that she thought about it, the more she figured that she would have felt the same way.

Instead, Randi immersed herself into her writing and was very close to getting a book deal. She knew that it was only because of Robert's connections that she stood a chance of being published so quickly, but she didn't care. It made no difference to her as to how she was published. Sometimes, she told herself, it's not what you know but who you know.

She'd been fighting a stomach bug since Thanksgiving weekend and was beginning to wonder if it was an ulcer. Robert insisted on making Randi an appointment with his doctor for a check-up. She finally agreed to go, mostly to get him off her back. The appointment was scheduled for that afternoon, and Randi planned on doing a little Christmas shopping afterward.

Before marrying Robert, Randi rarely shopped for others. She never had enough money, so birthdays and holidays were just a reminder of her poverty. In a way, she was thankful to have had so little for most of her life. She didn't take for granted the beautiful things that Robert gave to her. But she also knew that belongings didn't make a person better or worse.

There wasn't much of a wait at the doctor's office. The receptionist handed Randi a specimen cup when she arrived and pointed to the restroom door.

"Follow the directions on the chart, and leave your urine sample inside the closet."

As soon as Randi had finished in the restroom, the nurse ushered her to the scales. "You've gained a few pounds since your last visit!"

"That's probably a good thing!" Randi smiled and thought about Robert's complaints that she was starting to look like a skeleton.

"You'll be in here." The nurse opened an exam room and handed a gown to Randi.

Randi changed into the gown and plopped herself down into a chair. She flipped through the tattered magazines in the basket on the floor until she found one that interested her. After what seemed like a half an hour, the doctor knocked on the door and peeked his head in.

"How are you? What brings you in today?"

"I'm okay, I think. I've just been a little sick to my stomach for a week or so. And you know Robert, he insisted I come see you just to make sure I'm not dying of some strange disease!" Randi smiled at the doctor.

He pulled up his round stool and sat directly in front of Randi. It was difficult for Randi to read his expression. She hoped it wasn't serious.

"Well, what would you say if I told you that there is a reason for your upset tummy?"

"Oh? What is it? An ulcer?" She knew it! That was her first guess, but Robert had poo-pooed the idea.

"No, not an ulcer." The doctor smiled and said, "How does a baby sound?"

"But I can't get pregnant!" Randi didn't believe him. It wasn't possible. She wasn't supposed to be able to conceive; her fallopian tubes were all scarred up.

"Well, I guess your body sees it differently!" He patted her knee and said, "We'll do a sonogram to be sure everything is healthy and where it should be, but the urine test is positive."

"When can I get a sonogram?" She didn't believe it. It was too good to be true.

"We can do a sono right now. I'll just get our tech and we'll take a look before you leave today. Sound good?"

Later that afternoon, Randi had Madeleine prepare Robert's favorite dish for dinner. She wanted everything to be perfect when she shared the news with Robert. It took incredible restraint to keep the announcement to herself until the perfect moment.

"What did the doc say?" Robert asked between bites of Madeleine's delicious handmade ravioli.

"I'm fine. Nothing's wrong." If she kept her answer vague then she had a better chance of holding off until dessert. Madeleine just happened to be pouring more tea at that moment. She smiled and winked at Randi.

"So, how is the new film coming along?" Randi quickly changed the subject.

"Let's just say that the new girls aren't you, baby doll." Robert said woefully. "I wish you could teach them some acting skills. They seem to think that just getting naked is enough. I don't know what the problem is with this younger generation. Maybe lack of work ethic?"

Randi laughed and said, "Perhaps they don't take the business as seriously as you do honey. After all, most porn isn't quite as artistic as yours is!"

Robert shrugged his shoulders and chuckled. "Yeah, probably not."

He speared the last bite of ravioli and devoured it. On any other man, his mannerisms would have appeared brutish to Randi. But with Robert, his movements were sexy in a very masculine way.

"Are you ready for dessert?" Madeleine's sparkling eyes glittered with excitement. She had nearly suffocated Randi earlier with a hug in response to the news. Madeleine had no children, and this baby would be the closest thing to a grandchild that she would ever have.

"I am, if Robert is."

"Absolutely! I live for your desserts!"

"Oh my, Robbie! Flattery will get you everywhere!" Madeleine loved Robert as much as any mother could love her own son. She'd been with his family since he was in middle school.

Randi's heart beat faster while she waited for Madeleine to bring the dessert. She hoped it wouldn't be too silly. She'd never been very good at sentimental stuff but Madeleine didn't seem to think her idea was ridiculous.

"Here we are." Madeleine placed a small, frilly cake in front of Robert and stepped aside. Her eyes twinkled as she watched Robert's curious expression.

"One plus one equals three?" Robert appeared to be confused for a second or two. "Does this mean what I think it does, baby doll? Are you ready to start talking about adoption again?"

"No, you big oaf! I'm pregnant!" Randi squealed.

Robert almost knocked his chair backward to get to Randi. He swooped her up into a huge bear hug and peppered her face and neck with kisses. She'd expected him to be happy, but his over-the-top excitement was more than she could've hoped for.

"Oh, my God, baby doll! I am so in love with you right now!" Robert took a quick breath then began to question her. "When are you due? Is the baby okay? Did you have a sonogram?"

Randi giggled and kissed his forehead. "Yes, the baby is fine and I did have a sonogram – everything looks perfect! I'm about three months along."

"If only your momma could be here for this, Robbie." Madeleine sniffled into a hanky. "She'd be so thrilled!"

"You're going to be the best damned Grandma in the world, Miss Maddy." Robert called her by the pet name that he'd used as a child. "And we are going to be the best damned parents in the world!"

We'll be better parents than I ever had, Randi thought as she buried her face into Robert's chest.

# CHAPTER 81
## TEA AND HOPE

Lilly handed the last box of Halloween ornaments up to Gabe to place on the storage shelf in their garage. "That's the last of it," she said. "Thanks for all of your help today."

"No problem." Gabe climbed down and folded the aluminum ladder up, taking care to hang it back in its place. He brushed the dust off his hands onto his thighs and smiled at Lilly. For a moment, she went weak in the knees, as if she were a college girl again.

"Can I get you some iced tea?" She knew that she must sound desperate to him, always trying to find one more reason to keep him just a minute longer at the house. While Gabe had made no move to divorce Lilly, he also had shown no sign of desire to move back home.

Like a mushy fool, she'd allowed herself to become filled with hope during the time of her mother's death and funeral. Quick with a handkerchief and a strong arm, Gabe had made a proper public display of the supportive, loving husband. He even went so far as to stay at the house for the week following the funeral, to help with the children. She awoke one morning to find a note next to a box of fresh donuts. The note read, "Lil, I'll be at my place tonight if you need me. Give the kids a kiss for me."

Lilly refused to beg. Instead, she'd offered small gestures of goodwill. Most of the time, he turned her down. This time, Gabe frowned for a moment and massaged the back of his neck. "I guess I have time for a quick drink."

Lilly jumped up and down on the inside. This seemingly insignificant moment, a glass of tea accepted, was an enormous step in the right direction. She was willing to work her way back into Gabe's heart, one glass of tea at a time.

He followed her into the kitchen. He sat down in his old spot at the breakfast bar and watched her brew the tea. It was a familiar ritual. Lilly cherished every second. Not trusting herself to say the right words, she didn't speak. She placed the glass of tea in front of Gabe.

"Thank you," Gabe smiled. "I've missed your tea."

"You're welcome." She wished she could stop the hot flush spreading across her face. Her hands were shaking, so she shoved them into the front pockets of her jeans. After an awkward moment, Lilly busied herself with scrubbing out a perfectly clean sink.

"Lilly," Gabe said. "Can we talk?"

Lilly turned toward Gabe, still seated across from her at the breakfast bar. His expression was impossible to read. She nodded.

"I've been thinking about where we're going from here." He cleared his throat and waited a second or two before continuing. "I know I haven't made it easy for you over the past year or so, since the…rape."

The tears in his eyes gave Lilly an unexpected jolt of guilt. She offered up a silent prayer of pleading and waited for him to finish speaking.

"I am truly sorry for the rejection." A tear slipped down his cheek. "I'm not where I need to be yet with our marriage, but I don't want to throw it all away."

Lilly was afraid to speak, afraid to interrupt this flow of words that seemed to be leading in a direction that she'd prayed for. She rested her right hand over the top of Gabe's forearm and forced herself to wait patiently.

"I know that you haven't deserved the rejection that I've dished out. I'm not proud of myself." Gabe rested his head in his hands.

Lilly walked around the bar and turned him to face her. She cupped his face with both of her hands. "I understand. And I forgive you." These simple words were all that she could manage.

Gabe would never know the truth, never know that she was the one that needed forgiveness. She wanted to move a million miles down the road, past this disaster that she'd created. She knew they'd never forget it. But she hoped that in time, they would build something worth staying for.

# CHAPTER 82
# LOCKDOWN

"Miss Carter?"

Shanti continued to ignore the knocking. Talking was overrated, and she'd talked enough for a lifetime during the months that she'd been incarcerated. They'd sent a different person to interview her nearly every day. It was hard to keep track of time in the antiseptic little room that she'd been confined to since the day of Raine's arrest. Raine had deserted her – just up and left. True, Shanti did tell Raine that she would take care of the cops, but she hadn't meant for Raine to leave forever.

As always, when she didn't open the door, someone put a key in the lock and opened it. The ironic part was that she couldn't open it anyway, if they didn't unlock it on the other side. Stupid set up, she thought. Why bother knocking?

"Miss Carter?" The girl looked too young to be a doctor.

"Sure, why not?"

The Barbie Doll in the white coat looked scared, and Shanti felt a small amount of satisfaction. They all asked the same questions; "What do you recall from the day that your mother was murdered?", "What were you angry with your mother about?", or her personal favorite, "What is the meaning of the cross?" Of course, there were the more mundane questions, such as "Do you know what day it is?

Because she was bored out of her skull, Shanti entertained herself by fucking with them as much as possible. She didn't particularly feel like being helpful, and sometimes she felt like being confusing.

"How did you sleep last night?"

"Why do you ask?" Shanti watched the girl squirm. *She must be a student.*

"I'm wanting to check on your well-being."

"Well, Dr..." Shanti jutted her head forward to peer more closely at the girl's badge, "Dr. Calesso, how do you think my well-being is? I'm trapped in a ten by ten cage."

"I'd like to try something different today."

When Shanti didn't respond, the plasti-doc pulled some paper and colored pencils out of her bag and placed them in front of Shanti.

"I have some patients that have had great success with art therapy. Have you heard of it?"

"Sounds like something for an old folk's home." She scoffed and pushed the paper back toward the doctor. "No thanks."

"Well, I think I'll doodle a bit while we talk."

"Suit yourself." Shanti shrugged her shoulders.

The doctor scribbled for a little while before saying anything at all. Shanti found it soothing in a way. Every other person that had walked through her door seemed to feel it necessary to fill the air with chatter.

After a few minutes had passed, Shanti took a blank piece of paper from the stack. She looked through the box of colored pencils to find one that appealed to her. Shanti wasn't sure that she'd ever colored anything in her life. Most of the time, Raine was the one that did the fun stuff. Shanti did the hard stuff.

The colored pencil felt waxy as it slid across the paper, like a crayon only harder. The pencil seemed to have a mind of its own, so Shanti let it go where it wanted. Soon the blank sheet was filled with swirling, colorful shapes. Self-conscious, she tucked her creation under her legs and pulled another blank sheet from the table.

The doctor didn't ask to see Shanti's sketch. She didn't know whether to feel relieved or disappointed.

After the Barbie-doc left, Shanti sat crisscross style on the sterile little bed clutching her picture in her hands. She tried to make sense of the tornado-like shapes, but they looked like nothing tangible. Little angry bursts of color splattered about the paper as if someone had fired shots.

"Do you see this?" She asked Raine. Of course, Raine didn't answer. She hadn't said a word back for ages now.

At first, Shanti tried to coax Raine with the gentle loving words, "please Raine, I miss you. I'm so lonely". When her soft approach didn't work, Shanti used a different tactic.

"Goddammit Raine! Where the fuck are you!" Hoping to scare Raine out, she slammed her fist into the wall above her bed as hard as she could. *How long are you gonna stay away?* Shanti stifled back a sob and pressed her bloody knuckles into her lips. With her uninjured hand, she crumpled up the coloring page she'd made and threw it across the room.

She wanted to punch something else, but she knew it would only bruise her knuckles more and earn some additional time with the docs. Instead, she scooted back against the headboard and pulled her legs up to her chest. Pressing her eye sockets into her knees, she focused on the rhythm of her breathing. Neon-white webbing formed behind her eyelids, creating a welcome distraction from the reality she sat in. Shanti did her best thinking when she just let her mind go like this.

~ After Several Hours ~

Shanti woke still sitting, drenched in sweat. She had been smack dab in the middle of a dream and tried to go back to it because it all seemed very important. Raine was finally talking to her, telling her how to make things right. Hoping to return, she slid down under the thin sheet and blanket and closed her eyes. After a while, the brightly lit room took over, and Shanti gave up on the dream.

She wasn't sure what time it was, but judging from the lack of commotion outside the door, she guessed it was sometime after midnight. Regular sleep wasn't something that Shanti had been familiar with before the cage. Turns out she wasn't very good at it. No matter, her bladder was about to burst anyway, and she didn't want to piss the bed. It took forever to get a change of clean sheets.

The tile floor felt like a sheet of ice under her bare feet. *Why is it always so cold in here?* She shuffled her way to the bathroom which was only a few steps away, three to be exact. A passing glance in the metal mirror gave her an image even more distorted than she imagined herself to be. The patients weren't trusted with glass mirrors. While she relieved herself, she looked around for anything that she could use to follow Raine's instructions.

Nothing in the bathroom would work because there was nothing in the bathroom other than a toothbrush and a soap dispenser mounted on the shower wall. *Maybe prison would have better stuff.* She flushed the toilet and went back to the bed to think some more.

She pulled the meager bedding up over her shoulders and examined the room. To her left was a high window with the blinds built in between the panes of glass. A ridiculously large, utilitarian cabinet was screwed into the wall across from the bed with 7 plastic hangers that were permanently attached to the rod, which was also permanently attached. On the right side of the bed was a desk and chair that also functioned as a nightstand.

There were no personal things of Raine's in the room. Shanti wouldn't have known what to ask for anyway. And it's not like either one of Raine's bitch sisters would have taken the time to come see her. She was sure that one of them ratted her out. "Typical", she thought, "I take care of everyone else's problem and then they desert me".

With so little to work with, the decision was easy. Raine may not have given her a road map, but Shanti didn't need one. She dimmed the lights to create a shelter for the work at hand. She decided there was no sense in delaying. If she hurried, she could be out of this shit-hole by morning.

~ Finally All Together ~

"Shanti! Over here!" Raine called to her from the tree line. The sun was so bright that Shanti couldn't see her. She was swaying back and forth in the breeze, which made it even harder to focus her eyes toward the direction of Raine's voice. A rushing roar flooded her ears and receded just as quickly as it came. Bright flashes of light blinded her for a moment, and then there she was. Raine and Serenity both were just feet away. She could hear the others laughing and talking together.

If only I could stop this damned swinging, she thought. Shanti tried to stop the motion but her hands flailed about and grasped nothing. She tried to plant her feet on the ground, but they were caught up and so the swinging continued. The sight of Raine made her feel elated and she forced herself to be patient. She tried to call out to Raine to help her off the swing, but no words came out.

As if Raine could hear her thoughts, she appeared in front of Shanti. "You made it!" Shanti could smell Raine's hair and her vanilla scent. Raine wrapped her arms around Shanti and finally, the swinging began to slow down.

Shanti and Raine lay intertwined together, surrounded by soft green grass. Serenity sat next to them, making a necklace from clover flowers. The sun was brighter than she'd ever known but didn't burn like she thought it would. "Raine?"

"Hmmm?" Raine's eyes were closed and she had a contented smile on her face.

"Can we stay here?"

"We don't ever have to go back now. You did good."

Shanti already knew this.

# CHAPTER 83
# FREEDOM

Room 212 was a buzz of activity that morning starting from the moment Raine Carter's breakfast tray was delivered. The nurse's aide took two steps into the room, screamed, and dropped Raine's breakfast all over the floor, just like in the movies.

The day shift nurses had just started their shift and were still acclimating themselves to the tragedy of being at work when the aide ran out blubbering nonsense about the patient in room 212.

Too jaded to rush for anything, the charge nurse held the roster out at arm's length because her aging eyes didn't allow for near distance reading any longer. She cocked her right eyebrow up and assigned the room to the newest nurse. "Go see what all the fuss is about."

The new nurse grumbled as she left the nurse's station, and the charge nurse yelled to her back, "You're welcome." The rest of the group tittered and snickered. Laughing at the charge nurse's bullying was a requirement to survival in the ward.

Normally, the room would have been locked back up after the breakfast tray delivery. Instead, the door was left wide open with scrambled eggs, oatmeal and coffee splattered all over the entire entryway to the room. She didn't have to walk into the room to know that the patient was probably beyond help.

For a moment, before doing all the things that protocol required, the brand-new nurse stood in a frozen, horrified awe of the amazing job Raine Carter had done to end her life.

Fabric, sheets she assumed, had been torn into strips and tied together to make a long rope. The rope was tied repeatedly around the clothing rod in the sturdy cabinet and then wrapped and knotted around Miss Carter's

252

neck. The makeshift rope then went onto her ankles and was fastened securely. *It's almost as if she hog-tied herself.* She wondered how in the world the patient got up there without any help. As she walked into the room a little further, she could see that the desk chair had been knocked over onto the other side of the bed.

Inside on the cabinet floor where Miss Carter was hanging was a puddle of something, presumably urine. Next to the puddle was a crumpled-up piece of paper. The nurse pulled a pair of disposable gloves out of her pocket, put them on, and picked up the wad of paper. She smoothed it out as much as possible.

It was a drawing of two stick figures holding hands with the words "Raine and Shanti" printed in block across the top. *Must be a niece or something.* The nurse placed the picture on the bed and felt a moment of sadness for the child who had yet to find out that there would be no more "Raine and Shanti". She shrugged her shoulders and dialed security. Better get started, she thought. *This is gonna be a lot of paperwork.*

The End

# ABOUT THE AUTHOR

RaShell Danette Lashbrook was born in Wellington, Kansas, the eldest daughter of Lyle and Marcia Pope Lashbrook. Her parents threw the television away when she was just two years old, so she spent her childhood in Mulvane, Kansas reading, exploring, biting her nails, and picking her nose.

Her deep love of reading always fueled a small flame of desire to write, but it wasn't until 2012 that she began to practice the craft of throwing words onto paper and rearranging them repeatedly.

She is blessed to share her life with her first love, her six magnificent children and their friends, parents (including an awesome stepdad) that anyone would be envious of, Andee (her best friend since the eighth grade), the best siblings in the whole world, a crazy Australian Shepard, a psychotic Siberian Husky, and a "top-shelf" circle of extended family and friends.

RaShell's fascination with many different subjects has served her well in her writing. She prefers to think of her dabbling as "research". Her lasting passions have been organic gardening, music, cooking, murder, mysteries, aliens, and people with mental disorders.

Made in the USA
Las Vegas, NV
13 September 2022

55171732R00148